# HYPERSPACE RADIO

COLLECTED SHORT STORIES OF

JAMES M. BEACH

MIND
FU

HYPERSPACE RADIO

This is a work of fiction. All the characters and events portrayed, except for purposes of satire, are fictional and any resemblance to real people or incidents is purely coincidental.



A Mind Fu original book. 29 Grove St., #340 San Francisco, CA 94102

ISBN: 978-1-945451-02-7

LCCN: 2018903510

Cover design by James Beach

First printing. May 2018

v1.3.9

# CONTENTS

# CHANNEL WHIMSY

## 1

---

## CONTACT HIGH

Janice looked out onto the beauty of the desert. She loved all of it, the feel of the wool blanket and the ground beneath it, the fading stars, the coming dawn, and the stark beauty of the wild New Mexico horizon. She even liked her boyfriend John. She didn't know why sometimes; all he had to say was negative things. When he even paid attention to her, instead of the pipe he was stuffing.

"It sure is beautiful," said Janice.

"Absolutely. And a whole new kind of hydroponic too - you won't *believe* how strong it is."

She sighed. "John, I was talking about the - the sky, you know?"

"Hm? Oh yeah. Sure baby, it's great. Not like the city. Screw development." He took a hit and closed his eyes, savoring the smoke. "Ahh. Great stuff." He offered the pipe to her. "

Janice reached for it, and then saw something flash across the sky. "Look! Shooting star. Make a wish."

"What for? We're never gonna get better than this. We're young, hot and high." He leaned in to kiss her.

She dodged his lips for a second, and looked him in the eye. "It can't hurt to wish, can it? Don't you want more?"

"Baby, we got all we need right here. Just enjoy yourself."

Janice reluctantly took the pipe, and took a deep hit. She closed her eyes, and then opened them. "Okay," she admitted. "That is really good. Why weren't we smoking this from the start?"

At that exact moment, a flying saucer the size of a flatbed truck flew over their heads, and paused to hover. Readjusting course, it lowered to the earth right before their eyes.

John considered it for several seconds. "Holy. Fuckin. Fuck," he commented at last.

Janice turned to him. "You see it too?"

The dust blew as the ship settled. Lights whirled around its base, slowing with a sound that was much like an engine. The lights slowed, and then stopped.

Landing gear extended from beneath the craft, and then a ramp emerged. Two small creatures walked down it. They were about four feet tall, with gray skin. Their heads were narrow at the bottom and wide at the top, and they appeared to have no hair. It was tough to tell for sure, as they were dressed in late 1940's pinstriped double-breasted business suits and Homburg hats.

The alien on the left spoke first. "Greetings, Earth specimen primates. I am Boraxus, and my junior colleague here is Aaramaton. May we speak with your Eisenhower?"

Janice and John sat in silence broken only by the quiet background woosh of dawn desert winds.

At last Janice spoke. "Baby, that is some craaazy good shit."

"HELL yes," John agreed.

The alien who'd named himself Boraxus turned towards his companion. "Aaramaton, that made no sense. Is the translation device working?"

"It's in perfect working order. I just checked it."

"Check it again. Hello! Humans, we are here to claim your planet and meet with your Eisenhower."

Janice turned and took John's hand in hers. "Where DID you get this stuff?"

"Grandma's got the hookup. Good ol' Humboldt County. Damn."

The two aliens examined them, still seated on the blankets.

"Perhaps they are in need of some medication?" Boraxus said at last.

John and Janice burst into laughter.

"Hah!" said John. "Hah, no we're good bro! Ha hahahhah!"

Janice got up from the blanket, and wiped some of the desert sand from her bare legs. She opened and closed her eyes while looking at the aliens. She held a hand over first one eye, and then the other.

"These hallucinations don't seem like they're just inside my head."

"Yeah! They're not even changing shapes or anything. Awesome!"

"Of course we don't change shapes!" said Boraxus. "We are vertebrates like you! Do we look amoebic?"

Aaramaton tugged on Boraxus' suit sleeve. He turned off the translator machine. In their own language he asked, "I'm not sure if the primates even believe we're here?"

Boraxus imitated the primate gesture of holding one of his hands to his forehead. "By the Queen's Eggs! We travel all this way to meet them, and we meet two apes who are delusional?" He snarled. "We shall test them right away!"

"Must we, immediately? We might as well be polite. Let's see what they have to say?"

"You mean, before we enslave them with our mind-rays?"

Aaramaton sighed. "I so dislike that part of our work."

"It is why we are here for the Queen. If it weren't for our need for slave labor, we would leave these aliens to destroy themselves. Now focus. You're sure the translator is working?"

"Yes, yes."

"Good. Let's hope they have minds enough to enslave. Turn the translator back on." He turned to face John and Janice, who had witnessed their nonhuman language discussion with stunned fascination.

"Ahem! Greetings, primates. Listen closely. We can live in peace, but for that to happen we have demands."

Janice turned towards John, and suddenly a warm smile covered his face. She beckoned him to stand up from the blanket. When he stood, she leaned towards him. "I never shared a hallucination with someone before. It's kinda romantic."

"Oh yeah it is." He kissed her, and they began to make out.

"Hello!" Boraxus demanded. "Primates! Speaking to you!"

"I don't like that hallucination," said Janice. She pointed at the alien on the right and smiled. "He's kinda cute though. Seems sweet."

Boraxus stamped his foot into the dirt, scattering a small cloud of sand. "Primates. Listen carefully. We have an urgent message."

Aaramaton looked to at Janice, and imitated a human smile as he'd been coached. "Yes. We would like to see your Eisenhower."

Janice raised an eyebrow. "Oh, you wanna see my Eisenhower? I can show you." She playfully hiked up her skirt.

"Whoa," said John. "Janice, what the hell are you doing?"

"Oh, don't be jealous. He's just a hallucination!"

"Just, I don't know, it doesn't seem right to flirt with him like that."

"Listen I know this weed is amazing but you're not the boss of me."

"Stop!" declared Boraxus. "By Queen Zora of Zorax, stop your nonsensical primate monkey bickering and listen!"

The aliens look at the couple, examining them raptly. The couple stared back.

Janice chewed her bottom lip. "I wonder if..." She reached out and touched the alien on the right. Aaramaton jumped back. She jumped back as well.

"John! I think they're real!"

"No way!" John reached out as well. Both of the aliens stepped back this time.

Boraxus grabbed for a device on his belt. "Keep your distance, primate! I come from the Queen!"

"Whoa!" John exclaimed. "You two are real! And you're aliens! We're talking to aliens? This is amazing!"

With great effort, Boraxus restrained himself from stunning this primate with a mind-ray. Aaramaton had been right when spoke earlier - this was still the diplomatic stage. "Yes! We are real!

Congratulations, monkey. Truly your intellect is a wonder to behold."

John smiled smugly. "Ah, I watch a lot of Ancient Aliens."

"Do you have names?" Aaramaton asked.

"My name's John, and this desert flower is Janice."

Janice blushed. "Where are my manners. Here I'm about to show you my cooch and you're like, ambassadors from the universe or something!

"What is this...cooch?" Aaramaton asked.

Janice laughed and hung her head. "Kinda sounds like you'd love to know. "

Boraxus waved his fingers in front of Aarmaton's eyes. "My colleague! Focus. You, larger monkey with the shorter hair. Where is your nearest authority figure?

"Nowhere near here. Screw the system man. We're just here, enjoying some fine herb. Want a hit?" John offered them the pipe.

Boraxus pulled the device on his belt out all the way, and pointed it at John. "Do not threaten us!"

John offered his hands in a calming motion. "Naw, man! Jeez you're jumpy. Just offering you some of my special stash."

He carefully offered Boraxus his pipe and a lighter in his palm. Aaramaton leaned a scanning device over his hand. "By the galaxy!"

"What is it?" asked Boraxus.

"A substance that stuns minds!"

"You know it!" said John. "Wooooo!"

"By the stars. It would have almost the exact same effect as our mindslave rays!" Boraxus turned to John and Janice. "You ingest this voluntarily?"

John nodded. "Wake and bake, my brother."

Janice smiled. "It really can be fun."

Boraxus turned again to his companion. "How about you nice monkeys hold that thought." He signaled his colleague to turn off the translator again. "The last reports made no mention of this. This practice was perhaps less widespread. If they take ingest substances like that just for entertainment, our enslavement rays may have no effect at all!"

Aaramaton nodded happily. "So there's no way to conquer them cheaply. Our duty is clear. We must call off the invasion!"

"Yes," Boraxus admitted regretfully. "And we must leave at once to tell the queen!"

"What? We just got here! Another 60 years in space? After I've finally met an alien?"

His companion examined him thoughtfully, and then his face hardened. "You mean a human female."

Aaramaton tried to wave off the insight. "Details. Look, it's probably not safe for both of us to stay here. Someone must take his report back to the Queen, right?" He put on his best expression of brave magnanimity. "It's clear you don't enjoy their company. I will stay behind and maintain further scientific observation." He ruined the effect of this speech by looking over at Janice, who caught his eye and waved.

John saw this and scowled a bit, then took another puff from his pipe.

Boraxus sighed. "I'm leaving before I lose my mind like you."

"Great!" said his companion. "Ahem. Uh, you'll need to take a subject back with you to study, won't you?

"Let me guess. The male. You really want to make eggs with the female, don't you?"

"Please don't judge me."

"Fine. More of the Queen's delicious gruel for me, all the way back."

The alien on the right rolled his eyes. "Dream big..." he muttered under his breath.

"Is that some kind of derogatory comment against the nutrients excreted by our great queen?"

"No, no. It's terribly tasty. I'll miss it and I never grew tired of it."

"Just turn the translator back on. I will try my best to imitate the larger primate's speech patterns." The aliens turned to face John and Janice, the two very stoned ambassadors of the human race. "Hey, 'bro'. I think we'd love to try some of that 'wakeandbake'. Can you leave your monkey companion here, while we go try it behind that boulder?"

"Uh...ok, why there?"

The alien shrugged. "I'm shy."

Aaramaton smiled at Janice to reassure her, and motioned for her to stay there. John and the two aliens walked behind the boulder.

Janice heard John's voice come from behind the boulder. "Hey wait, what are you doin'?"

"Stand still primate!" came Boraxus' voice.

There was a flash of light and a thumping sound.

John came running out. "Get back, Janice! The alien tried to touch me. I defeated him quite well!"

Aaramaton emerged from behind rock, dazed and stunned. "Quickly!" Boraxus ordered. "Quickly, this way!" The dazed creature followed the second alien's orders back into the spaceship. The hatch closed, and it rose back into the night sky, leaving the couple behind.

Janice hugged John, and began examining him. "Are you okay baby? What happened?"

John shook his head. "I do not want to talk about it."

They watched the spaceship disappear into the growing dawn. "Did he try to touch you?" Janice said.

John watched her face for expressions. "Maybe."

"That's kinda hot," Janice admitted.

"Good." They moved in closer, and became preoccupied with nonverbal interactions.


INSIDE THE SPACESHIP, Boraxus completed what appeared to be Aaramaton into a study bed. He then pressed a button, and the creature's shape changed to reveal John.

"What'n hell's are you doing?" John asked.

"You have been selected as a test subject."

"Where's your buddy?"

"Aaramaton has selflessly volunteered to switch places with you, and study your species up close." He closed his eyes and held his hand over one of his small hearts. "The poor, brave son of an egg. He will be remembered."

"I knew he was hot for her! Dammit!"

"Good! Get your primate emotions worked up. That will give us more accurate readings."

"You gonna anal probe me or something?"

"Stars, no!" the alien shuddered.

"Oh."

"No, the machines do that. And we've got to get you good and terrified first. Such is science."

"Well, I don't know if it really terrifies me. I like to experiment. You know that thing you zapped me with behind the rock there, that was kinda neat. Felt a bit like shrooms."

"That was actually what we were going to probe you with."

John paused for a second. "Alright!! Wooohooo!! Bring it on!"

Boraxus sighed. "You are the most frightening creatures I have ever met." He turned off the translator, and stabbed a sequence of buttons on the console in front of him. "Scout ship X2 reporting, transmitting on the tachyon wave 6237B. We must halt the invasion of Sol 3 immediately. There doesn't appear to be much we can do to the humans that they aren't willingly doing to themselves."


BACK ON EARTH, Janice and the being who now looked like John sat down on their blanket. John picked up the loose bag of remaining weed that laid on the blanket, and dumped it out onto the dirt.

"You're done smoking for a bit?"

"It would only distract me from the beauty around me. Such as you."

Janice smiles kissed him on the cheek. "That might be the sweetest thing you've ever said to me."

John looked surprised. "It's simple truth. It's a shame he - I didn't appreciate you more. Let's work on that." He puts his arms around her, and she leaned into his side.

After a while she asked, "Think we should we tell anyone about them?"

"Who would believe you? I mean, us?" He smiled. "That is of course, if the aliens were even really here." He looked at the big, open sky before them. "Just look at that. All that space, and there's no other place I'd rather be."

2

## THE FIRST ART SHOW

Cave of the Moon Bear - 15,000 B.C.

It was a big day for Urghluk. He had been painting for a long time, in darkness, barely lit by torches, deep in the spell of creativity. Now it was time to shake that off, be social, and show the tribe what he had done. It was, at last, time for his art opening.

The painted bear skulls were arranged at the mouth of the cave, the tops holding small long-burning torches. Many berries had been gathered and sent off to the wine maker. Fern leaves had been braided and laid along the path. It was the night of the first moon. Word was spread around their little valley, and even into the next.

His good friend Flarg headed into the cave, with a large hunk of roasted boar over his shoulder. Good for people to pick at as they perused Urghluk's new works. Ordinarily they might have cooked it in the cave, but Urghluk didn't want it to distract from his paintings.

Flarg plunked it down on a waiting slab. "Hey Urghluk! How's it going?"

Urghluk grunted. "Weather looks good. Hope for a good turnout. Seen Ala yet?"

"That new girl from the far valley? I saw her around the fire earlier. Did you invite her?"

"I left a map drawn in antelope blood at her cavestep. Maybe she got it after she was done gathering for the day. It's very last minute. No big deal if she can't make it." She was the one person he really wanted to show up tonight. "Where is everybody?" said Urghluk, changing the subject. "It's already after sunset."

"Plenty of people will come tonight, I'm sure. I see you brought your new club."

"Yes! Just had it made. Ghwargulog makes a good club. I promised to use him as a mighty hunter with an erect penis in my next series."

"You're wearing new fur too. You look sharp as a tiger's tooth, my friend."

"Thanks, hunt brother."

"Ala will appreciate all that you have done to impress her." Urghluk looked pained. "What?" Flarg asked.

Urghluk sighed. "I didn't do all this just to impress her. I want her to see things that I see. I want to show things that others haven't seen or thought about. I want her and everyone to see these things I have deep inside me, that burn like…like the sun must burn, when it goes over the hills and hides in caves at night."

"The sun? What is that?"

"That's what I call that orange ball that rises in the day time and makes things warm. I think it hides in caves."

"Whatever you say," Flarg said, patting his shoulder. "Who is that old man?" He pointed towards the cave's entrance.

"Oh! Good. The winemaker's here." Urghluk put down his club and walked outside to help the old man and his children drag a sled in. He noted with approval that the sled was piled high with filled wineskins, and many drinking horns were along the side.

"Ah, Urghluk! I have a good batch of wine. This time I left them out in the rain. Added a fresh zing! You will make me a good painting for my cave as we agreed?"

"Of course. And we will have many thirsty people tonight, so your fame as a winemaker will spread." Urghluk looked around for where the wines could be set up. "Perhaps," Urghluck began, pointing to a spot near the entrance.

"...On the big rock over there," the old man said, pointing to a different location about halfway inside the cave.

Urghluk thought that spot might distract from his paintings and wanted a different place. But it was at that moment he noticed a spot of the old man's wine on his fresh bearskin tunic. He screamed and ran to the back of the cave where he hoped no one could see him, and tried to polish it out.

The stain didn't just stay, it spread. Did he have time to run back to his cave and change tunics? He looked to the entrance and his heart sank - people had started walking in. Sighing, he took a position near his favorite new pieces, holding his new club in front of the stain and trying to look casual.

The first attendees were an elderly couple, possibly even as old as thirty winters. They seemed well fed. They seemed to like his rendering of a mammoth hunt. Maybe he could get a commission to paint their cave. He was considering how to start up a conversation with them, when he happened to glance over at the winemaker. The old man's younger helpers were now carrying small woven baskets of....

Urghluk ran over. "What in the name of the bear god is that stuff?"

"Oh, this!" One of the winemaker's children picked up a chunk of dripping white stuff that resembled bloated flesh. "That's the milk fungus."

"What??" Urghluk looked around. No one had heard them. "Why would you bring such things to an art show? And...did you say milk?"

"Yes, yes," said the young man impatiently. "Don't you know, down at the tip of the river valley they've been keeping yaks in pens and drinking their milk."

"Ew!"

"I know, I know, it seems weird at first. But they left some of it out and it turned solid and I tasted it, and...it's not bad."

"Well actually it is bad. That's the whole point, it went bad. I don't want it at my show."

"You should try it," the old man said.

"Get that stuff away from me."

"Just try it! If you don't like it, the wine tonight is free. Here, as a matter of fact have it with the wine."

Against his better judgment, Urghluk took a bite and then a swig of wine. He was about to spit on the ground, when he paused.

"....huh!" The combination actually tasted quite good.

"I told you," said the winemaker. "Something about the combination goes well with paintings also." The old man nodded towards the mouth of the cave. "You will need every impressive thing you can find, now that he's here."

Urghluk looked over, and saw an older man approaching. He was about to ask who it was, when a hushed voice called out from the crowd "The Seer!"

Urghluk jumped in shock. The Seer?? Could it be, the Seer coming to his show? Fear and hope ran through him like bolts of lightning striking treetops. The Seer was a wise man known for his wisdom, which sometimes was harder for simpler people to understand at first but which was always explained later, also by the Seer. The man had known many winters and witnessed many different kinds of paintings and creations. His judgment could make Urghluk a famous painter, known throughout the land! It could also ruin his name forever, making him unfit for anything but decorating children's training spears!

The Seer had arrived with a younger woman in tow. Urghluk could not see her face. Perhaps this was one of his servants he called "interns". Such was the wisdom of the Seer.

Urghluk's eyes grew wide and softly focused, as if in a waking dream. "If he likes my paintings, why - I might not even have to join the hunt any more, I could make cave paintings full time!"

"Hey, what's so bad about hunting?" his friend Flarg asked.

Urghluk snapped back to the present. "Nothing, nothing - how do I look?"

"Same as before. Sharp, okay? Besides that wine stain - say, is that Ala?"

Urghluk looked where his friend was pointing, and cursed the sky. For the woman walking arm in arm with the Seer, was none other than Ala herself. He watched helplessly as they went over to the wine maker's rock and procured two horns of wine.

"It looks like - " Flarg began.

"They're on a date," said Urghluk. He leaned against the wall in dismay, resisting the urge to run and hide.

"Don't take it so bad!" Flarg said. He grabbed his friend by the shoulders. "This is your big night! You can't help but get some commissions for caves, your stuff looks great - and him even being here is a big thing. It puts you on the map!"

"What is a map?"

"It is a thing we use to track deer...it's not important. You're a big artist now. Don't let it get to you."

"I guess so," said Urghluk, from his voice clearly not guessing so.

"My baby!" Urhgluk heard a voice call out, and cringed. His parents had come.

"Mom!" he said. "Not so loud, okay?"

"But my darling! We're so proud of you!" his mother announced, embracing him like some kind of parental she-mammoth. "Such an artist!" She tried to pinch his cheek. He managed to dodge her right hand, but she was too quick with her left and pinched his other cheek.

"Mom, do you have to... to..."

"What? I'm not supposed to say hi to my little baby? We're so happy and proud for your big show! Isn't that right honey?" She turned to Urghluk's father.

His father gave a grunt indicating that he was in fact aware the show existed.

"Yes, yes of course," said Urghluk, recovering. "Have you seen the wine? There's some interesting new food that seems to go well with it...you might want to spend some time trying it out." He directed his parents towards the winemaker's rock.

The cave was filling up now. Urghluk stood next to what he considered his latest and most important series of cave-paintings. He waited for people to come over and talk to him. Or at least near him, so he could hear what they really thought about the art.

Many liked it, which made him feel quite good. He overheard a passing group of spear enthusiasts chatting lightly about the different paintings and their styles. How this series was from the Loose Eyes period, while those other paintings were the Blue Pigment period. Urghluk nodded. Yep, he'd had a concussion that nearly knocked his eye loose. Then he'd transitioned out of that period by finding some blue rock, while wandering dazed. Inspiration, really.

Other people might as well have not been seeing the art at all, and were just talking about their day. An older berry-gatherer compared Urghluk's piece on red deer to his own child's dirt-scrapings. That was unfair. Urghluk had his own entirely unique style of dirt scraping.

After a while the Seer approached. He appeared to be enjoying the milk fungus. So much the better, for Urghluk wanted the Seer to be in as good a mood as possible when viewing Urghluk's work. The man did appear rather satisfied, smug even, looking quite pompous in fact with his arm around...

"Urghy!" said Ala, so beautiful and smiling.

"Ala! I am so glad you could make it."

"I wouldn't miss it! Your paintings look so great in here!"

"Thank you. I've been working on them for so long, it's great to have people I want to see them - I mean finally show them to people."

"These are your works?" asked the Seer.

"Yes," said Urghluk. He nervously started his prepared statement. "I've been working on-"

"Tell me what you were thinking with this one." The Seer waved towards a series of antelope surrounded by hunters.

"I call it 'Hunt at Dawn'. They're, uh, hunting animals...."

"At dawn? Interesting." The Seer leaned in, and wrinkled his nose. "How are we supposed to know it's dawn?"

"I painted an orange circle for the big light that comes out in the morning and then hangs over us all day. See how it's low above the mountains there?"

"It could also be sunset though," the Seer pointed out.

"It looks pretty," said Ala.

"Yes, but it has to do more than look pretty," the Seer admonished.

"Why?" she asked.

"My dear, paintings have to draw in the spirits to accomplish a great hunt. They have to inspire us to live brave and free, and show our value to the gods." He looked at the paintings, and frowned. "I'm not sure these quite accomplish that. Let's see some others." They walked over to the next series of paintings. Urghluk followed. A small crowd gathered behind them as they walked, soon hanging on the Seer's every word.

"I kind of like how he makes things look," Ala persisted.

"And that's what's charming about you, my darling," said the Seer. Urghluk swallowed as the Seer walked to a series that he had just barely finished the night before. He almost hadn't done them, until he realized he simply needed more pieces to have a big enough show. This series depicted a group of hunters pursuing a herd of mammoths off a cliff while the hunters had huge erections.

"Ah," said the seer. "Intriguing." Urghluk realized that the entire cave had become quiet as everyone strained to hear the Seer's pronouncements.

"That's a bold choice..." said the Seer, leaning in.

Urghluk felt a flash of relief. "Yeah, I was going for the excitement of the hunt," he explained. "It feels really like a horny rut. You want the...the meat."

"Wow, I never thought of it like that," said Ala. She turned her eyes towards Urghluk with new respect.

"But this is really nothing new," said the Seer.

"What?" Urghluk sputtered. "I haven't seen it before. I came up with it myself."

The Seer sniffed. "I saw Galukluk did the same thing in his installation at the Hill Valley Bear Clan. And their penises were over their heads."

"Yes," Flarg jumped in, "but that wasn't the artist's idea. They actually try to stretch their penises over their heads. They're not the brightest."

"Anyway Seer," Urghluk rallied. "What does it matter who has done what before, or why? These are my paintings. What should matter is how they make us feel. How I felt when I made them, and the feelings they bring to others."

The Seer noticed that Ala's eyes were on Urhgluk. He could see that this cave painter's arguments were winning her over, and scowled. "You have not yet had enough winters to know this, so I shall instruct you. The point of art isn't to make people feel things. The point is to please the spirits so they help the hunt, and to appease the gods so we are not hunted."

"Mmm...I don't agree," Urghluk responded.

The Seer raised an eyebrow, and chuckled indulgently. "Well you're new to art, so I can see why you don't yet understand. But that's just pretentious bearshit - not unlike your paintings. You see," he began, and prepared to launch into a lengthy speech.

Urghluk's new club smashed down on the Seer's head, crushing his skull.

All the visitors looked over at Urghluk, Ala and the fallen bloody body of the Seer.

The cave hung in silence for a second, and then it filled with polite applause. The excitement of the moment over, the crowd returned to the winemaker's rock.

Urghluk's father caught his eye to nod approval, before the old man reached for another piece of yak milk fungus with his wine.

Urghluk turned towards Ala, and found he was enjoying the look in her eyes. He tried to seem less like a happy little boy. He decided to lean in. This was, in fact, the hunt. "So, what are you doing later tonight?"

And the rest of the show was also a smashing success.


### Exhibit at the Metropolitan Museum - 2015 A.D.

An entirely new branch of cave paintings had been discovered in the famed caves of Lascaux, France. "Stunning," was one academic assessment. Several careers were launched and would be maintained over decades, on the study of this one set of works from an artist who lived before history began.

The images were duplicated and sent on an international museum tour. They came to stop in an artificial cave known as the Metropolitan Museum of Art, where they attracted many viewers.

"Of some anthropological interest, perhaps," said one established art critic. "But certainly nothing compared to the art of our modern times." Being a particularly well-known modern art critic, a sage of art even, he appraised the mood of the gathered crowd with an expert eye and continued. "It's too representational, too simple, too direct. There isn't even any subtext."

"They look so primal though," said one particularly pretty young woman to his left. The critic guessed she was a recent college graduate. He could humor her.

"They do have a certain barbaric passion," he allowed. He did his best to smile sagely, "I do expect much better at a more modern show I'm reviewing tonight. One never knows, but there will be drinks at least. Perhaps you would be interested in accompanying me?"

The girl considered it. "Well, this guy I know gave me a flyer for his show tonight. I was thinking I might go to that if you want to come along."

He considered it. It sounded perfect. He would stand out in this crowd of lesser-knowns, and better his chances with her. What likelihood was there that the artist would actually be impressive, and thus a rival? He chuckled indulgently. "A nice, small show? It's been a while, it sounds quite fun."

3

———————

## ILLEGAL ALIEN BEINGS

Peter Myenfeld sat in an unfamiliar lobby, waiting for an explanation. He'd been enjoying his lunch break in the State Department cafeteria, getting ready the afternoon arraignments that he'd be prosecuting. Then two men in Homeland Security uniforms had shown up, requested his help with a top secret matter, and brought him here.

'Here' was a downtown building he'd walked past many times without giving it a second thought. The exterior was drab gray concrete with shaded lobby windows. The lobby interior was understated marble, glass and chrome, no more or less impressive than many lobbies. Peter watched people come and go, wondering when someone would emerge to tell him what was going on. For no reason he could put his finger on, he was beginning to feel that wearing his good suit today had been a good idea.

A man emerged from a row of elevator banks and walked towards him at a fast pace. He was slightly older than Peter, also in a suit, and carried several folders in his left hand. He extended his right hand to Peter. "Hello Mr. Myenfeld."

"Uh, yes, hi," said Peter as he automatically shook the man's hand. "And you are...?"

"That's classified. Call me Bill. Walk with me, we're in a bit of a hurry." The man had already turned and was speeding down a corridor to the left of the elevator banks.

Peter hurried to catch up with him. "Can you tell me what this all is about? Those officers wouldn't tell me anything."

"Good."

Peter blinked. "Look, perhaps there's some mix up. I'm a prosecutor for minor cases in the State Department..."

The man called Bill cut him off with a chop of his folders. "You mean you used to. You work for us now. Your new pay is quadrupled."

Peter's eyes went wide. "What? Why?"

"In return you will never tell anyone else what we do here, ever. Watch your head," he said, as they turned a corner. Peter nearly ran into a young woman rolling a device the size of a file cabinet with protruding and glowing wires.

"Uh...why can't I tell anyone? And what can't I tell them?"

"We're throwing you in the deep end of the pool, Myenfeld, so listen closely. A year ago the Earth was contacted by a galactic federation of planets." They rounded another corner and sped down a long hallway. "The US secured the right to be the main point of contact. Quite a coup, took a lot of wrangling. The downside is that, according to their blasted galactic law, we have to treat all alien creatures like we would treat human beings."

"But..." said Peter, his mind racing. "Look, I'm very happy to get that much more money. But why me?"

The older man slammed to a stop outside two large wooden doors. "Our lead counsel quit 30 minutes ago, and we have one day to try these cases or we forfeit. You're the best lawyer we could find on such short notice, who has any familiarity with immigration." Bill's expression hardened. "So buckle up, son! You're going to represent the US Department of Homeworld Security in immigration hearings about some aliens - who are actually aliens."

"Homeworld...?" Peter managed.

Bill thrust the folders he'd been carrying into Peter's hands. "Go get 'em and make the US of A proud, tiger!" He opened the double doors and pushed Peter in.

The courtroom interior was a mix of plastic and chrome that looked both space age from the fifties, and worn from frequent use. There were a handful of seats towards the back wall, with a couple of suited men who looked at him with curiosity.

Peter realized he knew one of them – a defense lawyer he'd tangled with a few times. Maxwell Carmichael, just as coiffed and dandy as any of his commercials. Peter had faced the man before, in much more ordinary high-profile immigration cases. The man was an attorney of the sleaziest sort, known to represent any Eastern Bloc oligarch who had just fled his country with a bucket of cash.

At the front of the room was what looked like a raised judge's bench and two tables right before it, one on each side. As Peter came closer he saw that the chairs at the tables were made of wood. They looked like they had been taken hastily from some other part of the building.

Bill indicated the table to the right. Peter picked a chair at the left end of the table, and put the folders on top of it. Bill sat next to him, and tapped the first folder. Peter began to read it as quickly as he could.

"All rise!" Peter saw a bailiff had come through a door to the right. They rose.

The judge entered and walked over to the bench. She was in her 50s, with streaks of gray and a mild expression belying a sharpness in her eyes. "Thank you, be seated. I'm Judge Magdalena Royce. Who is representing the US in this matter?"

Bill looked at Peter, and Peter coughed. "I am, your honor. My name is Peter Myenfeld, on behalf of the Department of Homeland - Homeworld Security." She looks reasonable at least, Peter thought to himself. He took a breath and tried to wrap his mind around the situation. Four times his current salary was....well, pretty great. Whatever the hell was going on here, he didn't want to lose a case if he could help it. Presumably there was a Department of Homeworld Security for a reason.

The judge smiled. "Just replaced Pierson, huh? That was quite a meltdown. Bill, is he up to speed? Otherwise Homeworld Security will have to forfeit."

Bill nodded. "He's all set and we have complete confidence in his abilities."

"Alright then. Looks like we still might be able to finish these cases this afternoon. Next case. Bailiffs, can you please bring before the court..." she put on her reading glasses and examined a tablet on her bench, "Shllshshhhhh Shlllelexershshhsn."

A door slid open to the right of the judge's bench. Several bailiffs walked in, warily surrounding a huge dark creature with no eyes, huge teeth, an elongated head, deadly claws, a menacing whip-like tail, and a glossy, bony and slimy exterior, that looked like...

"Oh my God," Peter blurted. "Is that the Alien from the movie Alien?"

"Nice, pal," said a voice to his left. "All aliens look the same to you?"

Peter looked over, to see his frequent courtroom opponent Carmicheal approaching the defense table. He laid his briefcase down, and with a sneer framed said "Myenfeld."

"Carmichael," Peter responded. It all clicked into place. New environment, same game. It was on.

"I'll let the government go first," said the judge. "What's the position on the claimant?"

Peter looked into the first folder. "Your honor, it seems pretty clear that Mr....Shllle...Shlelshl.... that he was not born on US or even Earth soil."

The alien produced a hiss. Flecks of spittle reached the plastic of the witness box it barely fit in, sizzling against and producing wisps of black smoke.

Carmichael nodded. "My client is requesting asylum for religious reasons. He's a born-again Christian. He has been a movie consultant and job creator for several years, and is an asset to the community. Please find as exhibit A from the defense, many testimonials as to his productive work ethic and God-fearing nature including from Rudy Giuliani, Pat Buchanan and Stephen Baldwin."

Peter looked through the folder further. "Your honor, I read here that he likes to eat humans."

"Profiling!" Carmichael shot back. "Your honor, my client is a vegetarian."

Peter held up a printout of a web page. "Your honor, here is a Facebook post that says, and I quote, 'I love the taste of humans who are basted in my acid saliva."

"Objection! Out of context."

Peter read the next passage, and then turned a mocking eye to Carmicheal as he spoke. "Your honor, the paragraphs before and after this describe a...flesh tenderizing method based on his larval young bursting through human chests."

Carmichael coughed. "May I confer with my client?"

The judge nodded. Carmichael took a small glass shield from his briefcase, walked to the witness stand and held the glass between his head and the alien's mouth as it whispered. Several drops of spit struck the glass and scored smoking trails as they dripped to the floor. Peter wondered idly what the maintenance budget of this room was.

Carmichael nodded and returned to the table. "My client says that was satire."

Peter's jaw dropped. "What? Your honor, come on now..."

The judge shook her head. "We have to respect free speech. The paperwork is in place. Deportation is denied. Mr. Shlllelexershshhhsn, we look forward to more of your creative work. Hollywood needs new ideas like yours."

Shlllelexershshhhsn was escorted out by several bailiffs, with a jovial pip to its skeletal slinking. Carmichael closed his briefcase and gave Peter a parting playful finger-gunshot.

Peter scowled, and turned to Bill. "Sorry," he said.

Bill shrugged. "Ah, you gave it your best, kid. We were screwed on that one from the start."

The judge looked down at the papers before her. "Next? A..." she squinted her eyes. "Greblieps? Braxas? Bailiff, which is it?"

"Your honor, it appears this being's street name is 'E.T.'"

Peter read the next folder, as the bailiffs brought in the next defendant. This time the bailiffs towered over the creature. It waddled along on paddled feet, its wrinkled grayish skin giving it an appearance of both age and harmlessness. Its oddly flattened head and large eyes looked almost like the outline a pair of binoculars would make if they were covered in papier-mâché.

Peter began. "So, 'E.T.'..." The judge scowled. Bill pulled on his sleeve, and Peter leaned down. "That term is offensive," Bill whispered. "Just say alien."

"But..."

"Just read what's in the folder."

Peter looked into the folder and started again. "Your honor, it appears that this alien's family name is Griebleps and Braxas is his... pseudonym. The Department of Homeworld Security became aware of him a couple of decades ago, and attempted to sign him up as a contractor. He refused, and was supposed to self-deport to his home planet. But instead..." Peter read on, and stopped.

He really didn't want to say this.

Bill coughed. The man's look reminded Peter that this was his new job.

Peter sighed, and continued reading from prepared text. "Mr. Greblieps proceeded to hang out near drug stores and hand out supposed prescription pills for various ailments that were actually Reese's Pieces."

The judge looked thoughtful. "But did the healing occur?"

Bill glared at her.

Peter flipped through the pages. "Well, apparently yes, but without a prescription. The actual healing was done by the physical contact of handing them the pieces. So this is fraud."

"I see," said the judge, tapping her fingers thoughtfully. "It does seem rather victimless though."

"The Department feels very strongly about this. For not registering with the government after his fraudulent self-deportation, but continuing to live with his host family and cut into the profits of local pharmaceutical companies, we request immediate deportation." Peter then looked over at the sad pathetic creature as it gazed back at him with its huge eyes. Then he noticed the empty table next to him.

"Uh, where's its counsel?" Peter asked.

Under the table, Bill kicked him.

The judge sighed. "The public defender didn't show up today either. Between you and me, he hasn't been the same since his wife was deported. Although I don't know how much you could miss someone named Vampirella...In any case, we have to move forward. So the government's position is to deport him?"

Peter looked over at Greblieps, who stared at him with pleading in his eyes. He looked into the folder. "Yes," he said sadly.

"I would be inclined to at least give him a waiting period. But the laws on this matter are pretty clear. Deportation, so ruled." The judge banged a gavel, and bailiffs took the sad and unprotesting alien away.

Peter ducked down and whispered to Bill, "How many more of these?"

"Easy there, bleeding heart," Bill whispered back. That was a slam dunk and you almost blew it. Just one more for the day, and you can go home to your new bonus."

The judge read again. "Finally, we have...Kal-el? Street name, 'Superman'?" She laughed. "Wow, some people have a very inflated opinion of themselves." After reading a bit further she frowned. "A very inflated opinion. Apparently he couldn't be bothered to make it to court himself today. He's being represented by a Mr....Kent."

"That's me, your honor." Peter turned to see the other man from the back of the room approaching the bench. He was a rather mild-mannered man in a cheap but presentable suit, that gave hints of a surprisingly muscular build. The man's glasses also didn't suit him at all.

The man reached the defense table. "Superman apologizes," the man continued, "but he doesn't consider it safe for others to see him. If he is examined too closely, his true secret identity could be revealed. It could make it difficult to save the world."

"That's no excuse," said the judge.

"Isn't it?" asked Kent.

"Well..." the judge considered it. "His job is to save the world? That's good and public-spirited, but we all have work. Court is important. It's part of his civic duty, if he wants to be a legal American - right, he does want that?"

"Of course he does," said Mr. Kent. "Superman is very proud of his adoptive country. His not appearing is intended to maintain his ability to protect it."

"Well, Counsel?" the judge asked. "What is the state's position on the citizenship of Mr. Kal-el? I'm not calling him by that ridiculous name."

Peter checked the folder, and his face fell. He said nothing. Bill coughed.

"Counsel?" the judge repeated. "I'm getting impatient."

Peter sighed. "Your honor, the department's position is that Mr. El has not declared himself an alien formally, and has thus been saving the world without benefit of a social security number. He has taken world-saving from ordinary working Americans."

Kent gasped and then gave an astonished chuckle. "I should think that in the case of saving a world, there might not be time to find a - a qualified US citizen who can save it. I - uh, Kal-el is uniquely qualified in this regard."

"Is he?" said Peter, feeling very guilty inside. "It's not a unique skillset, is it? It appears that..." he read some more, his eyebrows going up further. "Mr. El runs in a gang with several other aliens - including a woman from an enclosed nation of feminists near Greece, who is known to disrespect the free speech of Nazis. She also has no naturalization papers. Then there's a manhunter from Mars, and a man who claims to be 'King of the Seas' but has no passport and is known to be opposed to commercial ocean farming. Kal-El's illegal alien cousin even plays a part. They appear to be acting as some sort of 'Justice Gang'." Peter thought quickly. "That could even mean a RICO racketeering charge, or other felonies with gang enhancement."

"RICO? The Racketeer Influenced and Corrupt Organizations act is usually used towards organized crime, not organized crime-fighting."

"If they're illegal, then it would certainly apply, wouldn't it?" said Peter. He noticed Bill's quite approving glance and attempted to ignore the pit in his own stomach.

The judge considered this, and nodded her head. "That's an interesting possibility. Mr. Kent, your reply?"

Kent hung his head, appearing crestfallen. "Your honor...Mr. El loves the country of his adoption, as well as the planet that surrounds it. He arrived here as a refugee when he was just an infant, before he had even learned to speak. He was raised by kind people who taught him their timeless values of hard work, honesty, kindness to those who need help and justice towards those who would cause harm. He could have gone to work for the US government or a corporation, and received sponsorship. Instead he has just continued doing the best he could." Kent clasped his hands in front of his chest, in pleading. "If he were to leave the Earth, not only would his heart would be broken, but this country and world would be without his defense. Is there some other path to citizenship that the United States can create, so that he may gladly join this country and contribute legally and fully, to one day become a citizen recognized by the law?"

Peter did not answer. Bill nudged him, and shook his head.

The judge observed this, and waited. Several seconds passed. "State, you have a response?"

Peter looked at Kent, and nodded. "Yes, your honor. State drops all charges and any requests for deportation."

"What?" Bill stood up. "No!"

"Mr. Bill, you are here as observer but are not legally entitled to practice law. No more outbursts." She picked up the gavel. "Court notes that all charges have been dropped, and all reasons for deportation have been dropped. So moved." She banged the gavel.

Surprised and elated, Kent smiled. "Thank you sir! You won't regret it!"

"Yeah you will regret it," said Bill.

"Last case of the day," said the judge. "Lovely! A quick and easy day. Dismissed!" She smiled at Peter and left the courtroom.

Bill snatched the folders off the table and scowled. "What's the matter with you. That sanctimonious Kal-El character broke the law!"

"But - but he would get deported, while that first alien who was so awful gets to stay because he had connections? Why?"

Bill stuck a finger in his chest. "You know why. Because that's the job."

Peter looked at the room for a moment, and then back at Bill. Really he was just checking to be sure. He had already made up his mind a minute earlier. "Then I don't want the job."

Bill's mouth tightened. "Just like Pierson." Bill pointed at the door. "Get out. They'll drop you off back to your normal life, and you'll never have a chance like this again." He sat down, and pulled out a smartphone. "I advise you to never tell anyone about any of this, unless you want to end up in an institution. Good luck back in the minor leagues, you bleeding heart amateur." He turned his back on Peter, clearly dismissing him.

Peter Myenfeld walked out of the courtroom and into the hallway. He was stopped on his way out by Mr. Kent.

"That was a good thing you did in there," said Kent. "It takes courage to stand up. Kal-el would probably not leave, the world needs him. But it matters very much to him that he does the most he can within the law."

"Yeah," said Peter, and sighed. "Thanks. I just wish I'd been more...I guess, thinking right? During the case before Kal-el's, that grey little guy. But I was so rushed, and I wanted the job, and...I didn't do the right thing."

"I know someone else who might be able to help that guy out," said Kent. He put a hand on Peter's shoulder. "Every little bit that we do right moves the whole world forward. Which means the Universe."

4

CALLYPIGIAN PHILES EXEMPTED FROM
CALUMNY

Shelly had the spell for weeks, but it took a long time to work up the courage to use it. The last straw was her brothers teasing her about the boy she had the deepest crush on. His name was Tex, he was new to town and he was dreamy. She had finally gotten his attention, and they'd started hanging out after school. It had been weeks now, but their relationship hadn't gone to where she needed it go – for him to tell her the truth she hoped for deep inside: that he liked her.

She and Courteney had found the spell in their homeroom teacher's desk drawer, when trying to get back Shelly's phone. Their teacher had confiscated it for texting in class, and then died overnight. The spell itself said "This can only be used once." It was dated from the early 1940s. So apparently their teacher had brought this with her without using it for her whole life.

They chatted on Facebook for weeks until Shelly finally declared she'd use it.

The perfect night came – her parents and brothers left her home to go to a line-dancing competition. As soon as they were gone, she broke into her parents' liquor cabinet. A few full glass of rum and she was ready to go.

She went upstairs and logged into Facebook. As she did, she saw her butt in the mirror on the closet door. She didn't know if her butt was too big, just right, or not big enough. She felt like Tex liked it, and her, but she knew she also wanted to believe that. How could she know for sure?

According to her smirking brothers, no guy would ever tell the truth about a girl's butt to a girl. They were always complaining about no answer being alright for their girlfriends. Shelly had the support of her friends at least. Most of them were stuck home tonight too, but they could chat. They were interested in this spell too.

Once she confirmed that she was actually going to cast the spell tonight, the news spread like wildfire. It had been a slow night to begin with, and not much news in general. Interest kept expanding for this teenage girl who was about to cast a spell.

She pointed her laptop's camera for a good view of her, and pulled a folded-over piece of paper from her pocket. She opened it, revealing a torn-out notebook page covered with rainbow sparkles. It contained the spell she'd copied from an old book they'd found, underneath some scraps in the boiler room below the school library.

On the paper, in her purple ink writing dotted with hearts, was the formula of the spell: I risk the love of my life to know if my love is real! I declare it forfeit, to make _ not lie!

"I'm still not sure if I should put his name in," said Shelly.

"Does he like your butt?" asked her sassy friend Courteney. "That's the question here. He should, your butt's fantastic."

"Thanks Courteney – but how can I know that if he likes my big butt he won't lie about it anyway?"

"It shouldn't be just about him either," said Shelly's other close friend Audrey. "What about other guys too?"

Suddenly it came to Shelly. What was that song her brother was listening to the other day? "I got it!" In her rum-drunk state, it seemed like just the thing.

Her eyes closed, she held the note tight and whispered the incantation: "I risk the love of my life to know if my love is real! I declare it forfeit, to make sure people who like big butts cannot lie!"

She pulled out a pink lighter, held her thumb down and lit the notebook paper on fire. It quickly took to flame, and disappeared in a flash of rainbow glitter.

In Shelly's room, and then astonishingly in every room connected to the Internet around the world, a gathering force rose. It was felt first as hairs raising on the back of the neck, then goosebumps, and then as an electric current within one's own soul – a feeling amplified by all the people now witnessing this spell. In the olden days, it would have been rare to gather as many as twenty witches for such a spell. But this evening, there were hundreds of thousands.

The spell climaxed, and crashed like thunder.

Shelly thought it was just the rum, as she passed out. But, amplified by her pure innocence, the rum, and Facebook which amplified her spell to millions, the magic's effects spread like a shockwave throughout the world.

The next morning, and from that day forward, she found that all who liked big butts could not lie. Her brothers, and others' brothers, could deny. But when a girl walked in with an itty bitty waist and a round thing in their face they got sprung – from the cages of their own deceitfulness.

This shook society to it's foundations.

Most children could still lie, until around when they hit puberty. For the rest of humanity, politicians and peasants, police and criminals, employers and employees, pastors and flock – whatever their station in life, whether high low or middle, the very large percentage that liked big butts were forced to tell the truth.

Judges were soon selected based on their Internet browser history. Entire political careers became based on candidates selecting the preferred kind of porn. Parties and governments lost favor because of their sudden mass inability to lie to their voters – they could no longer claim there were easy, simple solutions to any number of different problems. On the other side of power, the voters who elected them had to face their own real impulses, because they could no longer lie to themselves. That is, as long as they liked big butts.

After all the social upheavals this brought the world, humanity settled into a deep and lasting prosperity and peace.

There are now full-size statues of Shelly in every major city. Behind these statues people are taken to swear oaths – for none can lie when they look upon her statue from the rear.

The bittersweet irony is, Shelly still didn't know how Tex actually felt. He was still able to lie, and did so to save her feelings. He revealed years later that he really preferred skinny men.

She did find out that Courteney had some interesting feelings for her, of an entirely different sort.

They were married behind Shelly's statue ten years later.

5

## THE WARTHOG SCHOOL OF VOCATIONAL MAGIC

Hey you! Yes you, reading this magical advertisement that only a select few can see. Tired of trying to make it in the mundane world?

We've all heard of the grand wizarding universities and magic academies. We know the stories of the wizards who've graduated and gone on to risky and ill-advised adventures.

But what if you couldn't get into that fancy wizarding academy? Or you just don't have the grades, the money or the connections?

Maybe you don't want to take on the debt of all those school loans? Or you don't want to apprentice to some wizard who'll probably die soon anyway, leaving you holding the bag of holding?

Have we got an alternative for you!

Don't just get magical skills - get a magical career!

Who keeps the castle nice and cool while the owners are off on adventures?

Who helps ensure sorcerers a good return on their magical gold - and if it's leprechaun gold, makes sure it's invested in the right leprechaun mutual funds?

Who polishes the gargoyles and tending the basilisks, while everyone else is off on some dangerous adventure to some deity-forsaken hellhole?

Maybe you! THEY can go ahead and risk their lives *and* have to pay off hefty school loans. YOU can put in your 8 hours plus lunch and breaks, go home and have a mead.


DEGREES INCLUDE:

### Magical Maintenance

- Warlocksmithing
- Lair Conditioning & Refrigeration
- Celestial Mechanics

- Golem Transmission Rebuilding
- Magic Carpet Cleaning


## Magical Business Administration (MBA)
- Certified Pagan Accountant
- Prophet Management
- Medical Billing with the AOCA (Affordable Occult Care Act)
- Supervillain Supervision
- Interdimensional Travel Agents
Specializations in:
- Astral Plane Reservations
- Magic Castle Accomodations
- Clairvoyant Cruises


## Cryptozoological Veterinary Science
- Familiar Care
- Feeding
- Training
- Exorcising
- Manimal Husbandry
- Centaur Grooming
- Service Cerberus Certification
- Dragon Obedience (a certain so-called mother of dragons might have benefited from this course)
- Care and Careful Feeding of Carnivorous Plants


Plus,


!NEW!


## Paranormal Culinary Arts

Learn how to create a filling and fabulous food experience for nonhuman clients, even if they're dining on human ones!

- All styles of preparation, including Cthulhu cuisine
- Dietary solutions for vegan vampires
- Smart new ways to prepare brains, to give the walking dead more pep in their step

*Remote Viewing classes available!*
*Free set of adjustable wands when you graduate!*

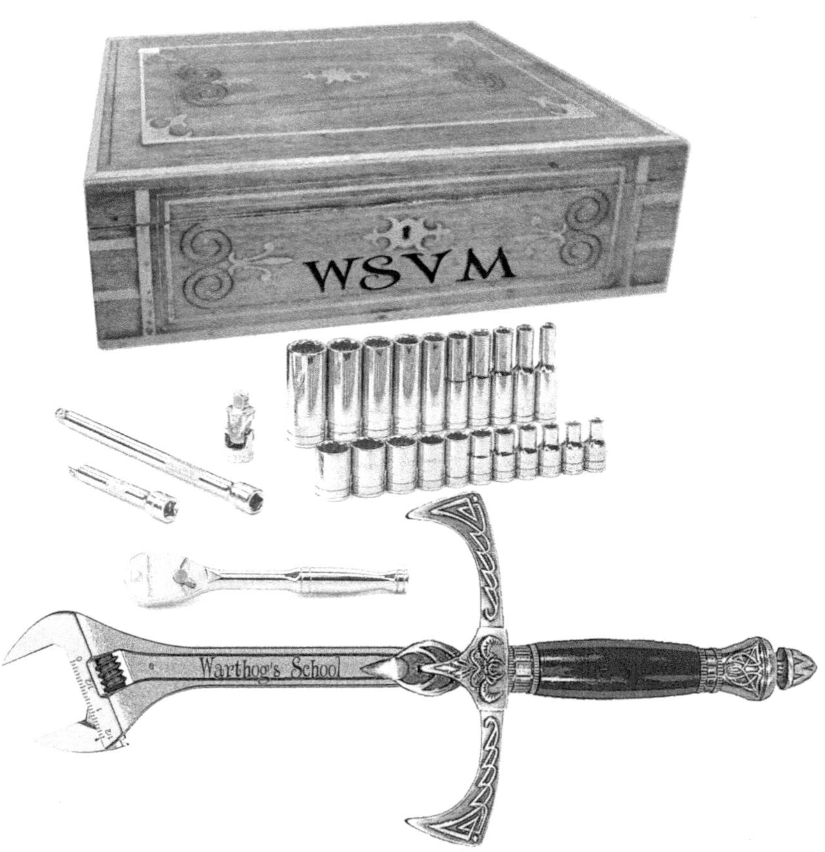

Not interested in mechanics or business, but still magically inclined? You might qualify for our sister school, the

**Merlin Monroe Institute of
Fey Fashion and Qabalistic Cosmetology**

# Merlin Monroe
### Institute of
## Fey Fashion and Qabalistic Cosmetology

*"Mirror mirror on the wall,
What's the school you've got to call?"*

GLAMOUR - DON'T JUST glamour vampire victims, glamour fashion victims! Learn how to put makeup on invisible clients!

<u>**Fashion Design**</u> - Capes, robes, boots, and all the accessories for snazzy supernatural flair.

<u>**Infernal decorating**</u> - Who do you think finds and cleans all those skulls for the villains' lairs? Not the villains - they've got evil schemes and minions on their minds!

Also includes: Fang Shui for discerning werewolves.

Entrance to both schools conveniently located at the loo in the petrol station across from King's Crossing. Just go between 12 and noon, and slip between the cracks in the floorboards.

Conjure us now! Mediums are standing by.

6

———

## GOD ON THE COUCH

Today felt stranger than usual. Philip Heynman, an experienced psychotherapist with no belief in the supernatural, had no idea why. The strangeness was palpable, and familiar too.

He had just sat down and was reviewing his calendar for today's appointments when the feeling came on. He shook his head - it must be a mistake.

Philip called out the door to his assistant. "Andrew! Who's my next client?"

In that instant a woman appeared on the client couch. "That would be me. I'm God. I'm a higher being and I'm feeling pretty low."

Phil stared at her for a second, his sanity scrambling. He found a hold on the one thing he could understand about this situation. "How did you get in here? Andrew! Come in here!"

His assistant came in, holding an iPad with the day's schedule. "Actually Mr. Heynman, for your next client I'm showing a... Jay Hovah."

"That's what I just told him. Phil, you need to keep up."

Philip fell back on a calm but firm demeanor. "Ma'am, you're not scheduled so I'm afraid you have to leave."

"Where would I go? I'm everywhere."

Phil glanced over at Andrew, who was maintaining a careful lack of expression. "...OK ma'am, so I can see you really need therapy. But you're just going to have to get an appointment like everyone else."

"Check your desk calendar again."

Phil stared at her, not wanting to take the dare. Something about her confidence unsettled him. He was unable to resist his curiosity, and saw now that...Jay Hovah was filled in with gold ink on the piece of paper that had been empty moments before.

"What..."

She leaned over the edge of the couch, sympathetic. "It's a fair amount to grasp, I know. But I need your informed perspective. I just added it. I could have changed your memory too, but that would go against the purpose."

The therapist leaned back in his desk, and blinked a couple of times. Either he'd lost his own mind or this was real. He decided to treat this as if it was real. "Thank you Andrew. That should be all for now."

"Thanks," said Andrew, a bit of relief in his voice as he closed the door behind him.

Philip turned towards the woman on his couch, who for now at least he was going to treat as God. Which meant...treating her? After this session he consider whether and how he might find some treatment for himself. "So what is this purpose you're talking about?"

"Thanks for rallying, Philip. I knew you had it in you. I guess I put it there. But let's just cut through the rest of this doubt. Your real last name is Irvine, you cheated on both of your wives, and you really don't like your son. You are have a prescription pill habit, and you really wish you were painting instead of doing this."

The gradual revelation of his inner secrets hit Philip like series of bombs.

"I can relate," she finished. "That's why I'm here." She made a fist and then held out a hand with a huge diamond in it. "If you help me out, you could get this. Or something better, your choice. Not big enough to be change the world on a large scale. But there's quite a few options before that."

"Oh," said Philip. "But then...why see me?" He spread his hands. "I'd love to be flattered, but I'd hardly believe I'm the best therapist in...in all of existence, forever."

"Time's ticking. Trust me, I picked you for a reason. Just jump right in and get to work."

"You being...who you say you are raises a lot of questions for me. But treating all of this as real...I can see that you're in pain."

She nodded. "Yes. Thank you. You have no idea.."

Feeling foolish, he persisted with what he did know. "How would you describe the pain? On a scale of 1 to 10?"

She smiled sadly. "Infinite."

Philip nodded, and thought. "I imagine it must be difficult, in your ... your job. If all the living things on Earth are all your children, then you are making choices that they die."

She nodded. "Yes, and that's hard. But that's not why I'm here. Life and free will means pain and randomness as well as justice and joy, and death gives meaning to life. That's just the way it has to work."

"Alright. Then why are you here?"

"Because I need someone to tell me the truth. Everyone just kisses my ass. Angels, feh. They're the worst for constructive criticism. I created the sun, that doesn't mean it shines out my every orifice."

"What do you need the truth about?

She puffed her cheeks, as if hesitant to let the words out. She shut here eyes and spoke. "Is it my fault you all are so hung up on perfection?"

Philip found himself a bit more angry than he expected. He saw her eyes peering deep into every thing he was feeling. He sighed. Like he told his other clients often, feelings were never the problem. What mattered was what you did, and what helped that was understanding where the feelings came from.

"I don't know if that's fair," he said at last. "A lot of things go wrong in this world, and a lot of bad things happen to good people, or even innocent people. A lot of things are just random. Our lives are so short...is being upset about that really being hung up on perfection?"

She nodded sadly. "I knew this would be hard for you to take. It's not just you. It's all of your civilization. It seems like in the past couple of thousand years or so, people have developed entirely the wrong idea about being made in my image."

He struggled to be fair to her as a therapist, and understand her perspective. "Are you disappointed that they - that we don't reach your perfection?"

She shook her head sharply. "No. See, that's exactly what I'm talking about. I made people in my image - that means I must not be perfect either. Perfection leaves no room for improvement, for growth. The universe is growing, humans are growing, I'm growing too. How can I not grow? I'm infinite!" She looked deep into him again, and laughed sharply. "Don't be shy, Harold. Say it."

"Wouldn't our being upset with you, as our creator, also be how you made us - to yearn for perfection?"

"So that's my fault too?" She frowned. "That can't be your point."

"What I'm trying to say is, if you made us in your image, wouldn't that also make us like you? Demanding perfection."

She leaned back and closed her eyes. "You could have a point there. My perfectionism made my own wife leave me."

"You were married?" he paused. "To a..."

"We tried counseling. I don't want to talk about it. Look, I sure don't need you giving me crap about it. We both know your history."

"Would it help if I talked to her? Hear her side of things?" Philip's mind went straight to how much money he could make, if he wrote the book of being God and his wife's couples therapist.

God shook his head vehemently. "I would not advise talking to her right now. She can probably hear your every thought too. She will let you know when she wants to talk."

"I'm just ... I didn't think of you having a wife."

"Few of you do, nowadays. Focus. I want to understand why you all can't just...just let me be who I am. I am that I am. And you all want so much from me." She coughed. "Is it that I'm missing something? So I've put myself in a finite space, and come here to you. Tell me what I'm missing." She sighed. "Now here, in this physical body, thinking slow limited thoughts like you, I'm not even sure what I want." She sighed. "Maybe this your chance to diagnose me. Tell me how I can be a better God."

Philip stared at her, his mind racing. How could he possibly be in the perspective of someone whose very intentions could change reality? "I have no idea what it's like to be you. Unless perhaps…"

God laughed and shook her head. "No, you can't give having my job a shot for a while and figure it out. You're a good guy but you're a bit of a control freak. Not happening. Move on."

Phil stood up from his desk, and faced the window as he gathered his thoughts. "Ok. So if I were to give a snap diagnosis - then please forgive me - it's safe to say you have all the same problems we have, except death, right?"

"Right. And no death means it also never ends. Great pep talk, doc."

"You wanted honesty." He began to pace. "Some of us think our biggest problems come from some sort of search for meaning. But from what I've seen, the biggest problems come from just being out of balance. What might be out of balance for you?"

"I…don't really know. Or at least I can't think of it while I'm dealing with human language."

"Okay!" said Phil, relieved. "So there's an action plan at least. Find out what might be out of balance. And I have a theory."

"Well don't keep me waiting, doc."

"It sounds like you might just need to forgive yourself."

She blinked at him. "For what?"

The therapist waved his hands around the room. "For all of this. For everything. Because you made us like you, but we at least have each other to blame. Or you - we can blame it all on you. But you don't really don't have anyone else you can blame your sorrows on, besides yourself."

God took that in. "Ok…how am I supposed to forgive myself?"

"If you're like us, it's going to take a lot of uncomfortable work.

But if you can imagine things like we can, then..." he struggled for the words. How to explain creative effort to an infinite being? This would be the one limitation an omnipotent and omniscient being could have...understanding and changing their infinite selves. God's own efforts could be a stone they could not lift, that they could then lift... and if it was an omnipotent psychological blockage, then they would have to lift it. "Maybe just try to imagine a way to...forgive yourself. Have compassion for yourself. Have loving kindness to, to the lonely parts of yourself. Where you hurt."

God was silent for another momentary eternity, that felt tinged with a lot of sadness. "I don't really know how to do that."

Humor came to Philip, and he smiled. "Just try to see infinity as half full."

She looked at him, and then she laughed. Her glorious laughter filling his heart, as it did for all eternity.

"You know what!" He decided to push his luck with the new thought he just had. "I know you are all-knowing and all-powerful, but that doesn't mean you should still have to take all of the emotional burden. In the stress of decision-making. Have you considered delegation? Having or creating some beings who can take over some of the decision-making from you?"

She looked at him, and began to cry. His heart sank.

"What do you think I created you humans for?" She wiped her eyes. "You're getting better than you used to be, but it's taking so long. I know I deal in eternity's. The pain is also every moment. And it's taking so many moments for you all to get it together." She sighed. "But that's motherhood. It means never giving up." She shook her head. "It just can't be soon enough."

"Even so, does it all have to be work?"

She got up from the couch. "Okay, you know what? Good stuff." She brushed some lint from her dress. "So many universes in the dust motes too...but laughter and love saves everything. Thank you for that. I'm glad I came to you. People make songs about having sympathy for my former employees. Not many people remind me that I can have some sympathy for myself."

Philip smiled. "We all deserve it. That means you too. Maybe even your former employees...but that's not exactly my call to make." He looked down again at his calendar. "Do you...want to schedule for next week?"

"Nah, I think I'm good. I'm gonna go have some fun. Turn some televangelists gay. I love what that does to their free will."

She walked over to Phil and put her hand on his arm. "You, you're about to forget this happened. I'm sorry, you've really done some good to me. I just don't feel like creating any new prophets this century, they usually cause religions and I feel like we're kind of full up right now." She held out her hand, and the giant diamond was again within it. "This or something else?

Phil looked at the diamond, and then in to her eyes. "Maybe..."

She laughed again. "Oh, my Me no. There's no way I'm going let you cheat on your wife with me! Come on now."

Phil smiled. "Alright. Then how about..."

"That's great. Great! Wise choice." The diamond disappeared. "I'll spare you the trouble of phrasing all that. If you apologize right now to your wife and pay more attention to your son, while keeping boundaries that are honest for what you really want, you will have a lumpy and very human form of happiness." She patted him on the cheek. "You will come to this conclusion if you let yourself paint something."

"Thanks God," he said. "I usually don't want my clients that deep in my personal life...but you're already there. Thanks."

She smiled sadly. "You won't mention it." She waved her hand.

Philip blinked. "Who are you?"

"Just someone like you. I was lost and now I'm feeling found. I'll show myself out."

Philip stared after her for a second. "Andrew?" he called.

"Yes?"

"How's my schedule look?"

"The strangest thing," said Andrew. "All of your patients just cancelled. The whole day."

Philip didn't know why it was okay, but that was okay too. He leaned back in his chair and put his hands behind his head. "Thanks Andrew. Take the rest of the day off. With pay."

"Thanks Phil! What are you going to do for the rest of today?"

Philip turned idly in his chair. For no conscious reason he could trace, he quoted one of his favorite parts of the Bible. "'Consider the lilies, how they grow: they toil not, they spin not; and yet I say unto you, that Solomon in all his glory was not arrayed like one of these...' I think I'll make some calls, and then...why, I just might get some paints."

# CHANNEL ADVENTURE

## 7

## GHOST MAGNET

The fading evening light glinted off the dying eyes of drug addicts, in a large and formerly beautiful house in the Sestoretsk district outlying St. Petersburg. The only sober man inside wondered how in hell he'd come to this.

Looking into his past, Aurelian Vyzhivshiy saw little fortune and none of it good. St. Petersburg had quickly given him a choice - steal or starve. He had become a thief, and a good one. Yet his rewards never seemed to match up with his efforts. The last of several scores, a robbery of antique gems from the State Hermitage Museum, had gone so wrong that he only barely escaped.

Now instead of being drunk in a fine hotel like a winning gambler, he hid here in a drug den. His childhood friend Pavel was letting him stay here, for a price – enough rubles for Pavel to get more of a new drug called Prizrak. It was said to be similar to Kokodril, so named because it had turned men's skins scaly like a crocodile before it killed them. Prizrak was simpler and more unsettling, as it seemed to make men rot from inside until they moved like wraiths. The drug had to bring some fantastic kind of high, because once someone got on it, they stayed on it for the rest of their shortened lives.

The door downstairs opened, and cold fresh outside air blew in.

Like any thief who made it to adulthood, he became fully alert. He leaned forward to see who entered. His heart calmed on seeing they were clearly not police, but private citizens – a thin man in his late 50s wearing an immaculate business suit, followed by three larger, younger men in cheap suits.

Those pathetic denizens lying on the floor who were still conscious moved weakly and wearily out of their way like dying and polluted rivers before Moses.

From the railing above, Aurelian watched with hooded eyes. Even though they were not police, their arrival was unsettling. They were all too healthy to be here for the drugs. The younger men all looked big. One was slim and seemed like a viper, another was of a medium size that would easily be ignored in a crowd. The third one who stood closest to the older man had a shaven head, and he looked even bigger than the others. Aurelian decided all three of them must be bodyguards, as they moved with the physical confidence of those used to winning fights.

The older man looked around, and barked an order. The largest of his apparent bodyguards, a shaven-headed hulk of a man, reached down and picked up a particular junkie. They began to ask the addict questions.

Aurelian couldn't hear the conversation, but the fact it was even happening at all was a sign of nothing good. He moved back from the railing and turned to a man seated on the floor, busy staring at nothing with his mind in numbing dreams.

"Pavel!" Aurelian whispered.

The man kept staring.

"Hey!" Aurelian whispered louder, risking alerting others to his presence. Pavel started, and regarded him with glazed and disapproving eyes.

"Who is that?" Aurelian whispered, and pointed to the group who'd just entered.

Pavel leaned forward with strange difficulty, and squinted. "That is Coba," he whispered back. "Mikhail Coba. This is his place."

Aurelian scowled. He had heard of the man. This was no good at all. Mikhail Coba had been a coroner for years, known among the underworld as a man who could make any death look accidental for a fee. Then his wife and children died. He retired from his official job, and found a new career that was entirely illegal - making inconvenient corpses disappear. He showed a legendary effectiveness in this useful service, and had carved out a niche business for St. Petersburg's most brutal crime groups. Grudging respect as a quiet and reliable player allowed him to develop a side business of selling drugs. It made sense that he would create his own lodging house for addicts— not out of sympathy, but as a place for customers to use the goods that slowly killed them, until their flesh gave out and it was time to make their dead husks disappear.

None of which was Aurelian's business. This was only supposed to be a convenient spot to avoid the long reach and cold grip of the St. Petersburg police. "You didn't say this was his place!"

"But it is." Pavel nodded at the wisdom of this, leaned back, and returned to the surcease of the drug.

Aurelian cursed under his breath. He had passage on a freighter to Odessa just before dawn. He had heard that the criminal world in Odessa was even worse than St. Petersburg's; still, there were not yet police waiting to catch him there.

Getting that passage had cost nearly all his hard-stolen money. He had given the remainder to Pavel in exchange for hiding here. All he needed was a simple and uncomplicated place to stay before he headed to the shipyards, and his junkie friend had led him to a drug lord's house. A man who was now going through the house and asking questions of people.

"Why is he asking them questions?" Aurelian whispered. With herculean effort, Pavel mustered enough energy to shrug. "Give me back my money!" Aurelian hissed.

"It's in my arm," Pavel giggled. "It is so good...you must try it."

Aurelian got up to a low crouch and picked up his backpack, with all his remaining possessions in the world. He watched as Coba made his way across the downstairs room, occasionally leaning down to talk to a junkie and then moving forward. Aurelian cursed further as he saw they were heading to the stairs. He stayed in a crouch as he slowly moved away from the top of the stairs. He accidentally stepped on someone's hand, only noticing this on hearing a low moan from a nearly comatose former workman lying in his own filth. Aurelian murmured a reflexive apology, realizing while saying it that the man was unlikely to even hear him. If he were a colder man he'd rob the pathetic bastard of what little he had left before he ran out of this place. He sighed. He never was smart.

He looked in the only open room off the landing, and cursed again. The room had no windows to escape through.

He made it around a corner, successfully out of sight. Mikhail Coba and his crew were halfway up the stairs by the sound of it. He heard an older voice say "That one." Aurelian realized that must be Coba. The man spoke in a flat, clipped Georgian accent. Aurelian liked this even less, if that were possible. Stalin had been a Georgian too. Someone else it hadn't been good to be noticed by.

Aurelian peeked around the corner to see the bald bodyguard and one of the smaller ones pick up an older addict in his sixties. Up close they looked distressingly large, especially next to the addict. His emaciated chest rose and fell with effort, and his arms looked like they could easily slip through their beefy fists. Like they were trying to hold a noodle. Coba took a metal case from his overcoat, about the size of a paperback book. It had old markings on it that looked like Soviet military. From the case he pulled out a hypodermic needle. Coba paused to look at it with great respect, and then moved a half-step forward towards the junkie. Aurelian turned away just as Coba sank the needle into the addict's arm and pushed the plunger.

That didn't make any sense. What drug dealer would give a free drug to someone already addicted?

"Stop wriggling, you old bastard," came one of the younger men's voices. Then Aurelian heard a sudden scream, followed by a rattling moan. That was all the confirmation he needed to decide it was far past time to leave. He put on his backpack and prepared to run.

"Tell me where the basket is," Coba demanded.

*Basket?* Aurelian wondered. Was that some kind of code word or something?

"We... we don't know..." said a scratchy voice. It must have been coming from the skinny old addict. It was unexpectedly coherent, and also strange, as if more than one person was speaking at once.

"Find where," said Coba, "and I will let you have this one."

The apparently crazy old junkie proceeded to argue with himself. The argument ceased, and then every single hair on Aurelian's neck leapt to attention. It felt as if someone stood right next to him, and was staring. He whirled around to check behind him, and saw only junkies gazing into space.

"He knows something about the basket," the addict outside said.

"Who?" said Coba impatiently. "You're pointing the body's arm at the upstairs wall."

"The young man just around the corner on the landing. Aurelian Vyzhivshiy."

Aurelian felt his own jaw drop. How could anyone here know his real name? Pavel didn't even know it!

The heavy footsteps of a bodyguard plodded up the stairs. With no other options, Aurelian stayed crouched and waited until the footsteps were just around the corner. Then he leaped blindly at where the man should be, and rammed his elbows into the chest of a man the size of a bear. Somehow his luck held for once. It had been the medium-sized bodyguard, and he was knocked off balance. The man stumbled, and Aurelian slammed a foot into his side and knocked him back a step. As he fumbled at the top of the stairs and lost his footing, Aurelian rushed past him down the stairs. The two other bodyguards still had their hands somewhat full with the addict they'd picked up off the stairs. The largest one of the three acted quickly enough to let go of the old junkie and throw a ham-sized fist at Aurelian's head, the wind whistling as it barely missed and raising Aurelian's adrenalin. He barely managed to not be there for its intended follow up, and sank a punch right into the guard's crotch in return. By this time the third bodyguard had let go of the old man and pulled out a gun, letting the addict fall like a sack of paste.

Aurelian jumped over the side of the banister. Used to second story exits, he rolled with the impact and shot to his feet, already heading for the front door. "Wait!" Aurelian heard Coba bellow from the stairs. Whatever the coroner-turned-pusher was about to say, Aurelian didn't even waste time to wonder. He hit the cold air of dusk and kept running.

The area was poor and suburban, and offered little cover. It was time to zigzag through the roads and woods and disappear.

If only the damned museum job hadn't gone so bad. He had a place to stay above the store of his mentor in thieving, Volya. It was not much, just a cot in a locked room. Now he couldn't even trust his own bed from police surveillance. It also was just not right to risk police attention on the old man. Volya hadn't exactly saved him out of kindness, but a debt was still a debt. The place didn't have much besides the cot, just some clothes and some books Aurelian had planned someday to read. He could get more books someday. What he missed right now was its warmth.

An hour and a half and nearly two miles later, Aurelian had made it to a more populated area with various soviet-area housing projects. He saw no immediate police, pursuers or robbers, so he felt it safe to slow his pace and start to seek a hole to hide in. Curse this city. He'd been stuck in St. Petersburg for ten years. Russia was supposed to no longer be a dictatorship, yet still there was no way to even leave one city without an official passport to another. He could not even apply, or they would find out he didn't have a passport for St. Petersburg.

All he wanted was a way to get to Moscow. There were gangsters there too, like everywhere. Especially in the government. Still, there he could make real money. Maybe even go legitimate and find work that wasn't hurting others or himself. Here, too much risk for far too little reward. Moscow, that was the dream. Moscow was the gold medal, St. Petersburg was the silver, and there was no bronze.

Frostbite and exposure could kill him just as dead as any bullet. He needed some place to stay warm enough to live until dawn. If this were an American movie about Russia, he might come across some strangers congregating around a fire in a barrel. It must not be that cold in America. No one stayed out at night in alleys here, let alone with barrels to indulge in luxurious public fires. His best bet was to find a stairwell and work from there.

He began to search the block of apartment buildings. Eventually he found one that looked occupied and not too posh, with a trash alley up the side blocked by a fence. It would not do to go in the front entrance. He checked and saw no one observing him, then hopped the fence and ran along the building's side until he reached a fire exit. A quick picked lock and he found himself inside a dark stairwell. He closed his eyes completely for a few seconds so they would adjust, and opened them.

There appeared to be no basement, so he went the opposite direction and headed for the roof. Near the top was a side door that yielded easily to Aurelian's skills. Inside there was a fairly large and empty space. The floor was dirty, but it was at least dry. At the far end was apparently a maintenance man's refuge - a crate, a couple of pornographic magazines and what looked like an electric space heater. That should give off enough heat that he would not die of the cold. He should be happy his luck held this far at all. He plugged in the heater, set down his backpack and leaned against the wall to drink in the heater's comforting warmth. In just a few more hours he could at least be free of this city.

He had just leaned his head back to try and catch some rest, when he was shocked upright by a crawling sensation all over his neck and head. It was the same feeling as he'd had in the drug house. He looked around frantically. There was no one and nothing near him that he could see.

"There," he heard a voice outside, just past the room's door. A moment later it was kicked open.

It was Coba and his three bears. The bodyguards drew guns, and fixed them on Aurelian. The largest one, the one he'd kicked at the top of the stairs, came towards him. He looked rather angry, probably at how easily Aurelian had slipped past him.

Aurelian had no option but to look unsurprised. "Help you?" he asked, rising to his feet as nonchalantly as he could.

Coba looked at him for a second, and then laughed. "So cool, so cool," he added. "Mr. Vyzhivshiy, let's talk about some things."

"And spread your arms in the air while you do it," growled the biggest bodyguard. "You won't be able to sneak a punch this time."

Aurelian felt his defiance rise, even as he raised his hands. "What, I should give you warning? Have you seen how big you are?"

"I'm not here to discuss boxing rules," said Coba. "Where is the basket?"

Aurelian shook his head. "No bullshit. I really don't know what you're talking about."

Coba sighed, and pointed to the bodyguard Aurelian had kicked at the top of the stairs. "Vasily, check his backpack."

Aurelian examined the man as he holstered his gun and walked over. He was clearly professional, taking care not to cross the first bear's line of sight. Pragmatic, Aurelian gave the man no resistance as he took off Aurelian's backpack and dumped its contents onto the room's filthy floor.

The man poked through all Aurelian had in the world. It didn't take long. "Not here," he said.

"Disappointing," said Coba. "Where is it?"

"I don't even know what you're looking for, how can I know where it is?"

Coba shook his head impatiently. "Don't waste my time. I have it on very good authority you are connected to the basket."

Aurelian laughed as if the matter were light as falling snow. "What authority? Because they apparently know something I don't know."

"That authority with no reason to lie," growled the larger, angrier bodyguard. "The dead, who you will soon join."

"Nikolai, be quiet," said Coba. "Aurelian, just tell us where the basket is, and I will let you leave my city on the *Visigoth* at dawn."

Aurelian tried to keep his face from showing the shock he felt. How had this man known his plans to that degree—down to the name of the ship? He attempted to master his growing dismay. "If there is some connection I have to some basket, I am not aware of it. If you know my plans to that degree, you should know that too."

Coba considered him. "It is strange that there aren't more details for that," he admitted. "Still my...sources have never lied." He nodded to his men. "Bring him. We will sort this out." The ex-coroner turned his back and ventured to leave.

Aurelian looked at the approaching bodyguards as calmly as he could. His odds were bad enough in this enclosed room. Once they took him God knows where, his odds of survival shrank to microscopic levels.

The giant Nikolai pointed his gun at Aurelian's legs, and smiled. "Try to run," he sneered. "I would quite enjoy that." The bodyguard named Vasily approached behind him, took Aurelian's left arm down from its raised position, and then took his right arm to cuff it.

Aurelian dropped and then spun to his right, grabbing and pulling the second bodyguard with him. Nikolai fired, but didn't hit Aurelian. Instead a wet splash of blood erupted from the side of Vasily's kneecap. He screamed in pain as Aurelian threw him at the first bear and ran for his life.

For once Aurelian's luck almost held. But as he sprinted past the third bodyguard, the man reached backwards with just enough impact to push him into the room's wall. This gave Nikolai enough time to catch him by the back of his head and then pull his arm behind his back.

The bastard increased pressure on Aurelian's arm until it almost broke. Aurelian gasped.

"You like that, bug?" the giant asked, smiling as if he was picking flowers.

"Fuck your mother!" Aurelian said through gritted teeth.

"Your grandmother Irina says hello," said Nikolai, and laughed.

Aurelian stared. He hadn't spoken of his grandmother to anyone in almost ten years! How did this stranger know her name?

"Good night, cockroach." Their conversation concluded, he introduced Aurelian's head to the wall and then to darkness.

AURELIAN AWOKE TO find himself looking at a broken vial held in a soft and slender hand. The vial was the sort that was used to wake people up. The hand looked female. The world was also on its side.

He realized he was lying on a bed. His eyes trailed from the hand up its arm to the hand's owner, a slim young woman with a graceful form. Her long black hair fell on either side of a simple white dress. Her deep brown eyes looked back at him.

As his consciousness returned she moved back, sat in a nearby chair and looked away, examining her nails. "You're a mess," she said.

He moved his head first, and then his arms. His hands weren't tied. He looked down at his own jacket. Apparently some of the floor's filth had gotten on it, as well as some dried blood. He touched the side of his head, and winced. He felt it again, more carefully. A rather nasty scrape, but nothing seemed broken.

"Yes, he is a mess," agreed the voice to his left. Aurelian was disappointed but not surprised to see the bodyguard who'd knocked him out. There he was, as sure as life's injustice. "Go tell Mikhail he is awake," the bear ordered.

"I woke him up. You go tell him," she responded, and began filing her nails.

Nikolai growled. "Do you want to find out who is in charge here?"

She returned his gaze with cold indifference. "I believe I already know. Would you like to find out which of us he would replace?"

Aurelian saw a vein start to pulse in the man's forehead, but heard only silence. After a moment Nikolai stood up and left the room.

"What do you do here?" asked Aurelian.

"What I don't do is answer your questions," she said.

Mikhail Coba entered the room. Nikolai followed, pushing a decrepit man who moved with awkward, shuffling steps. This walking husk looked even worse than the last addict Aurelian had seen them interrogating.

He realized it was someone he knew. "Pavel?" Aurelian asked softly.

Coba chuckled. "You knew him? Well there's not much of him left. But we'll get as much as we can before we start a new one."

Pavel's skin was turning colors as they spoke, spots of deep unhealthy red spreading and slowly changing at the edges to greens and purples. From his mouth came short puffs of breath, each seeming another gasp of life fleeing his body.

"Those inside, come to the surface," Coba commanded.

"Aurelian," the voice came from the addict's mouth. "You must tell them." Pavel's voice sounded more than a little odd. Yet some part of the oddness was so familiar. Aurelian didn't like it at all.

"Pavel, stop playing around to get your fix. These guys are serious," He faced Mikhail. "What garbage is this? This junkie knows nothing about me."

"The junkie isn't talking," Coba said. "Listen harder."

"Aurelian," the voice continued to emerge from Pavel's sinking face. "Remember our summers in the country? Before I had to die." The voice broke. "Do as this Coba says. Let me leave this world to find peace. Don't make me see you die too."

Aurelian's jaw dropped.

It was his grandmother's voice. He had attended her funeral ten years ago, before he ran away from his so-called home, never to return.

"Tell us, idiot!" Nikolai bellowed. Aurelian turned towards the sound of the bodyguard's voice out of instinct, but the words didn't really register. He slowly turned back to Pavel's dying form.

"Tell him!" continued the voice of his long-dead grandmother, continuing to mix oddly with Pavel's voice. "Tell him where the basket is, so I can be free!"

Aurelian shook his head. "What kind of shit is—?"

"Yes, this is really happening," Coba cut in, with a bored tone of having said things many times before. "Where is the basket?"

Aurelian swallowed. "What?"

Coba slapped him. "You don't appear to be concussed. Try harder."

Aurelian stared. He tried to speak, and words failed him. He tried again. "You bring me here—after teaching that, that crawling, crippled snake to reproduce the voice of my dead grandmother? And you ask me about a basket?"

"He is not too quick, this one," the girl said.

Defiance rose in Aurelian's mind, giving him an anchor to cling to in this storm of unreality. "Fuck you, bitch, no one asked you shit. Maybe you should hear a cheap imitation of your dead grandmother and have stupid questions thrown at you, then you can talk."

"I hear everyone's dead grandmother," she said, and went back to filing her nails.

"Good for you," said Aurelian. He faced Coba. "I don't have any reason to lie to you, and I don't have any idea what you're talking about. However you're doing these stupid parlor tricks, they're a waste of time. I'm a thief, and a good one. I don't steal baskets."

Coba examined him thoughtfully. "You inside the husk, he seems to be telling the truth. Explain this."

Another voice spoke from Pavel's voice box. "He knows something he does not know. He is connected. Perhaps someone else he knows, knows more. We have done all we can. Let us feed!"

"Stop playing games, Pavel, or I'll break your fucking neck!" Aurelian yelled.

Coba caught Nikolai's eye, and indicated Aurelian. "Go to my police contacts, and find his known associates."

Nikolai looked a bit relieved. "I shall go check right now."

Mikhail held up a finger. "Not just yet. See this before you go. It's a little different every time." He smiled at Aurelian. "You watch also, thief. It is most instructive." He addressed what Aurelian had once known as Pavel. "Our bargain is complete. You may feed."

A deep sigh emerged from Pavel's face, that Aurelian could swear had the tone of many voices. Pavel's body then began to crumble from within. A smoke emerged from his form as the bones beneath his skin fell in on themselves. His body didn't drop so much as it gradually lost the mass to stand. The smell was the most disturbing of all—a dry, ashy smell, with no life left in it. The last to go was his skin, some of which remained in a pile mixed in with the man's clothes.

Aurelian looked at the remains, and then to the bodyguard. Their eyes met, for once without anger or contempt. Nikolai's face held a deep revulsion that could only come from seeing such a thing many times before.

Coba smiled with satisfaction. "Just so you know what kind of man I am, and what I can do."

"What those you deal with can do," the girl corrected.

Coba glared at her for a moment, then resumed as if she hadn't spoken. "Thief, you had better search that scrambled young mind of yours and tell me how to find this. It is a wicker basket, brown, and about sixty years old. It will have a bit of red paint on the inside near the handle, which covers a hidden pocket."

The girl spoke. "You will have a better chance of surviving if you accept that this is real. Not a great chance, but at least better."

Aurelian put a great amount of effort into it, and managed to clear his mind. "I need to speak again with that—that thing that says it is my grandmother," he said finally.

"You should not have asked for that," said the girl.

Coba smiled. "We can arrange that. But we don't want to do that just yet. Lyita, it is time for you to earn some of your keep."

Lyita stood, and put her fingernail file on the chair behind her. "I hate you," she said, in the same flat tone as a butcher might say "That slice of meat will cost you seven rubles."

"What is this even about?" asked an agitated Aurelian. "You can at least tell me that! How will that harm you?"

"Very well," Coba's eyes sparkled. "One day, when I was still a coroner, a body came across my table - so old and melted, it seemed it must have laid there for centuries. Yet from a journal in his coat pocket, he had lived up until the day before. In his notes I read rumors and hints of a project long ago. With the help of my current associates, I broke into his apartment and found the drug which killed him. Used sparingly, it enables me to do this." He waved at Pavel's remains. "Summon ghosts to worthless flesh like this. Where, in return for the joy of human sensation, they follow my commands." he rubbed his hands. "If a man like cannot be useful while living, he will be made useful before he is consumed. This fate awaits you, if you keep me from what I want."

The older man reached inside his coat.

Aurelian launched off the cot to grab what Coba reached for, and barely caught it by his fingertips. It was the same case he'd seen back at Coba's drug house. Coba dived to grab it back but missed. Aurelian scrambled to open it, and retrieved the only syringe inside. Just in time he held it needle first at Coba, who backed away.

Fear bloomed in the old man's eyes. "Be careful. You don't know what you're doing with that."

"Just stay back!" warned Aurelian. "Or you'll see how much you like it!"

"Get out of the way, sir!" Nikolai declared as he drew his gun.

"That's the last one, don't let him waste it!" Coba demanded.

Aurelian held the needle against the wall. "I'll smash it, how's that? You'd better let me out of here."

The bodyguard placed a large hand on Coba's shoulder and easily moved him to the side, pointing the gun in his other hand at Aurelian's face. He held it still and advanced slowly. "How are you going to get out of here and keep that needle against the wall, cockroach?"

"I'll trade you the gun for it."

The bodyguard gave vent to a short bark of laughter. "I'm not an idiot."

Aurelian didn't argue the point. "Drop your ammo clip, and give me the gun. I'll give you the needle and leave. I don't need to be a part of any of this crap."

"Just get the needle back, dammit!" Coba screamed.

Nikolai paused. He held his free hand out to Aurelian palm forward, and pointed the gun to the ceiling. He pressed the clip release on the gun with his other hand, grabbed the clip and pocketed it. Then he flipped the gun, and offered it grip-first to Aurelian.

Aurelian very carefully reached forward for the gun, with his other hand still holding the needle against the wall.

The bodyguard dropped the gun, grabbed Aurelian's wrist, and yanked him forward.

Guessing what was coming next, Aurelian got the needle in front of his face just before the giant's fist came in. The needle stabbed deep into the flesh between Nikolai's knuckles and the plunger was pushed in from the force.

"No!" said the man, jumping back with sudden shock and staring at the syringe now protruding from his hand. "No!"

"Damn you!" said Coba.

The bodyguard fell to the ground and began to twitch. Just as with the old junkie in the drug house, he gave vent to a bloodcurdling scream.

Aurelian grabbed the gun, snatched the ammo clip from the twitching man's pocket, and slammed it back in the gun. He aimed at Coba. "Get out of the way. I'm leaving."

"You wasted it!" cried Coba. "You'll pay for this!"

"Keep talking. I have the gun." Aurelian turned to the girl. "Let's go!"

She blinked. "What for? He will just find you again. Your grandmother's ghost will know."

"How did you get involved in this?" Aurelian demanded.

"He has my parents' souls under his thumb. Same as your grandmother."

Aurelian went pale. "Is that what you are doing, you damn vulture? The one good woman in my life?"

Coba sneered. "Yes. Kill me and she doesn't even go to Hell. She stays unliving and alone in St. Petersburg for all eternity."

Aurelian's finger tightened on the trigger. He just couldn't bring himself to do it. Coba smiled.

"Just stay away from me!" Aurelian yelled, and fled upstairs.

It was the same drug dacha. Here was the same living room he'd run through last night. The other two bodyguards were lounging on couches, engaged with a couple of low-grade whores. The kind who didn't mind the ambiance of people dying in their own filth as long as they weren't competition for the coke. The slightly larger of the two, the bodyguard named Vasily, now had a heavy bandage on his leg. He saw Aurelian and reached for his gun, to be stopped by a warning motion from Aurelian.

"I'd check on your boss if I were you!" he yelled at them. That seemed to stall them just long enough for him to make the corner of the hallway and hit the door.

Out he ran. This time it was into morning sunlight. This time there were a couple of civilians on the street, probably on their way to jobs that might even be honest. He put the gun inside his jacket and walked quickly, looking for a crowd he might be able to fade into. He found small but sufficient amount of people waiting at a bus stop. A bus pulled up and he entered by the back door, hoping that he would not be asked to pay.

The bus was headed to the center of the city. He found a seat and gathered his thoughts as best he could. Once again he was out in the open, this time without even any of his possessions. His last way out of the city was gone — the ship must have sailed hours ago. His old cot above Volya's place was as bad a thought as ever.

There was only one thing he could try. Find the first payphone he could, and call the Finnlander. He lacked even the coin to pay for this bus ride. Could his luck let up on him once? What kind of gypsy had he fucked over to deserve this? This brought him uncomfortably close to thinking about his dead grandmother. He stuffed those thoughts deep inside. They were useless right now.

He needed to contact the Finnlander. How?

He placed his hand over the gun's cold metal in his coat pocket. It gave him a feeling of security. It was the only thing he had that was worth any money at all. He was either going to have to rob someone with it or he was going to have to sell it. Both by personal preference and by skills, he was a thief but not a robber.

He got off just outside the city center, and began to look. It was harder to find fellow criminals in the morning, but after some time he was able to find a man interested in his stolen .45. The money was an insulting pittance, but he now could make a call. He found one of the few remaining payphone booths in a dumpy bar that was just opening for an incoming crowd of laborers, and called the Finnlander. The man picked up on the third ring.

"Hello," said Aurelian. "Is Alexandra there?" This was their prearranged code if they got separated after the robbery, which they had been—by police that came way too quickly, thanks to the Finnlander's failure to retrieve the right alarm codes.

"She's at the opera. Can I help you with something?"

"There's a book I need. Can you bring it to the corner of Gubina and Promyshlennya?" By previous agreement, any places mentioned on the phone were off by five blocks north and three blocks west.

"Sure," said the Finnlander, in a baffled sort of tone. "What book?"

"Any book," Aurelian snapped. "Just bring it." Then he realized something. "Do you happen to have any baskets?"

"No," the surprised voice said. "Just—well this old wicker thing that came with the apartment. You've seen it before."

"Bullshit!" said Aurelian.

"On the mantelpiece. You knocked it over when you were drunk, and complained about how old and dirty it was. Why?"

Aurelian did remember it—a worthless-looking wicker piece of shit, dry and cracking with age.

"Burn that basket," he said. "I'm not joking. Do it right now."

"Why?"

"You wouldn't believe me if I told you. Just do it! And stay away from Coba!"

"Coba? Are you involved with him?"

Aurelian closed his eyes. "I don't want to be."

"That's good, don't contact him," said the Finn. "I hear he has many contacts in the police. Also it's whispered he killed his wife and daughter to make his life more simple. You're better off if he never even learns your name."

"I'll keep that in mind," Aurelian said numbly. "Just meet me in half an hour."

He hung up and left the bar. By hurrying, he was able to reach a viewing point near the meeting spot in fifteen minutes. He bided his time in constant movement, walking around to peer around the corner at the meeting site every few minutes until the time came.

Seven minutes before they were supposed to meet, he saw the Finnlander arrive. The man was wisely doing the same thing that Aurelian had been, checking around to see if anyone else might be seeing them.

The Finn also held a brown paper bag. Aurelian was about to wave and catch his eye—when he saw the Finn glance to his right and give a light nod. Aurelian followed his glance, and saw a parked black van. Of the shadowy shapes showing through the windshield, one looked just like...

Aurelian's fists clenched. The bastard had sold him out to Coba. From the mere mention of Coba's name! Had Finn just sold them all out at the museum robbery too? Was that why the alarms had gone off, and why the Finn himself hadn't gone into hiding?

Then Aurelian felt that cold feeling all along the back of his neck again. He ran through the city's streets, not knowing where he should even go.

After another fifteen minutes of running his side began to ache. He found a place behind a parked delivery truck. He hoped at least to have a few minutes here before he would need to run again.

Where previously he had been in the position of choosing between jail or starting over in Odessa...he was now in the position of choosing between jail and death.

They could apparently find him no matter what. If he was in jail, at least Coba might not be able to get to him. Perhaps Aurelian would only get a couple of years, and not be put in with too many murderers. Maybe, just maybe, if his luck held to a degree it never had before, whatever this strangeness was would be all blown over by the time his sentence would be done.

There was nothing else to it. Any other decision was just increasing the chance Coba would catch him first.

He sighed and walked towards the nearest police station. He knew where it was by heart, after having avoided it as much as he could since he'd first come to this city. It took less time to get there than he'd expected. Or maybe he was just enjoying his last breaths of free air too much.

On the last corner before the station stood Lyita, waiting for him. He knew what else must be waiting, and looked around until he found it. At the opposite corner was a black van, with Vasily leaning against it on his good leg as he smoked. Inside the van there would no doubt be Coba himself, and perhaps the Finnlander was well.

They were still in public and in daylight. Even with Coba's police connections, Aurelian doubted they would try to kidnap or shoot him here. In any case his best odds still applied. Jail over death.

"Out of my way," he said to Lyita as he walked forward.

"I cannot," Lyita said. "He has my parents."

"Not my problem."

"He has your grandmother too."

"Bullshit!" Aurelian snarled. "Out of my way!"

"You now will see why Coba keeps me." She stiffened, and her eyes rolled back in her head to show pure white. Her posture softened to that of an old woman stooped with the weight of hard years.

"Aurelian," he heard his grandmother's voice again. This time it was mixed with Lyita's voice, and with less harshness. "You must not go to jail. You will die!"

"I will fucking kill you, Lyita!" Aurelian shouted. A couple of passersby looked their way. "I don't care anymore. I'm going to jail anyway!"

"Everyone must die, Grandson," the voice continued. "But you must not so soon, and not for this. If you die now, then this girl will also die, and many others will die, all for nothing - and then be trapped like me."

He could only accept that that was his grandmother's voice. No one could have possibly known her mannerisms, her tones, the look in her eyes. So many things he had not even remembered until now, shown on this younger woman's frame like a movie on a screen. "How can this be? What has been done to you?"

"I am stuck between worlds," his grandmother's voice sad with sadness. "After my death I could feel the beyond freedom, whether it was something or nothingness. Before I could reach out to it, I was drawn into a prison instead. I touch nothing, taste nothing, feel nothing, see and hear nothing. I can only break free to inhabit someone else's flesh, like I am now." Lyita's solid white eyes began to wet. "You cannot imagine what this is like. You cannot let him keep doing this to me. You cannot let him do this to others. We dead cannot rest until we're free." Tears that were not Lyita's rolled down her cheeks. "I named you, you know."

He laughed in spite of himself, tears starting in his own eyes. He remembered that story now. "You said 'Aurelian' was from church Latin. I was your little golden one."

She pointed a finger at him. "Aurelian was a Roman emperor as well, towards the end of their empire. He tried as best he could. You were a good boy once. Do the right thing. Do not die and the join us in our torture as one ashamed." Her voice softened. "I would not have that for you, Grandson. I will not allow it."

Aurelian said nothing as Lyita's posture returned to that of a young woman, now a bit shaken. Her eyes returned to normal, and she wiped away the tears that were not hers.

They stood staring at each other for a second.

Wearily, Aurelian walked to the waiting van.

Vasily the bodyguard sneered, tossed aside his cigarette, and winced as he put weight back on his wounded leg. The cigarette died with a quick puff in the snow as he hobbled over to the side of the van and slid the back door open. Aurelian stepped in, to find waiting for him on bench seats Coba, the Finnlander as he'd half-expected… and what was once Nikolai.

"He knows we're not who this body was," a voice cackled. The eyes of Nikolai's former body were bloodshot, and the skin around them had begun to take on a greenish tinge. "Hee hee! The fear he has! We love this! It's been so long…please more healthy bodies Coba…"

Vasily slid the door shut, and made his way to the driver's seat. "Straight to the dig," Coba declared. They took off. It was too late for Aurelian to reconsider now.

Coba faced Aurelian. "I didn't expect you would think of going straight to jail. That was almost clever. It still would not have stopped me of course."

Aurelian tried to shrug, hemmed in as he was by hopelessness. "Why do you even need me along?"

"You will find out soon enough."

"Fuck you, you pimp of the dead."

Far from offended, Coba laughed. He turned to the Finnlander. "Do you have it?"

The Finn opened the bag to show the crappy wicker basket Aurelian had seen when he was drunk.

"I told you to get rid of that, you fool!" Aurelian exclaimed.

The Finn gave him a superior smile. "You never did understand business." He handed the tired-looking object to Coba, who produced a pocket knife and began to probe inside it.

Something else clicked into place for Aurelian. "You went back after the bust, and stole for yourself!"

"Yes, after the police took care of the partners I'd have to split it with." The Finn laughed. "You all thought yourselves so smart."

Aurelian itched to stuff that laugh down his throat with his fists. He lunged at Coba, and was pushed back by the Nikolai-thing's big hands.

Coba laughed. "The squabbles of petty thieves, as we near the potential of such a great reward...Ah! " He ripped open the dried and brittle wicker, to reveal a strip of paper. It had a series of numbers in faded black ink. "At last!" Coba looked at it for a moment with pure love, and put it inside his suit. He rubbed his hands. "This will all work so well!"

The van slowed to a stop. The bodyguard named Vasily turned around from the driver's seat, to point a gun straight at him. Coba took this moment to hand Aurelian some handcuffs.

"Put these on. Behind your back." Aurelian hesitated only as long as it took for the bodyguard to nudge the air with his gun. "You too, Lyita. It will make those pretty breasts of yours pop out quite appealingly." She looked at Coba as if he was some entirely new form of filth she'd found stuck to her shoe.

The Finn coughed. "Now, about my payment."

"Indeed." Coba produced another pair of handcuffs and tossed them onto the Finn's lap.

Aurelian had the small but still substantial satisfaction of seeing the Finn's eyes gape wide. "We had a deal!"

Coba shrugged. "You are a young snake. An old snake does not keep deals with young snakes. That is how a snake gets to be old."

"Can I just kill him?" asked the altered Nikolai. It giggled in childish glee. "I so would like to kill him!"

"If he doesn't put those cuffs on, do whatever you like." Coba fixed the Finn with a stare. Red-faced, the Finn put on the handcuffs.

The three of them were led out of the van in the now late-morning sun. It was warm for a winter's day in St. Petersburg, only ten degrees below freezing. They were in the courtyard of some abandoned apartment complex among many at the eastern edge of the city, where few even bothered to squat.

"In there." Coba pointed to a doorway. Aurelian wondered if they were being marched in to die.

They came into the small living room of some Soviet bureaucrat's former apartment. On an abandoned bookcase lay several miner's helmets. In the middle of the room was a large hole cut through the floor and into apparent dirt below, with a cheap ladder poking out. A hint of a smell came up from the hole, a vile perfume that mixed mildew and...the smell Pavel's body had given as he was eaten by the ghosts.

Coba pointed to the bodyguard named Vasily. "Lead the way."

"On this leg?" he protested.

"Do you want to partake in the rewards or not?"

The wounded bodyguard cursed, and hobbled over to the abandoned bookcase. He took one of the miner's helmets, and threw the other to Coba.

"What happened to your third bear?" asked Aurelian, with nothing to lose.

"Shut it," Vasily snarled.

"We'll find him soon enough," said Coba. "First things first."

"He didn't like what we do with this body," said the thing called Nikolai. It giggled. "Maybe he will die soon and join us in this feast."

Vasily turned his helmet light on, holstered his pistol and started awkwardly down the ladder, favoring his wounded leg.

"Go on." Coba motioned with his own pistol.

This was worse than the last time Aurelian had been trapped in a room with them. If he had to die, he would rather it was up here. Lyita's eyes pleaded with him. His grandmother's most recent words stayed with him.

Silently Aurelian went over to the pit in the middle of the room, and climbed down the ladder. He was followed by Lyita. Behind her was the Finn, the ghoulish remains of Nikolai, and finally Coba.

The ladder descended through a rough dirt tunnel into a chamber. Aurelian jumped the last ten feet and whirled around, hoping to catch Vasily by surprise. The bodyguard was ready for him, and sneered from across the room with his pistol back in his hand. Aurelian sighed and examined the rest of the room. Vasily's helmet lamp illuminated concrete floors and a roughly poured concrete floor. At the far end of the room was a spiral staircase made of aged lumber.

The rest of their strange company came down the ladder. Vasily went first down the stairs, and with without words they followed, deeper into the earth. Aurelian wondered if the creaking wooden staircase would continue to withstand their weight. He and Lyita were light at least. If Coba, his servants or Finn fell through it wouldn't exactly break his heart. After a story or two the lumber gave way to painted steel. It was still rusty in some places, but altogether much more sturdy.

He began to hear giggling from the thing that once was Nikolai. "It's here, we're almost here. Our body can get in, we can free our souls!"

"Do be quiet," Coba commanded.

"Or what?" a second voice from the giant body muttered. It was immediately answered by another voice from the same body, "Shh, not now." "We're so close," a third agreed. Aurelian wondered if Coba heard the exchange. He had no idea what their deal was, but if he were Coba that would begin to concern him.

Then something occurred to him which concerned him more directly. The ghosts might soon want another meal after this bodyguard. That meal could be him.

One last flight and they came to the end of the stairs. Coba flicked on a battery-powered work light, illuminating a concrete sub-basement reinforced with steel girders. The walls nearest them were covered in Stalin-era posters, including a rather grim mural showing the Supreme Soviet encircling the world. At the other end of the room from stood a door that would do credit to a bank vault. The smell of death was slightly stronger – unless it was just that they were in close quarters with Coba's ghoulish bodyguard.

"What's this?" asked the Finn.

"This is where you die, hee hee," said the bodyguard.

"Shush," said Coba, in bored tones. He pointed to Aurelian and the Finn. "You two fools get against the vault."

"Like shit!" said Aurelian. Vasily slammed the butt of his pistol into the side of Aurelian's head. Dazed, he fell halfway to the ground. He twisted and jumped back up, ramming his shoulder directly into the man's gut right below his sternum. Vasily flew backward, slamming into the wall himself. His pistol went off, ricocheting the bullet around the room. Everyone ducked as the bullet bounced and chips of concrete went flying.

Aurelian kicked at the man's bandaged kneecap. The man screamed in pain and leveled a gun directly at Aurelian.

"Stop!" said Coba. "Don't kill him yet. Are you crazy? We need them both alive. Unless you want to take his place?"

"Stop with your bullshit," growled Vasily. "I don't understand every crazy thing that's going on here, but this street trash dies now."

The massive bodyguard now owned by ghosts stepped between them. It reached out with blinding speed to grab the guard's hand holding the gun. "It feels so good to move flesh!" a voice said. "Careful, you'll rip the muscles moving them that fast," came another. "So use them up!" added a third. "It feels so good to have flesh again!" chimed in yet another voice.

Vasily tried to free his hand from the possessed giant's fist, and found he could not. With his free arm he punched the creature in the stomach. A volume of air emerged from its open mouth, and then a small bit of puke.

The giant's only reaction was to smile. "Yes! Make us feel some more! Pain is wonderful. Feeling anything is wonderful."

"Later," said Coba. "Give me Vasily's gun and let him go."

The giant sighed in several voices at once, took the gun and tossed it to Coba. It then shoved the bodyguard away and laughed to see him bounce unsteadily off the wall to the floor. Nikolai's head swung down to examine the hands of the body they possessed, and smiled in satisfaction as it closed them into fists. Nikolai's head then smiled at the downed bodyguard.

Coba addressed the downed bodyguard. "You. You! Cripple. Look at me." Vasily dragged his eyes away from the horror's smile with some effort. "Get up and uncuff Aurelian and that Finnlander, if you know what's good for you."

The bodyguard managed to climb to his feet, hobbled over and uncuffed Aurelian and then the Finn.

"Now, each of you fools stand on one of those plates." Coba pointed at the floor near the vault door. Aurelian saw two metal semi-circles that extended from beneath the vault's door.

"You stand there," said Aurelian.

Coba sighed and addressed the giant. "Hold them there. I promise you all the bodies you could ever want. If this succeeds, we will all have our needs fulfilled."

The former bodyguards' former hands grabbed Aurelian and the Finnlander each by the neck, and held them against the wall over the plates. "Like this?" it said, the body's corrupted breath washing across Aurelian's face and roiled his stomach.

"Yes," said Coba. He went over to a steel beam and examined it briefly, then pressed on a particular rivet. He smiled in satisfaction as, in front of Aurelian and the Finnlander two metal panels slid aside. They held a series of switches with numbers painted next to them.

"Some kind of fuse box?" said Aurelian, baffled.

"Of a sort," Coba chuckled unpleasantly as he produced the strip of paper he'd retrieved from the basket. "Two of the poor bastards who built this made a way they could sneak back again, if their fortunes changed and they were locked out by their superiors. Now you two peasants have one chance to live through this. Each of you set each switch to the right number at the same time, and then pull down the final switch. If you have set it wrong then you will both be electrocuted."

"And what if we don't?" said Aurelian.

Coba shrugged. "Then we shoot you both, and Vasily and Lyita give it a try."

Vasily growled. "I strongly advise you to do as he says."

"We had a deal!" the Finnlander said.

"Don't live in the past." Silence filled the small space. "All discussions finished?" Coba turned to the strip of paper. "Enter 5, 17, 7! Then wait for my mark."

Aurelian and the Finn followed his orders. Hating that his life depended on the Finnlander, Aurelian watched his eyes carefully. "Listen to me Coba, you son of a bitch," said Aurelian. "My ass is on the line, so I give the mark."

Coba smiled and nodded, indulgently. "Why not."

Aurelian faced the Finn. "You pull that switch down right when I say 'four'. Not after 'four', but exactly at the same time 'four' leaves my lips. Got it?"

Too fearful for wisecracks or betrayal, the Finn nodded.

"One, two, three, *four*!"

A light charge of electricity came through Aurelian's fingers. He leaped back off of the pad.

In a few seconds there came a light rumbling. Lights turned in the ceiling above the doorway flickered on, and the vault slid back to reveal a cavernous space, close to 50 feet high and 200 feet across.

The possessed bodyguard contemptuously pushed them backward, and they stumbled in.

It had the still air of decades to it—and the same smell that had come from the old junkie, from Pavel and now from Nikolai, mixed in with the choking remains of easily a dozen bodies, long desiccated. They had not been reached by rats or maggots, and seemed to have mostly melted into the floor.

Beyond the bodies lay what appeared to be some kind of electronics laboratory. In the middle of the room stood a half sphere about thirty feet in height. Around its base were several large stacks of wires and components, consisting of wires and tubes and the occasional jumping spark. Above, the rest of the sphere was completed by a shimmering blue light. Arcs of something that looked similar to electricity swirled around it.

The sphere itself contained fluid that seemed very much like what Aurelian had seen inside Coba's hypodermics. Wisps shot through it, at least tens of thousands, numbers impossible to count, moving with what seemed to be their own will. Many of the quick-moving flashes would bang repeatedly into the shimmering blue light surface of the sphere, to strike sparks which then repelled them back to the center. Behind it was a large semi-circle of sheet-metal housings, and a console connected to the sphere with a series of conduits running along the floor.

Every few moments a wisp would break through and get a few feet past the sphere and then stay there, flickering as if striving against an intense pull. They too would be sucked back into the sphere. At the edge of the shell new wisps would also wink into visibility, while they were already being pulled in.

Aurelian turned and noted Lyita's face. Her eyes were on the sphere itself, and were filled with longing.

"Is that...?" he began.

"Yes, that is where her parents, your grandmother, and many others are kept," said Coba. "Is it not magnificent!"

"What the hell is it?"

Coba laughed. "The Ghost Magnet. I knew it was real!" He

rubbed his hands together and practically skipped over several mummified corpses to see the device more closely. He briefly basked in its light, and then lovingly ran his hands over the surface of an instrument panel. Aurelian noticed that the entire time he never got closer than a certain radius from the sphere that also was clear of bodies. He sighed happily. "At last I am here!"

Lyita spoke, her voice flat. "Stalin had many secret projects. As he aged, he became particularly fascinated with death. He knew how to properly motivate his lessers—he set scientists to conquer death or die. All failed. This one group found an interesting something by accident — a way to attract and harness the power of ghosts."

"And here we are," Vasily said at last. "Now we can really get some power."

"You sons of bitches should rot in seven separate hells," Lyita said without emotion.

Coba walked over to Lyita and took her chin in his hand. "Come now! Don't be petty. Respect the beauty of this moment! Many thousands of psychics were spared execution, to give their worthless lives for this. Their brains harvested for the compounds that help ghosts enter their brains. Now we have not only a new source of that serum - we have the sphere that traps them within itself! An army of ghosts to do our will!" He let go of Lyita, and frowned at Aurelian. "And we almost didn't get here at all, after you wasted that syringe on Nikolai," he added reproachfully.

Aurelian laughed incredulously. "Am I supposed to feel bad about that?"

"It is fine," said Coba, in a tone magnanimous with victory. "It has all worked out for the best."

"My grandmother died in a hospital in St. Petersburg," Aurelian said with dawning comprehension. "Is that how her soul..."

Coba gave an abrupt dismissal with his hand. "I can't say soul or spirit. But her ghost is in there. She can only escape temporarily to another body, if a mind is open to her—and when that connection ends she is drawn straight back to the Ghost Magnet."

Aurelian saw that the corpses littering the floor wore moldering lab coats. Some appeared to have been partially eaten, perhaps by others. "Whatever happened here, it doesn't seem to have worked out well for these people."

Coba chuckled. "Indeed. When Stalin died, direct knowledge of this facility went with him. These scientists starved to death with no one to come and let them out. Their ghosts must still be in that sphere as well. That basket held the only code in. Any wrong code, and the entire place would blow." He shook his head. "So much work to at last find someone living who had seen that basket, and to find had a ghost who knew them. If you had made it onto that freighter the other night, we might not be here at all." Coba shrugged. "I guess that hardly seems lucky to you, now does it? My wife and children also did not feel lucky, when I showed them who was master. The silly debutante found out about my interest, and threatened to report me. A gas accident does wonders for disobedient wives and their child parasites." He gazed off in fond recollection. "I received so much sympathy too—I did enjoy that."

"We are impatient. What of your promise?" said the voices coming from Nikolai's dying body.

"All will occur as we agreed," said Coba. He looked up at the dark majesty of the sphere and its swirling energies. "With this I can do more than just stay ahead of the criminals and their packs of rats. Perhaps I can even learn to possess a new body." He looked at Lyita. "You could do nicely." Coba grabbed her.

Aurelian jumped forward. He was stopped by the sight of Coba's pointed gun.

"What of these two thieves?" asked the thing.

"We're done with them," the coroner said. "Enjoy yourself."

The bodyguard grinned from ear to ear. He faced Aurelian, and his right arm reached forward so quickly his fist was a blur— punching the Finn so hard in the throat it sounded like his neck snapped. The Finn sank to the floor dead.

It/they looked at Aurelian and smiled wider.

Aurelian stepped back.

"Yes, do run," said a voice from within the bodyguard's frame as it advanced toward Aurelian. "I want to chase him. It's been so long since I felt a body run!"

"I want to feel what it's like kill him with my bare hands!" said another voice. "I never got to do that while I was alive!"

"I did. It wasn't as fun as I thought," said a third voice.

"Shut up! No one asked you," said the first.

"Grandmother, are you in there?" Aurelian asked as he kept moving backward.

"She's not in right now," the first voice said as it followed. It took a deliberate, leisurely pace, as if it were savoring the entire experience.

Aurelian had an idea. "Wait! You want to experience sensation again, right? What if you just pleasured yourself?"

The bodyguard's form stopped advancing as they considered this. "You mean...physically?" said one voice.

"Yes, exactly. It must have been a long time since you felt that pleasure," Aurelian said, his voice hopeful.

"He has a point," said another voice.

"We could just rape him," said a third

"True," said the first voice.

"Either during or after we've murdered him?" said a new voice that sounded suspiciously like...

"Pavel?" Aurelian asked. "You son of a bitch!"

"Yes, fine idea," concluded the first voice. The voices having reached agreement, they moved Nikolai's body forward towards Aurelian.

Aurelian searching around for something, anything he could use. Coba settled into a bench at the wall, forcing Lyita down next to him. Vasily leaned against an instrument panel and lit a cigarette with an interested expression. He leaned towards Coba and said something too low to hear. Coba laughed and nodded agreement. Lyita's eyes were developing a blank and inward look, before she let her head drop to hide her face in her hair.

Aurelian found a loose section of pipe rusted to the floor, near the outstretched hand of a mummified corpse. He scrambled to pull it loose. The giant nearly caught him just as he pried it free. Aurelian began to swing it. The giant chuckled and tried to grab for it with his arms. Aurelian connected solidly with his forearm. "Yes! The sensation! My arm hurts!" it said joyously.

Hopeless but with not much else to try, Aurelian swung again at the same arm. This time it smacked into the forearm at the elbow. A bone cracked loose, pushing out the cheap suit sleeve at an odd angle. The bodyguard then ran at Aurelian, who barely managed to sidestep it. Nikolai's husk stumbled forward to the wall and put its broken arm in front of it, breaking it further. Either enjoying the pain or paying it no mind, it spun and charged at Aurelian again.

Aurelian ran and dodged around the room, as the thing lunged at him with a now useless forearm. Aurelian realized the pipe had a sharp end. Maybe he could stab the thing?

Aurelian noticed a sudden motion across the room. Lyita's head snapped back, her eyes now white orbs. She looked at him and he knew that his grandmother was in there.

"Hit the switch!" she cried.

"What switch?" Aurelian demanded. The giant blind-sided him with a rush, and laid a fist across his temple. The force knocked him sideways and left him dazed, causing him to drop the pipe. The creature laughed as it grappled Aurelian and dragged him to the floor.

"With our bare hands now, yes?" the first voice asked.

"Oh yes!" the second voice agreed. The thing's rotting breath washed across his face as it grinned from ear to ear, wrapped its good hand around Aurelian's neck and closing like a vice. Aurelian gasped and struggled, kicking helplessly. His hands couldn't budge the thing's grip by so much as millimeter.

Aurelian's flailing hand found the pipe again and brought it across the creature's head. It laughed. "Yes! Feeling that! Yes!"

Aurelian swung again, and the thing gave vent to another yelp of joy. His vision started to fade at the edges. He got one knee up under the giant's body, but could not budge his grip. He swung the pipe into the thing's good arm, and felt the pressure loosen. He was dismayed to realize this wasn't due to the impact of the pipe. The thing had been distracted by trying to use the fingers at the end of its broken left arm to loosen its belt and fly.

Swinging again in sheer desperation, Aurelian connected solidly with the thing's good arm at the elbow. The grip on his throat was shaken loose. Gasping for air, Aurelian turned the pipe around and jammed it into the thing's eye. The jagged end slammed through the lower orbital socket, crushing the eye and spreading blood and viscous fluid across the former bodyguard's face.

It jumped back. "I never felt that sensation when I lived!" said a voice excitedly.

"But now we have less vision!" said another. "The bastard has robbed us of half a sense!"

Panicking, Aurelian reversed the pipe and ran the sharp end into the formerly human stomach. Blood began to pour out and down its front.

"That has harmed this body."

"Yes! All that pain, it is delicious!"

"We can still kill him before this dies."

It leaned in. Aurelian struggled desperately to pull the pipe loose, but it was firmly lodged inside the former bodyguard's torso.

"Don't kill him just yet!" Pavel's voice came from the former Nikolai's throat. "We can go into his body, if we drag him near the sphere!"

"The switch, Aurelian, the switch!" the voice from Lyita cried. Dazed, Aurelian turned his head to see a large switch on the console next to him. It was just out of reach. The giant began to pick him up. He pulled the pipe free. He could either swing at the creature again, or...

With a prayer from his earliest church-school days on his lips, Aurelian threw the pipe at the switch on the console. It connected, and knocked the switch upwards. Instead of turning it off, Aurelian had increased the power.

The giant lunged for him as the sphere expanded.

The sphere surround the bodyguard's frame, and the creature lurched and froze. It twisted as voices gripped the throat in protest. One by one short wisps were sucked from the body back into the sphere. The body they had inhabited fell to the ground. Aurelian ran over to it to finish it, and was stopped by its unexpected human eyes.

"Thank you..." said Nikolai, as one living being to another, before he died. Then a last, new wisp emerged from the body and was pulled into the sphere to join the others.

Coba gave a sardonic clap. "Ah, you are a resourceful rat. You've cost me a little bit of money." He took a money clip from his pocket, and gave Vasily what looked like 20 rubles. Then Coba drew his gun. "I don't like losing bets. And I definitely don't like rats in my home." He took aim.

"The other way!" his grandmother's voice came from Lyita again. "What you should have done the first time! Set us free!"

Aurelian ran over to the switch, and pulled it all the way down. As he did, something slammed into his back.

The sphere shuddered for a moment, and then stopped all motion.

Then it released. The force exploded across the room, knocking all the living into unconsciousness.

AURELIAN AWOKE FIRST. He saw a somehow familiar floating light flash about him, love and gratitude emanating from it.

He tried to get up, and found his left arm wasn't working right. In the next instant a searing pain revealed itself in his upper back. That bastard Coba must have shot him there.

Above him, all of the fluid was draining from the sphere into gratings in the floor. The blue energetic shell around faded in size intensity. More and more wisps were breaking free.

Moving solely from fear and will, he picked up the pipe in his good arm and wrecked every breakable part of the machinery he could. Then he hurried over to where Coba, the two bodyguards, and Lyita lay.

She was alive. Unfortunately, Coba and Vasily were both still breathing too. Not much justice in this world, but he would take what he could get.

He'd seen firsthand how gunshots affect people. It was a serious thing. He might not have much time left before he went into shock. He retrieved the handcuff keys from Coba's pocket and uncuffed her. Then he slapped her. "Wake up!" He picked up Coba's gun with his good hand.

A group of wisps that had once been inside the sphere shot into the coroner's body. Coba's eyes opened. "There are enough of us!" said a voice that was not his. "We have him without the serum!"

"Yes!" said another. "Him and his servant. We can make them last. We shall taste our vengeance before we go to freedom!"

"No wait," said a voice that was actually Coba's. "You can't! I'll - I'll give you other people!"

At this moment Vasily's eyes sprang open. "Get out of me!" he screamed.

Lyita came to, and had her own brown eyes again. "What..." She had a couple of wisps around her head as well. Some other flashes of light came near, before her own wisps knocked them away. From the corner of Aurelian's eye, he saw a similar light doing this for him.

"We have to go Lyita," said Aurelian. "Now."

"No!" said Coba's own voice, as the flesh of his face began to wilt. "Don't let them do this. You have to - turn it back on! Suck them back into the machine."

"Or kill us!" said Vasily. "Just don't let us die like this!"

Another voice resumed from Coba's throat. "I think with you two, perhaps we will take our time."

More of the floating lights encircled Coba, and fell into his flesh to disappear. He had no apparent ghosts to fend the others off.

"Maybe your wife and children are already inside you, taking some vengeance," Aurelian said. "Maybe there is some justice."

Aurelian helped Lyita to her feet, nearly falling himself. They walked towards the chamber's door. His vision almost went black for a moment, and she steadied him. They made it into the hall outside, and she saw the pairs of fallen handcuffs next to the dead Finn. "One moment!" she said. She ran back inside with them before he could stop her. He lifted the gun and aimed back into the chamber, hoped he wouldn't hit her if he fired. She handcuffed Coba and Vasily together.

She ran back. "Now let's shut the door."

Aurelian agreed, and lent his body to moving the massive vault door closed. Mechanical locks turned, sealing it into place.

The two wisps were circling her head more and more slowly, dancing lightly. They faded into the air like smoke. "No!" she cried.

Aurelian closed his eyes, and wished his own grandmother love and good travels to wherever she might go. He could swear he heard or felt a loving farewell.

Then he found he had held his eyes closed for too long, for he started to feel faint. Something stopped his fall. He opened his eyes to find he was still upright, and Lyita had put her shoulder under his. "Not yet," she said. "Let's get out of here. Upstairs. We can make it."

He looked wearily the way they had come. "Up those stairs?"

"Yes. Up."

She took off his shirt and wrapped around his wound as best she could. They made it all the way back up the stairs, and then the ladder. She uprighted an overturned chair and sat him down in it, then pulled the improvised bandage off to look at his wound. "We'd better get you to a hospital."

That meant the police could find him. He laughed at such a mundane concern. "I have had some...misunderstandings with the law. Perhaps we can find a veterinarian."

Lyita nodded, not saying anything.

"Thank you," he said at last.

"Don't thank me," she said. "We had our reasons. My parents are free now."

"As is my grandmother." He shook his head. "But you helped her, and you helped me. So I'm thanking you, and there's nothing you can do about it."

In spite of herself, she smiled. Then her expression became

thoughtful. She was thinking what to say, and something told him to leave her be until she said it.

She found her words. "Sometimes I can talk to the dead who stay. When they stay it is because they have regrets. "

"I'm not even staying in St. Petersburg."

She laughed. "The best way to not stay, is to let go of your regrets."

"Or to have no regrets at all." He kissed her.

## 8

## WISHFUL THINKING

The startup company that could one day change the universe was born from a weekend sidewalk sale in the Mission District of San Francisco. Ray MacKinnon, a recent transplant in his twenties, was looking for distraction. He had just found himself unlucky in work as well as love .

Having moved from New York in a mix of whim and desperation, he found he rather liked San Francisco. His most recent firing made him wonder if it much liked him. As he pondered why he was once again having a hard time staying on his feet, his eyes were snared by an especially tacky brass imitation of an oil lamp.

Something about the boldness of its kitschy absurdity appealed to him. The cheesy thing could have come right from a 1970s version of "Aladdin". Ray leaned in to take a closer look. A voice to his left stated "Beware."

Surprised, Ray turned to the source of the voice. He hadn't noticed anyone standing there – let alone this guy. A fit man in his apparent late 50's, he had on a blue turban, a blue jacket with one of those odd wingless tubular collars he had seen in pictures of the Beatles – what was it called, a Nehru collar? - and loose black pants that would have been excessive for MC Hammer. His questionable taste and striking visual impact ended in a pair of blue curled-tip boots.

"Beware," the stranger repeated. The distraction irritated Ray, and he let himself go full East Coast on this stranger.

"Who the fuck asked you?" Ray demanded. "What are you, the fucking genie of the lamp?"

The man bowed slightly. "Such is my honor."

Ray blinked. He hadn't expected the guy to just go along with him. "Uh-huh. What's the warning for? Are you selling this stuff?"

The man laughed. "I sell no wares. All I have is a boon to give. To be fair I must warn you – engaging with the lamp can have unpredictable consequences."

"Like what? You think I'll break it or something?" Feeling dared, Ray picked it up. The lamp was cool to the touch, and surprised Ray with its lightness.

The man laughed and clasped his hands in joy. Ray had not expected that reaction. "See? No damage." Ray continued. He tried to put the lamp back on the table.

"Not so fast, young man," the stranger said. Ray was stunned to see this guy actually wag his finger. "Now you must make a wish!" The strange man declared with glee.

"Not interested, have a nice day." What was with this guy?

The man raised an eyebrow, his tone filled with scorn. "You are not understanding me, my friend. It does not matter if you choose to keep the lamp. The lamp has chosen to keep you."

"Oh boy." Ray sighed. "Straight up. Are you pushing some sort of personal development seminar or something?" He hadn't even been unemployed a full day yet. Did he already have "desperate for cash" smeared all over his face?

"I push nothing, human. It is you who have been pushed, by the universe. The Lamp of the Genie sits now in your hands. It has been swept from one estate to the next, unseen for centuries, seeking for a wisher to receive a wish– until at last this day."

"A wish? Not three?"

"No. I don't know who keeps telling people that! Only one. You can't wish for more wishes either. Nor time travel – I do not have the power or the authority. Nor can any wish result in my or another genie's harm or end." His face assumed an impassive magnanimity. "Excepting those conditions, you can wish for anything you want in the known or unknown universe."

Ray looked close at the man and saw no obvious signs of delusion or stench of alcohol, nor even a very deadpan joke. This could be a much deeper kind of crazy. That disturbed him. Having lived in both New York and San Francisco, he considered himself rather experienced in the delusional.

He was really starting to not like this.

"Supposing this was real, and not some web video prank," said Ray. "What if I don't want a wish?"

It was the genie's turn to blink. "Why would you not want a wish?"

"I don't know," Ray said slowly. "But now that I think about it, every story I've ever heard has everything going straight to shit and the wisher gets completely screwed. After which they're lucky to keep any what of what they had in the first place."

"There is nothing that you want?" the so-called genie said. "Are things so good for you right now?" He added, with an amount of insight that made Ray even more uncomfortable.

"Let's say they aren't the best," Ray allowed. "I don't want to go through enough shit that my current situation looks good." He held the lamp towards the guy in the strange turban and MC Hammer pants. "Whatever you're selling, find another sucker."

The man crossed his arms and refused to take the lamp. "You do not understand. You're going to make a wish. This can occur in an easy way or a difficult one."

"Whatever, buddy," said Ray. He went to drop the lamp on the table - and found that he could not let go. He shook it. The lamp stayed connected to his palm. "What the fuck?"

The man smiled. "As I said."

" You better get this thing off my hand before I fucking clown you with it!" Ray reasoned.

The man spread his hands in mild acceptance. "Perhaps you should do as you feel is right."

Ray shoved the lamp into the man's chest. The lamp and Ray's hand passed right through him. Off balance at meeting no resistance, Ray stumbled and then blinked. Some kind of hologram?

Ray swung the lamp straight at his head. It passed through him just as easily.

Ray went to scratch his head, and knocked the lamp against his own head. "Ow!" He looked at the lamp on his hand, and tried very hard to shake it. It would not even budge. He started to wonder if he was losing it. He looked around him. "Whoever's doing this, turn off the stupid hologram before I call the cops, you freak!"

The genie smiled patronizingly. "I am no hologram." He shrugged. "If you consider this unfair and want it to stop, all you need do is make that wish."

"Maybe I should just wish you to get fucked by a telephone pole."

The genie shrugged. "If you wish to spend a wish on something like that, so it shall be."

"Excuse me sir," said the woman running the sidewalk sale. "Could you take your call down the street..." Her eyes widened. Ray realized she'd thought he was having a cell phone conversation, and had just now seen he had no phone.

Feeling very awkward, Ray held up the lamp in his hand, and pointed at it. "I'm just getting this."

"Uh huh..." her eyes widened, and her face stayed very noncommittal. "Your hand is empty sir."

Ray began to experience a sinking feeling. "So you don't see a lamp at all." She shook her head. "How about this guy, is he buying anything?" He pointed at the Genie, who smiled.

She looked where he pointed, and looked back at him. "Uh..."

"You're not seeing anyone there, huh?" said Ray, his stomach sinking further into itself. She shook her head again. "And so I'm kind of freaking you out and you're wondering if I'm off my meds?"

She nodded. "Yep. And about to call the cops."

"Thanks for the honesty." Ray darted away, trying to shake the lamp off his hand as he walked. It wouldn't budge. As he expected and feared, the damn genie walked beside him.

"So, what are you inclined to wish for?" the genie asked. "There are many who would kill for the chance you have before you."

"What do you get out of this, anyway?"

The genie's face became noncommittal. "Nothing that need concern you."

Ray stopped, and sat on a house's front steps. He attempted to fold his arms, and grimaced as the lamp banged into his ribs.

He had either completely lost his mind at once, or this was really happening. He'd never had a dream hurt like that lamp just did to his ribs. Okay, until he found out different, it seemed the most sane thing to do was treat this like it was really happening.

"Ready for your wish yet?" the genie asked with oozing solicitousness.

Ray set his jaw. "I am not wishing for a single thing until I know why you're doing this."

The genie started back at him in silence.

"Alright, buddy. You know what? I'm in no hurry either. I'm unemployed." Ray sighed. "All this, and I haven't even had a coffee yet."

"Is that your wish?"

Ray focused on the genie with a gaze that said *What do you think I am, an asshole?* "Are you for real? What would you do, go straight to Starbucks? I can do that on my own, thanks."

"I could make you the best coffee any human ever tasted."

"Wouldn't every coffee I had after that taste like shit, for the rest of my life?"

The Genie continued looking at him with no visible change in expression.

"No comment?" said Ray.

"You could have it right now, and it would taste so very good."

"You're kind of a dick, aren't you?" said Ray. The genie did not respond.

A cup of coffee could help him think this through. He walked over to a nearby coffee shop. He ordered it to go and then reached for his wallet - forgetting that the nearly weightless lamp was still attached to his right hand. Several items on the counter went flying. He apologized through the stares and struggled to pull his wallet from his right front pocket with his left hand. Once after a seeming eternity that was achieved, he then had to figure out how to pull out his money one-handed.

He then grabbed the coffee, stepped over to the creamers and tried to add milk. The lamp that was stuck to his right hand slammed into the counter, knocking over a pitcher as it nearly obliterated the ceramic counter. He cursed and hurriedly grabbed for napkins under the weight of silent stares and, worse, by people politely looking away.

He wanted to sit now and take stock of things. He hurried to a table near the wall. The genie appeared next to him, sitting in empty air.

Ray pulled some ear buds from his pocket and put them in his ears, so he could pretend he was on the telephone. He was sure it would still sound crazy.

"There is much I can help you with," said the genie. "I can create employment for you. One wish, and you can have the job of your dreams."

"Which I'll then probably lose in a couple of months anyway," Ray answered, eyes glum. "Even if you didn't go and pull a Monkey's Paw on me."

The genie shook his head in dismay. "So cynical for one so young."

"How'm I supposed to trust you, when I don't even know what you get out of it?"

Irritation flashed across the genie's face. "That is quite enough questioning, monkey. I am a boon to you, and you test me at your peril. You must make a wish."

The lamp on the end of Ray's hand suddenly grew to the size of a wheelbarrow, tipping over the cheap table and launching his coffee into the air. On reflex Ray grabbed for the coffee with his right hand – knocking into it with the lamp. The force of the blow was too much for the flimsy paper cup and its cheap plastic lid, which sprayed coffee all over Ray's shirt - and onto the two startup mavens at the next table.

"Sorry!" Ray declared to the shocked denizens of the upscale coffee shop.

"Hey, what about my MacBook! " the startup geek nearest him exclaimed.

Ray froze a second. "It's just chemtrails, chemtrails!" he exclaimed. "Obama's the Antichrist, don't vaccinate!"

The first geek backed away, looking alarmed. The other scoffed. "Don't try and play the crazy card, man. Are you gonna pay for new laptops if we need them?"

"Yeah, I'm sorry – It's just..." well, what could sound crazier than the truth? "This invisible genie put an invisible genie lamp on my hand, and he just made it suddenly bigger because I refused to make a wish."

The guys looked at Ray, and then at each other.

"I said chemtrails! Chemtrails!" Ray then screamed ran out the door. He didn't look back until he was around the corner. So much for ever showing his face in there again.

"You will make a wish," the genie said. "And soon. I long for freedom from this lamp."

"That's quite a shame for you, then," Ray snarled. "'Cause you just fucked up. You tried to bully me a bit too far."

"I have just begun," the genie smiled. He bowed and disappeared.

The lamp remained its current absurd size. Ray barely managed to squeeze sideways through the door of his tiny apartment. He navigated through most of his roommates' various possessions that cluttered up the living room, and brought down a group of law textbooks piled on the back of their couch. His roommate Sara glared up at him from the couch, and pointedly put her headphones on.

He made it into his room and closed the door. The sparse furnishings were a bit of a relief. Even more relieving, the genie was still gone. He flopped onto his bed, and let his mind reel for a second at what was apparently actually happening.

As he considered it, all the television shows, movies, and stories he'd read involving genies confirmed his initial instinct. The one common thread all the stories had, was that the wishes always failed by some key technicality. Even in Aladdin where the genie was on the wisher's side.

He scowled. This meant a successful wish would require the kind of detail-oriented nitpicking that just wasn't his strong suit.

But he knew who was. He realized the perfect person he could ask about loopholes. One of the nitpickingest people he knew.

He went back into the living room. "Hey, so, Sara."

She took off her headphones. "I know, you got fired." She placed her headphones on top of her textbook, and somehow looked down on him from a sitting position. "I saw it on Faceplant."

"It's Facebook."

"For you, it's Faceplant. What's up with you and steady work?"

Ray sighed, and then chose to make a joke of it. "Oh, I'm too handsome, I'm too brilliant, I have too much charisma...so many gifts, so many different possibilities. It's irresponsible to speculate."

"Uh-huh. I hope you don't speculate that you'll be late with the rent again. Let alone doing again what you did to the toilet last week. My girlfriend almost left me that night."

"Sara, you know how sorry I am. Almost as much as I appreciate you bringing it up at every time we talk."

"Then what's up? I'm studying."

"Well...." Ray paused, and realized the full truth could be the last straw in convincing Sara he had truly lost it. "I'm writing a....story. Yeah."

"Oh, okay," said Sara. "I love stories. What's it about?"

"It's about an awesome, dynamically handsome, rugged and brilliant individualist named Richard, who gets a genie lamp." The genie flashed into being next to Ray, looking at him with a quizzical expression. "He has to make a wish, or the genie just won't leave him alone. So I'm wondering - why would a genie even be in a lamp? Let alone have this weird thing with a wish? What would the genie get out of it?"

"You know, that's an interesting angle," Sara admitted. "All the stories I know of, including the Disney thing, the genie's had some sort of curse put on him that he has to give wishes to get out of. So it's like the genie's either some kind of demon who's trying to trick any poor sap who rubs the lamp, or the genie's some sort of freaking idiot who got stuck in the lamp out of his own stupidity."

"Which could just mean he's too literal-minded to interpret something with a lick of common sense," said Ray. He looked directly into the genie's eyes. "So the genie has either the ethics of a weasel, or the brains of a toddler," The genie's face began to glower.

"Yeah, exactly," Sara agreed. The genie's face tightened, attempting to show no expression. Right there, this conversation had become well worth Ray's effort.

Ray turned back to his roommate. "And you know, getting the wish wouldn't be the only way to benefit from the lamp. Can you imagine? Real proof of magic? The first guy to show that evidence wouldn't need a wish. He could make a freaking mint!"

"Ha!" said the genie, a bit relieved. "Nice try, monkey. That is why the lamp and I are invisible to everyone else. You and your friend are both fools. "

"Let's say the genie has already thought of that. The lamp and the genie are both invisible to everyone but – the character," Ray continued. "The genie is just straight-up demanding that a wish be made, before he'll go away. And it's still only one wish, with no take-backs or anything."

"Well that would be easy enough to get around though."

"What?" the genie blurted, then hastened to regain his composure.

"Unless the genie made the guy sign a contract that's, like, *tens* of pages long, there's no way the possibilities are covered enough." Sara drummed her fingers on her law textbook as she considered. "Any number of things could trip the genie up. Just the actual length of the wish could be enough. If the genie didn't specify any restrictions, the wish could be hundreds of pages. Thousands. It could be a wish that keeps being written as it's being wished, over years! Any number of different things."

"He did say you can't wish for more wishes, though. In the story, I mean."

"Listen, you're talking to a law student," Sara said. "Without very specific contracts, people can get around all kinds of conditions. They do all the time."

"What if the genie didn't agree to a wish that had that much detail? Wouldn't it be too long?"

"Then the genie would be refusing to grant a wish. Which is his whole job, right? So the character could then reasonably claim breach of verbal agreement."

The genie snorted. "Best of luck finding agreement with a court of my fellow djinn."

"That's a lot to think about," said Ray.

"When did you get into writing, anyway?"

"Huh? Oh you know, just filling the time while I send out resumes. Seems like a good way to keep my mind sharp."

"Good call." Sara coughed. "Well, that's my degree calling me back. Been fun talking about your story. You might try and learn some more job skills. Like how to keep a job."

"Don't remind me." He went back to his room.

The genie followed. "Life is a river, always flowing, and passing you by. You would do well to make your decision soon."

Ray pointed at the genie with the lamp stuck to his hand. "Fuck you, and fuck your high-pressure sales bullshit. I'll just do everything left-handed until I goddamn feel like asking for my wish."

The genie raised an eyebrow, smiled, and disappeared.

Ray spent the rest of the evening trying to update his resume to send out.

Typing one-handed with this left hand didn't work too well for the Internet. It was hard to find a place to rest his hand with the lamp attached, so it didn't result in a cramp. At long last he found himself back to his cellphone, this time looking at pictures of his ex Abbie.

The pictures that he just couldn't bring himself to delete. Even though they hurt to see. There was a further mystery for him here also. Even though they hurt to see, sometimes he would look at them. Sometimes when he was saddest. It was almost as if he wanted to feel the pain further. It was like probing a hurt tooth with his tongue.

He remembered the last time he saw her, before he had dropped his job and apartment and gotten on a plane the other side of the country. He had asked her why.

"My feelings have just changed," she said. Her hair shining at the edges, a halo of streetlight coming through the rain-covered window behind her. The subdued lighting of the restaurant playing off her face, her skin. "I don't know...I just...I just don't feel the way I did. I can't explain it. I'm sorry."

The genie appeared. "Ahhh, I understand..."

"Don't you even," Ray growled.

"However you want things to be with her, is how they can be." The genie's voice took on tones of the generous and even magnanimous. "You can have her love you again, more deeply than a woman ever has a man. You can be revenged against her, and have her suffer exquisite tortures. You can snuff out her existence now, and no one will even remember her from this point forward."

"You've got to be shitting me," said Ray. "Is that what people usually ask for?"

"Quite often, yes."

"And you grant those wishes?"

"Do I detect a spark of interest?" The genie leaned in. "I don't like discussing the extent of my abilities, but...if it will help you come to your decision, yes. I can do any one of those three."

Ray shook his head, amazed. "People are such assholes sometimes."

The genie nodded agreement. "You really have no idea."

Ray turned on his PlayStation. He soon found a way to use his game controller one-handed. He brought up his favorite first-person shooter game. That killed a few hours, until the genie appeared before him and yawned, just happening to block his view. Ray's game ended in a hail of bullets he was used to dodging with ease.

"Goddammit," said Ray. "I'm not going to make some wish right away just to please you. Will you just take this lamp off my hand?"

"Is that your wish?" the genie smiled.

"No, fucko!" Ray threw away the controller he'd been attempting to use with one hand. It went through the genie to the wall.

"Ray, what is up with you?" he heard Sara complain through the wall. "I'm still trying to study!"

"Sorry! Uh, on the phone!" Ray turned to the genie. "How am I supposed to know you're even telling the truth?"

"Is it your wish to know that?"

"Do I look that stupid?"

"Is it your wish to know that instead?"

Ray started to retort, and stopped. An idea was forming in his mind. "I want you to know - paying attention, fucko?"

"That is not my name. I am known as-"

"From now on you're Fucko. How do I know you're telling me the truth?"

"Is it your wish to know that?"

"For the love of...." Ray attempted to ball his fists. This caused the tip of the huge lamp to knock against his chin. "Ow! Look. I refuse to make any wishes until I know how much I can trust you. The sooner I know that, the sooner you get to get out of that lamp. Haven't you been in there for a long time?"

The genie's composure slipped just a bit, to show an ancient weariness. "Ages," the genie said.

"Then how about you help me trust you, instead of just being a dick? That's not my wish - that's the only way you can get any wish out of me."

The genie considered, and sighed. "If it will help you decide on a wish sooner. The conditions of my...situation are that I cannot lie, and I cannot directly affect your or any other being's will. Until a wish is asked, I can only control the size and visibility of the lamp. If I violate any of these rules, my existence will cease. It will be as if I had never been."

"Sounds almost like parole."

The genie went silent again.

"If you can't lie to me, the most you can do is be silent," Ray confirmed.

The genie was silent a bit longer, and then gave vent to a very human-sounding sigh. "Yes."

Ray strained his utmost to keep his joy from showing in his face. The idea was nearing full form. He loved it so much. He went to bury his face in his hands so the genie might think he was despondent, while he thought it over. Unfortunately this resulted in him whacking himself in the skull with the lamp quite hard.

He rubbed his head. At least his elation was successfully masked by the pain. He looked over at the genie, seeing no change on his face. It just might work, if the genie couldn't read his mind.

He looked at the genie's face, and thought something particularly insulting and obscene about the genie's hypothetical parents. The genie's expression did not change from its current exasperation.

"Right on, dawg," said Ray, feeling saucy. This was more fun than he'd thought it could be.

He sat down at his desk, and created a new ad for Kickstarter.

**STARTUP INVESTMENT OPPORTUNITY – working name: the DJINNTERNET**

Are you willing to test something that seems impossible, and prove it wrong if you possibly can?

I'm sure you get contacted by a lot of people, with a lot of nonsense. This is very simple – try your hardest to disprove it.

Once you've tried this, you are free to enter into one of the following tiers.

...

Ray paused in drafting the Kickstarter ad, and turned back towards the genie.

"Have you taken leave of your senses?" asked the genie. "I thought I was quite clear that I will not let you prove the lamp or my existence to anybody else."

"Oh don't worry. You were very clear." Ray went to rub his hands, but couldn't as the lamp was in the way. For once he was glad the lamp was there -this involuntary motion could have given him away. He turned back to the Kickstarter ad. As he labored with his left hand typing, he fought the urge to grin broadly.

Ray posted the Kickstarter ad to the most skeptical places of the Internet, to draw the kinds of critical thinkers who would be the most offended. As he'd hoped, very skeptical young techs flush with startup money and sarcasm began demanding proof. Ray invited them all to an event where any and all questions could be asked of him, at a Mission district coffee shop where he hadn't yet worn out his welcome.

Ten minutes after the appointed hour, most of the attendees had arrived. Ray was surprised and encouraged by this level of punctuality on the West Coast. They in turn expressed surprise at how sane Ray seemed. Some proclaimed in voices intended to be overheard that he must be a prankster, a huckster or both.

Ray stepped up to the cashier to get a final cup of coffee. He used his left hand to pull out his wallet and then his credit card in a series of movements that had become a habit.

The card was declined.

The cashier looked away, embarrassed as if Ray had suddenly exposed himself. Ray realized in a sense he had - he'd exposed how broke he was. The clerk looked away, and mumbled something about the connection sometimes being down. Ray appreciated the out, and produced another card. It was his only other card. If this didn't work, he'd have to see about filing for disability for being unable to use his right hand.

He sighed. Like so many things in life, if he could just get credit for how hard he was trying. But then wouldn't everyone else get that credit too? Ray put the card back in his wallet with his other plastic cards...and a new idea came to him. Unbidden.

It was an idea that could be the perfect wish.

It was so good. It was even better than his current plan with the genie. It could solve it all. Not content to just hope, he turned it over in his mind and looked at it from every angle. He grinned. It was perfect! And it wouldn't have even come to him if he hadn't been here just now.

One of the waiting skeptics coughed. Ray looked at the clock on the wall behind the counter. It was time to go ahead with his previous plan.

Holding his coffee in his left hand, he walked back to address the crowd.

"Hi everyone, thanks for taking your time out. No need for foreplay. Let's jump straight to it. I hope you all have brought your video cameras, or will use your smart phones?" The gathered crowd nodded assent.

"Great! I want you all to shoot this from all angles, so anyone who sees this can be sure it's not some CGI effects or something. Ready?"

"Yup," said one particularly fat and long-haired programmer in a dirty t-shirt, who Ray guessed might make $300,000 a year. "Let's get your humiliation over with, huckster."

"Man, I salute you!" Ray said. "That's the exact right attitude." A bit disconcerted, the man glared harder. "Okay, the proof is pretty simple," Ray held out both of his hands, and pointed to him. "Why don't you walk towards me until you can't walk forward any more. Make sure your hands are in front of your face," he added, "I don't want you to get hurt."

A satisfied smirk on his face, the hirsute and surly programmer approached while waving his arms and saying "Wooooo..." - until he touched the lamp and stopped. There he was, touching something he could not see, nearly a yard from Ray's outstretched hand.

"There's something there?" the man said.

"Oh, come on," said another voice from the crowd. "This guy's an obvious plant."

"You try it, asshole," the fat programmer retorted. "Must be some really transparent glass or something."

The second man walked over, and also found himself pushing against empty air. He also was bemused.

The genie appeared, and turned to Ray. "Nice try, primate." The lamp began to shrink.

"Oh yeah?" said Ray grabbed a cup of coffee and dumped it on the lamp. The crowd watched in amazement as the shape outlined by dripping coffee shrank into nothing.

"Oh my God!" gasped one former skeptic.

"Alright then, " Ray smiled as he announced. "You all saw and recorded that, right?"

"No!" the genie gasped, too late.

"Yeah I did!" said one older video geek. "I even got it in infra-red and UV!"

"How the hell did you do that?" the larger of the skeptics marveled.

"A genie attached a lamp to my left hand, because I refused to make a wish. Now he's a bit mad at me," Ray turned to see the genie, who was actually incandescent with rage. "He's shrunk the lamp too small to test now. So let's go over the video."

The infra-red was particularly fascinating. It showed some sort of an object with absolutely zero heat signature. A freeze-frame of the hot coffee poured over it yielded a nearly perfect silhouette of a stereotypical genie's lamp.

Over the next two hours, every single person in the room tried to disprove what they had seen, and what the videos showed. Ray was happy to comply with every single question. Eventually, the genie began calling for his attention. "Pardon me," said Ray. "The genie wants to say something." He turned to face the disconcerted figure in the turban who only he could see.

"You can't do this!" the genie cried. "You can't benefit unless you make a wish!"

"This is just the beginning," said Ray. "You can leave me any time you want. Up for declaring defeat yet?"

The genie scowled, and disappeared in fury. Ray smiled, and turned back to the now less-skeptical skeptics before him.

"Now then," said Ray. "Here's the deal. This genie has refused to leave me unless I make a wish. So, it really has to be a good one."

"Then why let anyone else in on it?" asked the first programmer, who had become somewhat less argumentative but remained skeptical.

"Because every story I've ever read about this situation, there is always has some loophole in the wish that doesn't work for the wisher. But knowledge advances! So, I'm very sure that if we pool our minds and resources together, we can create a wish that's big and airtight enough to benefit us all."

"Crowdsourcing," said the second programmer.

"Crowdwishing, maybe," the first said, warming up to the idea.

"Exactly!" said Ray. "It would be pretty crappy for me to just claim this wish for myself anyway – and just throw away a chance to help the whole world. But the wish could also hurt the world. Making sure it doesn't means using a lot of resources and knowledge I don't have. Probably lawyers, logicians, ethicists and other philosophers, experts on economics on any big wish's impact, and other things I can't even think of. So, how about we put our heads together, and make something real with this opportunity?"

The crowd murmured, and more and more of them began to nod. One of them laughed outright. "Best Kickstarter ever!"

"Right on brother! High five!" Ray raised his left hand, and the clap resounded through the room. "So, anybody has any further requests for any kind of test, I'm totally down. Who's with me?"

The room cheered.

In that moment, Ray realized he felt more fulfilled than he ever had before. It wasn't the cheering alone. It was that it was people were coming alive with the power they'd seen in his idea – and this time he could see a way to make it happen.

At long last, he wasn't just making someone else's idea work. He was making his own idea really happen in the world.

At that point, unbeknownst to all of them and the genie as well, a genuine wish occurred to him that could really help him save the world.

Several whirlwind months later, Ray met with his startup staff in a very crowded, rented startup space in the SOMA district. The company name had come to him from his one philosophy class in his aborted run at college. The teacher had a favorite song he would reference every now and then – "Cold Lampin'."

"Alright, people!" Ray waved his hands. The crowd quieted down. "Welcome to Lampin'!" the crowd cheered. "You all know the deal. The Djinn you can't see - " Ray indicated him, the genie scowled at him and then the gathered crowd, "-is waiting. We have one chance to ask the perfect wish, and make any one thing on Earth happen. So! Legal, you have your conditions. Health, your sector's represented and staffed. Physics and Philosophy, you are all set to go as well?" Their bright and fresh young college-fresh faces smiled, shining with optimism. Next to them, they're more grizzled elder stuff smiled as well, ready to bring the perspective of experience to salt and season their enthusiasm. "We're running scrum teams. We're set to go. We want the perfect wish. Let's make it happen!" They cheered, and set to work.

Teams reported. Days turned into weeks as the different possible aspects of the wish were refined, tested in simulations, then reviewed by Ray. The genie always stood by, sometimes attempting to keep a poker face and other times eagerly happy to grant one of the possible wishes. Ray interpreted and tracked all of these varied reactions, then checking against previous evasions or flat refusals to answer until a matrix emerged.

The genie himself grew angrier and more frustrated, as, far from being a hindrance, the lamp on Ray's hand began to beckon many interesting people into Ray's life. As Lampin's development continued and they passed a first round of startup investment funding, Tech-Crunch, Engadget and other sites began requesting interviews. The assembled skeptic's testimony and video footage were released to the Internet, and withstood increasing scrutiny. There was a growing list of scientists who were curious in studying the lamp. The Amazing Randi, who had a standing $1 million offer for proof of the supernatural, was oddly unavailable for comment.

National governments had been slow to move towards taking Ray's lamp, but he had hired a security detail just in case. Several interesting and attractive women had come into his life as well, who were casually available and fascinated with what he was setting up. Some even pretended they could see the lamp, which amused Ray quite a bit. He couldn't help but wonder if Abbie was starting to see the news on him, whatever she was doing back in New York.

It was all coming together well. For his own part, without anyone's knowledge, Ray had broken down his ideal wish into different parts, reserving knowledge of the whole wish to himself. Legal experts had looked over some parts of it; other aspects were reviewed by economists, physicists, and experts in ethics. None had any objections. It remained his favorite of all the wishes that were suggested.

It was that idea he'd had in the coffee shop so many months before. Refined as it now was, he could conceive of no way it would be a downside for him, or for any of the humanity that had, in the course of this journey, helped him feel inspired and hopeful again.

He scheduled a meeting with his employees, advisors and investors for the next morning, to at long last reveal the wish that he would ask for. This long journey could be completed. After months of what had been a long and satisfying run of having his own company work his way, with no one else to answer to, and good ideas put to the test and passing through the fire stronger, Ray went home. Eager and also filled with trepidation, at long last he found his way to sleep.

In the middle of the night, the genie roused him from his slumber.

"You will do my will! You accept that you have to make a choice, like any other mortal!"

"Sure I will – tomorrow." Ray smiled. "And it will make the world a better place for everyone."

"I do not trust your smile, monkey. You will make your wish now! You must select your heart's desire!"

"Buddy, I don't have to do any such thing," said Ray. "And humans are apes. Monkeys are more like distant cousins. I Googled it."

"You have driven me to this. I have seen your type before, many times over many centuries. You are resourceful and put up a brave and defiant front, because when you were still a youngling your heart was broken."

Ray yawned in a loud and sarcastic fashion. Inside he was unsettled.

"You must have lost your mother first. Most likely she died...yes, probably around when you were ten. You blamed your father for most of your ensuing problems with the world and yourself. And then, at last, after you had become a young man, you found a woman. One who you thought could be your mate, your friend everything. One you thought could fix you-"

"Fuck you!" said Ray.

"Here is a wish you must want!" The genie conjured a dream of living a life raised by people he could have trusted.

"I refuse everything in this dream!" Ray declared, as soon as he had form enough to speak.

"What do you have planned?" the genie demanded.

"You'll have to find out like everyone else," said Ray, a glee in his eyes that grew as he saw it gave the genie pause.

"Instead of a direct replacement for your mother, perhaps a woman then. Another to fill that wound." The genie grinned in triumph now. Ray wondered what his face had shown – had the genie's words had an impact he didn't know? "There was one you tried to give the love you wouldn't grant yourself. But it didn't work, and she left you. Which in a way to you felt worse - she left by choice. She decided she didn't want you."

"Oh, big deal," Ray snarled. "You read our emails. Congratulations, you're as omniscient as a teenager who guessed my password."

"I have no need to read your electronic correspondence, mortal. Your wounded soul sings it from your eyes." The genie folded his arms and leaned back in smug triumph. His voice took on a magnanimous tone. "Things need not be this way, your heart radiating its painful brokenness, broadcasting over your armored walls so others' sleeping minds can hear it and stay away, even if their waking minds don't know why. I can repair this with one wish."

"How?"

"I can bring your Abbie back to you, of course. Or find you someone better."

"But...but I know a simple wish like that won't work! That's how all this genie lamp shit is!"

"Are you sure of that? Or are you just afraid?" For once, Ray had nothing to say. The genie pressed his advantage. "What would you not do, to have someone you love? How many more chances do you have for true love, in the shortness of your mortal life?"

"The answer's no!" Ray yelled. Behind his bravado, he was beginning to feel quite conflicted.

"Ah-hah," said the genie. He displayed his second smile for many months. "The love of your life. Do not pretend you are not very, very interested."

"I've made promises," said Ray weakly. "The company, the people, they are..."

"I can show you what it could be like, in a dream."

"Will that commit me to the wish?" asked Ray.

"No," the genie sighed. "Not since you have asked. But you will see. And it will change your mind."

"Alright," said Ray. "Show me." He bowed and raised his hands palm up.

Ray fell back asleep. And like that, he had a new girlfriend. Her name was Olivia. She'd started working for the startup last week, and the chemistry had been clear from the beginning. Best of all, she believed Ray, so he had no need to hide these conversations that, for all she could see, he was having with the air.

She was everything he ever wanted, and more things he didn't realize he wanted. She was an artist and a scientist, an empath and a massage therapist, and a red belt at Kung Fu. They lived long and well, and in the span of Ray's dream they had many years and many children.

He woke up.

"That life can be yours," said the genie.

"See, that's why I don't trust you," said Ray. "That's infatuation. That's not love. Being around someone *all* of the time, without even having any breaks? It doesn't matter who it is. That's just weird and won't work."

"You have to choose a wish!" the genie declared.

"I will tomorrow."

"You will now! I will show you how well things can truly be, with your long-lost Abbie!"

"Hey, wait. I'm not even asking-"

Ray fell into a deep sleep. He awoke in the Mission, the same day that, many months ago, around the corner the sidewalk sale that had bound him to this genie.

This time, he turned right instead of left - and ran straight into Abbie instead.

"Hi!" she said, surprised. "Wow, what a coincidence running into you. What are you doing in SF?" She looked more beautiful than ever. Her eyes sparked with that way she had, he'd never seen in anybody else.

"I moved here about 9 months ago. Just looking around for work now."

"How've you been?"

"Alright, I guess." He looked at her. "I have to admit you look fantastic."

She laughed, pleased. "Why do you have to admit that?"

"It's the truth."

She punched his shoulder. "Always such a stickler, that's something that gets you into trouble."

They sat down at a dinner table. "There's so much going on right now," he began, as he reached for a glass of wine.

She put her hand on his hand. He saw that, even though this was a dream, the lamp was attached to it. "I know. I know about the genie. He brought me here to your dream."

Ray's heart leaped into his throat. He looked at the glass in his other hand, and decided to drain it. This dream's construction was quite thorough; he could feel the effects of the alcohol as well.

"And?" Ray's bitterness overcame him. "Am I all that you want, now that I can make any wish?"

The hurt showed in her eyes. He was glad to see it, and he felt ashamed to have put it there.

"Of course not," Abbie said. "That would make me a pretty cheap hooker, wouldn't it?" She leaned in conspiratorially. "I know I'm the wish that is before you."

She leaned back and laughed, as he stared in surprise. He realized her laugh sounded like sparking diamonds to him, still.

"Then why are you here?" he demanded. "You already pushed me away."

"Because the genie showed me who you are." She placed her other hand on the table before him. "I understand now what I saw in you at first, and how I – I lost that thread. How that changed us." She took a breath in, and let it out. "I think we can do it again, and not go that way. I think we can make something strong and new."

He put his freed hand on hers.

She continued. "And I miss you. I want to have us again. I understand you better now too, as well as myself, and…"

Ray saw a waiter approaching. Dream or no, Ray thought, if that waiter interrupts us right now, I will murder him on this table with the butter knife. The dream waiter quickly walked away.

"I want what we could have had," she finished. "I want to have it again, so we can make it even better. Make it last forever."

Ray's eyes developed a discomforting wetness. He closed his eyes and let his tears flow a bit. "I so appreciate you coming here," he said at last. "To my dream. I appreciate you even being open to us being possible, again." He breathed out, a little troubled. His voice cracked with a bit of emotion and he didn't even care.

A part of him couldn't believe he was about to say his next words. "But I've got a bigger thing to do now. I really can change the world for the better. For the future. And what happened between us, is the past. That's where that 'us' belongs. Anything else is not the good kind of dream. It's the kind that in the morning, just falls apart." He sighed, as more tears ran down his face. They felt so real, perhaps they were running down his sleeping face as well.

"I thought you might say something like that," she sighed, and cried with him.

The dream faded into blackness.

Ray woke up to his alarm. He cleaned the sand from his eyes, shaved and dressed. It was time to go to the main offices of Lampin' and make the wish.

The boardroom was filled with all the members of his startup. Teleconference cameras and monitors showed other interested investors, from Swiss bankers to Chinese hedge fund managers to Russian oligarchs and more, from all over the world. Ray had been surprised one day to find their ranks had been joined by Vasily Ulyanin himself.

At the far end of the room, Lampin's employees finished carrying in box after box. They were stacked against the wall in columns, at last numbering twenty-two.

The receptionist called. "Ray, there's a Sara here for you?"

"Great! Send her right here, and you come too." Ray adjusted his tie. He couldn't believe he'd put on one of the things. But somehow this event seemed to call for it.

Sara arrived, with her characteristic and for once blessed bluntness.

"Can you tell me the deal yet?" asked Sara.

"You'll have to find out with everyone else. Glad you could make it. Really wanted you to see this too." He looked around. "Grab a spot over there." Sara made a face but wandered over to the spot without complaint. Ray realized it might be a bit weird for her to see him in confidently in charge. It would have seemed weird for him too, if he actually felt at all confident.

"Is that everyone?" asked Ray. The receptionist nodded. "Then we're all set," said Ray. "Now we can at last get past the secrecy, and put the different parts of the wish together, and tell you what we've got."

"Yes, mortal," said the genie. "Let's hear your wish at last."

"Alright!" said Ray. He rubbed his hands. "As you all know, it's taken a lot of work to get here. To come up with this wish, we had to balance a lot of things together. Making sure a wish works for just one person is hard enough. Making a wish that can change the world for the better is really complicated. Just wishing for a lot of money could unbalance the world economy. A cure for sickness could destabilize nations and start wars. There aren't a lot of really big wishes that wouldn't be destructive just as much as, or perhaps even more, than the intended good they might cause."

He paused, and looked at all the faces gazing back at him with hope and expectation. He continued.

"I've had a lot of different proposals, which we've all discussed. Any one of them would work great with a genie we can trust. But not one has been as, for lack of a better phrase, 'genie-proof' as the first one I came up with. I've had the individual parts of it vetted from every angle. Rather than give the genie time to prepare a way around things, I've held back the complete wish until now." He paused again, still hesitant about this final step.

"What is it, already?" asked his office manager.

"Yeah," said one of the skeptic programmers who had earned Ray's trust. "Spit it out man."

"Okay. Here it is. There is one aspect of the world that can be vastly improved – being able to show what people really tend to do. Everyone – from rulers to peasants, from CEOs to the mailroom. What this world is missing, is a product that shows everyone how other people are inside. What kind of people they are, and why, without the possibility of denial.

"So, the startup wish is for a product I like to call 'Namastecard'. Basically, it shows the balance each person's own individual karma, based on a measure of what they intend *and* how what they do affects others in the real world. People won't be able to hide the right and wrong they've done. When they do something that benefits others, they will show more karma. When they do something that hurts others, they will show a loss. We won't be able to hide the effects of what we do any more. We will at last know how just the universe is - or isn't. And we will be able to live and adjust accordingly."

The genie said nothing. His shocked face showed Ray everything he wanted to know.

"Wow," said the office manager. Similar comments came from around the room. The investors who had teleconferenced in hit mute and engaged in some off-screen conversations, before returning.

"Go on," said Vasily Ulyanin. The other investors nodded their agreement.

"One second." Ray turned towards the being that only he could see, and smiled. "Have you heard something like that before?"

"I must admit I have not," the genie said at last. "Is that your wish?"

"That's the gist of it. The full wish is in those boxes over there." He pointed to the twenty-three boxes that took up the far side of the conference room.

The genie turned pale. "I'm beginning to wish that lamp had not been found for another seven centuries," he declared.

Ray turned to his lead researcher. "Why don't you assemble the Word version of that wish, and email it to our investors? It's on the shared drive in separate sections, coded by-"

"Can we talk outside for a second?" Sara asked.

Ray looked up, surprised. "Huh? Why? We're kind of busy."

"We need to talk outside. Now."

Surprised and a little annoyed, he nodded. She walked briskly out of the room, with him behind her. She made sure he shut the door. "Are you sure that wish is a good idea?" she whispered.

"Of course I am. Why?"

"Let's say karma is a real thing, or this genie could make it a real thing. I'd think there are many people with a lot of power, who would never want anyone to know how badly in karma debt their souls are."

"Right you are," said Ray.

"So you aren't going to wish for that?" asked the genie, relieved.

"Nope," said Ray. "Oh Sara, sorry. Talking to the genie again. Nope, that's what I think I'm going to wish for. It's worth it." Ray beamed. "This is something I really want to do."

"But that will change everything!" the genie began. "You can't-"

The office manager poked his head out of the boardroom. "Sir! The investors responded with an offer to buy us out."

"What?" Ray looked, startled. "So they can make the wish themselves, I guess?"

"They won't say."

"What's the number?" asked Sara.

"About....$57 million total, in US dollars."

"Absolutely not, for any price!" declared Ray. "We can do this. We can change the world! We can make it a better place!"

Through the doorway, he saw the rest of Lampin's faces. Some were still with him, but others were starting to waver.

Ray stepped back into the boardroom, and faced the investors on the teleconference screen. Ulyanin the oligarch looked square back at him.

"There is no way I will sell my wish," said Ray.

The eyes in the man's otherwise bland face were piercing in their anger. They were practically burning through the screen. "There is no way we will allow you to make that wish. It would destroy our lives."

"If it will hurt you that much, then by definition it's what you deserve!"

"Then also by definition, we will happily commit more damage to keep it from occurring!" Vasily Ulyanin snarled back. "Do you think we will care about more bad marks against us, when those we love know without a doubt who we are? What makes you think we won't do *more* of what we've already done to stop you?"

Ray blinked. The rest of the startup looked back at him in silence.

"I've got a family," Sara said at last. "That's what I was trying to tell you. I have a girlfriend. You've got family too, Ray. Even if you don't talk to them much. Friends."

"I...I can include in my wish..."

"What?" asked the libertarian skeptic. "That no harm will come to any of us because of this wish? Is that even possible?"

Ray looked over to the genie, who shook his head. The genie's eyes gave away nothing.

Ray turned back towards the oligarch. His heart was breaking.

"It's not right for you to take that risk with our lives, Ray," Sara said.

After moments that felt like years, Ray hung his head. "Will you do $300 million, so that I won't make this wish?" He asked, in a voice that held no room for hope.

The office manager began to run back to his computer. He barely had time to turn around before was interrupted again by Ulyanin speaking from overseas, his face exploding with one single, guttural bark:

"Done."

"Alright," said Ray, his voice as flat as a grave. "Any conditions?"

"You know there are," he growled.

"Let's have 'em," said Ray.

"That you never, ever make that wish, or any other wish like it."

The genie gasped. "NO!" he shrieked. "No! You must make a wish!"

"As long as it's understood that if anything suspicious happens to me, any of us, or anyone we care about, the original wish will go into full effect. The genie will know." Ray waited.

The oligarch gritted his teeth, but nodded. "I would do the same. We have a deal."

Ray nodded, hung his head and looked away. "Finalize the contract and send it on over. We'll finish this today."

Ulyanin agreed, and disconnected with a stabbing finger motion. The other investors followed suit.

Ray sat down hard in an empty chair, as silence filled the room.

"And guess what, people," Sara said into the silence. "We're all cut in on that! We'll each get tens of millions – after taxes!"

The group gave vent to a growing cheer that quickly became deafening, and subsiding into excited chatter, high fives and backslaps.

"How much are you taking, Ray?" Sara asked. "Enough for a separate bathroom?" She tried to joke him out of the mood he was sinking into.

"Whatever is fair," said Ray, despondence in his eyes.

She looked close at him. "Jesus, Ray." She put her hand on his shoulder.

"I've never seen you like this. Not even when you first moved in, after that Abbie bitch dumped you.

Ray looked away, saying nothing.

"Why are you sad, human?" the Genie asked. "This has never happened before – you have found a way to get a benefit without having to make a wish! I was only in there for 700 years!...what in the 97 million Hells happened to you apes while I was stuck inside that lamp? "

Ray shrugged, unmoved. "Maybe capitalism. That's taught us to watch our backs. It's kind of been a genie's lamp too, I guess – material wishes granted at a risky price...." his voice trailed. He ground a fist into his palm. "Dammit! I thought I had it!" He stood up, and looked outside the boardroom's window, over the San Francisco skyline.

"I have some money now at least, I guess," he said softly.

"No," said the genie. "You will not."

"Says who?"

"You will. Once you have thought this through." The genie waited a moment, his face impassive. "I know you apes. Not everyone will believe you have forgone this wish. Someone somewhere will try to force you. And you will either die without making the wish – or you will make a different wish, and the oligarchs will kill you and those you love to get back their money."

Ray's face became engulfed with anger, and then with sorrow.

"So now, you know what you must do."

"God dammit," said Ray.

"Yes."

"My only chance is....to wish that all memory of these events be erased."

The genie nodded. "That should resolve this all."

"Can I ask for money too?" Ray said hopefully.

The genie shook his head. "That's another wish. Perhaps you could find a way to phrase that. But the clock is ticking now."

"I can find a way out of this!"

"Every minute you try, is more risk."

Ray put his head in his hands. At last he nodded.

"If I wish that everyone else's memory of these events are replaced with a startup that failed – will that be sufficient?"

"Yes."

Ray drew in a deep breath, and breathed out. "I so wish."

The lamp fell off Ray's right hand, and shrank back to its original size upon the floor. Ray stretched his arm.

"Well played, Raymond Quinn MacKinnon of the less-hairy Earth apes." The genie snapped his fingers and the room around them disappeared, to be replaced with a blurred and flashing colored void. "You have shown me something new, an event I thought impossible."

"What are you talking about. I blew it." Ray surprised himself by realizing he was holding back tears. "I could have wished to feed the world. I could have at least just wished for ten million dollars." He looked straight at the genie. "But you probably would have found some way to make it go to shit."

"Not me," said the genie. "It is fascinating to see you mortals try to wriggle out of it. The universe would not be in alignment with it. That is why wishes do not work as planned. You have to make things, and if they are big things, you have to make them in many tiny steps. This way, you gradually create the support within the universe to make it work. Nonetheless yours is very nearly the most successful effort I know of. Perhaps your species will find a way to make all your wishes true someday."

"Well...thanks." It was almost uncomfortable seeing the genie acting this magnanimous. Also, it was uncomfortably off from something Ray considered an important point. "So, just so we're clear. You're saying there's absolutely no way I am getting out of this without at least getting to keep that money."

The genie shook his head. "No."

"People do that all the time! What the Hell do you think most Internet startups actually are?"

"Wishes that did not come true." The red void around them began to settle into solid forms. "We have a limited amount of time left to interact. Do you have any other questions?

Ray looked around him. "Will I even remember all of this?"

The genie looked at him with curiosity. "Would you prefer to forget as well? Many mortals would. They would be tortured to have a life that lacks what they think they could have had".

"Glad to be different then." Ray laughed suddenly. "You know what? I gave it my best. What should I feel bad about?" Ray looked at the genie. "Will this hurt your parole, or whatever?"

The genie filled the air with booming laughter. "Your guess was quite wrong there."

"Then why did you do this?"

"My kind have great powers and intellects, but they are still as nothing before the universe's infinite mysteries. We find the intersection of short life spans and free will fascinating. So among beings of my kind, you can say I am a researcher. Among your kind, I am a tester." The genie coughed. "In some rare cases, I may also grant a boon. I would do so now, if you will it. You are free to reject this also."

Ray sighed. "Oh, come on. We were getting along so well. Not this crap again."

"It is no 'crap'. This is a boon I grant you, not a wish. I give you my word it has no negatives which I can see, and even if those develop, you can choose to reverse or reject this boon at any time."

Ray studied his eyes. "Really?"

"As you know, I cannot lie."

"What's the boon?"

"I cannot tell you beforehand."

Ray thought about it. "You know what? Sure."

The genie smiled and laughed. "Truly? As I said, I cannot guarantee your future happiness with this in any way."

"That's makes me even surer – that's a realistic promise. Let's do this."

The genie clasped his hands in joy. "So be it!"

The genie opened his eyes, bowed to Ray, and disappeared.

Ray opened his eyes, and found himself back in the Mission. It was late afternoon on that same eventual Saturday, with a couple more hours before the sun began to set.

He was back to being quite recently unemployed. But things were different this time. He laughed aloud as he realized, he may have found his true calling -

Solving problems of the unexplained.

Now that he knew there could be entities as strange as genies, he knew there had to be other things just as strange or more. With all the tech startups coming around, and the way that information was beginning to encroach upon a world he now knew also held magic, there were bound to be more and more of these kinds of situations.

This was just the tip of the weirdberg.

He could help people, and be his own boss, and get paid well besides. He wouldn't have to deal with bosses who felt threatened, or coworkers who just didn't get what he was saying or wanted to do. And maybe, just maybe, he could change the world for the better. Like he very nearly had, before the foiling of his wish.

He went to the same coffee shop where he had once upended a table. His business card was quickly developed that afternoon, in between sips of expertly crafted coffee.

**Ray Q. MacKinnon | Quantum Mechanic**
**Troubleshooter of the Unexplained**

**(415) xxx xxxx | xxxxxx@xx.com**

It wasn't all the way there yet, but it was good. Maybe the logo could be a digitized bolt of lightning, in an eye of Horus. Might have to get a graphic designer. Maybe he could look up a girl he'd met at Lampin'. Her memory of the whole company would be fuzzy now, so she'd have to meet her all over again.

Considering it was all even more delicious than the coffee he could now hold in his right hand.

But what was the boon the genie had granted him? He didn't notice anything new until the amount of coffee he'd consumed led him to the bathroom.

There he noticed that his red hair was now shot through with streaks of green - straight from the roots.

Ray was angry at first. That was it? That was the boon?

Then he laughed. Well, the genie said nothing about it being useful.

There was the much deeper gift of the whole affair. Deeper even than his new career.

It really seemed now that he had been given a place that he could be. San Francisco liked him.

9

---

## LESSONS LEARNED

**B**illy Short woke up one morning, with an enormous green pod growing out of his left ear. It was slick with some dripping fluid. As he tried to turn over, he could feel a creature rustling inside it.

"Mom!" Billy screamed.

"What is it?" his Mom replied from downstairs.

"It happened again! It's bigger!"

"Oh dear." She set down a carton of orange juice on the table, and turned her still face towards her husband. She was proud of how unchanged her expression was; it had taken years to be come this well-adjusted. She maintained her frozen smile. "Phil, perhaps we should help him. Do you know where the head clippers are?"

"I don't have time for this. You're coddling that boy," said Mr. Short, as he mopped the remains of his eggs with the corner of his toast. "Carrying on like that! At his age."

"Phil..." she said cautiously, "growing up can take some getting used to."

"We still need to get done what we need to get done. We're not supposed to complain about - things!" Mr. Short exclaimed. "If everyone complained, then -" Something ruffled angrily ruffled beneath his dress shirt, around his shoulders. His face twisted in a momentary spasm of pain and shock. "Then no one would want to work!"

"Calm down, dear."

"I'm calm!" His face resumed its normal placidity. He swallowed the last bite of toast, and pushed his plate away. "But if he's going to have a job when he grows up, then he's got to learn to *take* it." He reached for the reassurance of his morning mug of Coffee.

"You're right, of course," Billy's Mom sighed.

Billy could feel the creature move more purposefully. It was waking. He started to cry.

"Mom! MOM! HELP!" came Billy's voice from upstairs.

Billy's Dad leaned forward to refill his Coffee. He put down the mug, stood up and walked over to the downstairs bathroom. He began adjusting his tie in the mirror, as the thing beneath his shirt firmly wrapped its tentacles around his neck and tightened the reins. The tie was soon tied perfectly; 13 twists to the left, and one backwards. Billy's Dad patted it approvingly, and the thing agreed. They returned to the kitchen.

"You just have to let him go through it," Billy's Dad continued. "He won't carry on so much in the morning, once he knows there's no way out."

"Yes, dear." She readjusted her mask, and pecked him on the

cheek. The cracks at her temples faded, and were soon indistinguishable from the rest of her skin.

Mr. Short put on his suit jacket, and picked up his briefcase. The thing beneath his shirt adjusted briefly under the new weight, and settled in as they both went out the door.

Billy lay in bed, crying, praying for someone, anyone to come and save him.

Billy's Mom finished clearing the table, and sighed. She went down into the basement to find the head clippers.

After a while, Billy stopped screaming. He lay there without the energy to shiver. Tears dripped off his face onto his pillow. The more he had screamed, the more this thing had inflated. Now it was the size of a cat. It was dripping its fluid, of mucous pus and sweat.

And it was moving.

*Hello, Billy,* it said softly and slow. The flesh they shared transferred its muffled speech. Its murmuring voice was the sound of dirty things burrowing in rotting leaves; the sound of blood cracking as it dried from rich red life into blackness. It was smooth and sweet, seductive and terrifying, some strange mixture of chocolate and gangrene.

*I'mmm you're newww friendddd, Billy.*

Billy found the strength to gasp, "Go away! Leave me alone! I don't want you here!"

*But I want youuuu, Billyyyy,* it responded with mocking sweetnees. *Whyyy would I ever wanttt to leavvvvve?* Billy could feel it chuckling as some sort of inhuman digit started exploring where the parasitic creature was attached - the fleshy inside of Billy's ear. It scratched and picked at this barrier of skin between Billy's brain and the outside world.

*Just relaxxxx, Billyyy. We're going to be gooooood friendsssssss. For the rest of your life, yesssss, yesssss....*

Billy lay crying, helpless. He wanted to run but he couldn't move. His head was too heavy with this thing attached. And anyway, where could he even run? He would just bring it with him.

And the louder he screamed, the more desperate he became, the bigger and stronger it grew. Like his fear and his pain wasn't fighting it, but feeding it.

"Somebody," he called out quietly. It was all he could do. Just keep hoping someone, somehow, could reach him. That someone could save him, because he couldn't save himself. "Help. Me. Please."

Downstairs, Billy's Mom sighed. Her face strained not to reveal and encourage emotions. Still, some came through. She made a decision.

"Now *where* did I put those?" Billy's Mom scratched her head. She opened the basement door to look under the stairwell.

Back in Billy's room, the thing attached to his head extended its exploring digits. They found the purchase they were looking for. They dug in and gripped his ear. In the sudden flood of pain, Billy began flailing and fell off the bed, landing roughly on his back. He reached up and tried to get his arms around the creature, and rip it off. The loose bag of filth and tissue easily flowed out of his grasp.

*Whyyyy do you fighttt?* Billy's ear tore in an instant of excruciating pain. It began to reach inside.

"Aaagghh!"

*Fighttt if you wantttt. Soonnn, I will be youuu.....*

Billy's Mom broke in the door.

Billy felt the enormous sac of fluid start to shake and shudder. Strange nailed tentacles further ripped and pinned his ear open wide, and he screamed as the slimy thing reared back in preparation to launch all the way inside his head.

Just as the creature began to surge forward, Billy's Mom shoved the head clippers between them and clipped off what remained of Billy's ear.

Billy cried out in surprise. The creature, disconnected and suddenly unbalanced, fell onto the floor with a wet thud. Its momentum caused it to roll away from Billy. Billy scrambled to the far wall as, with expert speed, Mrs. Short grasped the sac at its top and twisted. The creature was entangled in its own casing.

She bent down and tied a bow knot in the top of the sack. Inside, the creature made wheezing sounds and shuddered as it began to fade without its host.

"Well, Billy," she said, picking up the wet pod and wiping some stray mucous on her apron, "I hope you're ready to go to school now. You've wasted a lot of time this morning."

She slung the pod over her shoulder, and headed downstairs lightly humming a tune.

Billy looked around the room, dazed, and huddling in the room's far corner. He realized something. "Mom! MOM!"

She turned around sharply. "Oh, what is it *now*?! You're almost late for school."

"I still have to go to school?" Billy asked incredulously.

"Of course you do!" said his Mom. "Don't you want to be able to get a job one day, like your father?"

"But – what about my ear?"

"Oh, honestly, Billy. Can't you do anything for yourself? I still have to make your sandwiches."

She sighed, and her expression softened slightly. "I'll sew it back on for you. But make sure you listen up in school today." She gripped the slick, green sac tightly as she turned and stepped down the stairs. The stairs protested creakily, but knew better than to make a fuss.

Billy stood up. He shook his head, but it refused to clear. He walked on shaky legs into the bathroom. As he brushed his teeth, his breathing slowed down to a more normal rate. Soon, he was able to bring himself to look at blood, greenish fluid and flecks of Pod on his neck and wipe it off.

He hoped school would be a little easier than this.

BILLY WENT DOWNSTAIRS, **and found his mother in the kitchen, hard at work over the sink.** She was pounding the remains of the Pod with a meat tenderizer. Green mucous occasionally sprayed onto the soothing blue of the kitchen walls, and did not clash.

She saw him and smiled distractedly. "Go sit in the living room. I'll have your lunch ready in just a second." Billy left the kitchen and did as he was told. She hefted up the dead creature in its sac, and drained it into a colander. Wax paper was set on the counter, and next to it, two slices of whitebread. She brought a carving knife back to the sink.

A few minutes later she came into the living room. "Go sit by the sewing machine," she said. Billy went over. "Now put your head down under the needle." He did so. She put his ear on top of his head, and began to stitch it back.

"Stop squirming," his mom said curtly. He gripped the bottom of his chair, and tried his best not to scream. Mrs. Short resumed humming, as her foot worked the speed control pedal. "There. That should do it." She stood up, and holding Billy's chin to the left, surveyed her work with pride. His ear was now reattached to his head with the new herringbone double-stitch pattern. "Perfect," she said.

Billy's Mom went to the kitchen, and returned with a brown bag.

"Here's your lunch," she said. She handed him a neatly wrapped brown bag with a perfect fold at the top. "And don't forget your hat." She put his favorite red baseball cap on his head.

"Today's lunch is made fresh. You should really like it."

Billy looked up at her for a second, and watched the sides of her face, at the cheekbones. Her face was doing that weird thing, where it almost seemed like there was another realer face beneath it. She noticed his look, and returned what seemed like a genuine smile.

"Mom...why..." He looked down. "I mean, I'm grateful, but can't you and Dad help me get rid of it all the way? There's some kind of a - seed or something in my head. And it seems like it gets worse every day I'm at school. Can't we just get rid of it all the way?"

Her mask shook a bit, around her eyes. Billy could have been imagining it, when he saw just a hint of sadness. "There's only so long we can do things we want to. Growing up means giving all that up, for your own good." She kissed his cheek. "Now hurry up. You don't want the bus to miss you."


BILLY WALKED DOWN THEIR DRIVEWAY, **and waited for the bus.** He looked up and down the road; no one else was outside. For the moment, he could relax. He somehow had the whole world to himself.

It was such a relief to not have to pretend that everything was fine. To not have to figure out how many questions he could dare.

Billy had noticed awhile ago that his Dad had something strange underneath his suit-jacket, which seemed to tell him what to do. More recently, Billy had noticed his Mom also had some weird look to her face, almost like there was another face layered on top. That looked exactly like her face, but smiled the same way every time. Whenever Billy asked them about it, they always just changed the subject. It was all so strange. They both acted like everything was absolutely normal.

Maybe it was. He was just a kid. It sure didn't seem normal. Any more than how his Dad would dress up in a suit and risk his life on the highway, just to work inside an office making phone calls and answering emails. Or how his mom dressed up just to stay inside the house.

And then that...thing had started whispering from inside his ear. And last night when he'd slept, it had grown big enough to almost take him over. Whatever it even was! And worst of all, it looked a bit like what he'd seen on some of the other grownups, including his dad.

Bad enough he had to go to school 5 days a week. He kicked a rock, and sighed. At least Mom had fixed his ear. Billy touched his ear gingerly. It still hurt. He was lucky it hadn't been his entire head. The thing had been letting Billy restore his confidence, lulling him into a false sense of security...Good thing there was still enough of his Mom behind that thing on her face to save him. Even though she just couldn't go beyond that and help him completely finish it off. Or even tell him what was really going on.

Were there any other grownups who would tell him? It was hard to trust adults, let alone teachers. But his teacher Mr. Murple seemed different. Not only was he less mean and weird than most of the other grownups, he actually seemed able to listen. Billy came to a decision. Billy was going to risk it, and ask him what was really going on.

Until then, Billy felt it was wisest to hold back the questions that burned inside him.

Billy breathed out, and tried to just enjoy the quiet before the bus. He tried to look on the bright side. At least they lived outside the Developments. Sure, some sort of inhuman creature no one would talk about, was trying to take Billy over from the inside and turn him into its unthinking slave. But in the Developments there wasn't any space between the houses. At least where Billy lived they had a yard, some trees and even nearby forests.

Tees and grass could grow unplanned and free. Squirrels ran around without explanation. The lack of asphalt helped the morning be both cool and bright. The fall leaves turned both sides of the road into carnivals of color. He sat down on his favorite rock, right behind their mailbox, and watched it all.

It really was amazing. Whenever he tried to talk with his parents about things like this, about this beauty, they kind of just patted his head. Grownups never seemed to see the world, just move through it. Billy sighed, and closed his eyes, and felt the peace around him. His hair felt warm and snug under his hat. The brisk fall air caressed his face. Leaves fell around him in delicate, multicolored spirals. On trees and telephone wires, birds swapped notes. Small animals danced along the grass and in trees along the road.

He couldn't even feel the pain of his ear. He temporarily forgot about the thing that had tried to invade his head. Everything was real, and beautiful. Sound, and sight, and touch and smell. And all of it was just as it should be.

That was the thing. Life really was beautiful. This world really was beautiful. He could feel it inside his own chest. It was the furthest feeling from that creature that he could imagine. It was all connected, and he was a part of it.

An idea started to come to him, inspired by the rush of openness, of sights and smells and sounds. Maybe there was a way! Maybe he could-

AN ENORMOUS YELLOW **beast** suddenly screamed to a halt, knocking a nearby mailbox into splinters. Shards of wood sprayed through the air, some of it glancing off Billy as he stood there stunned.

It was the schoolbus. It had missed him by inches.

Billy was in shock. He tried to shake it off and return to that lovely state of mind. It was shattered.

The bus door slammed open, and one red eye glared down at him over nicotine-stained lips. Where the man's other eye should have been was only a patch. The man's beard was filthy, and his shaven head was scarred with ancient surgery.

"Are you our new bus driver?" asked Billy.

"No, I'm your pig-sucking uncle!" he roared. "Ya getting in or not?!"

"Yessir," said Billy. He meekly made his way down the aisle to his usual seat. Billy's friend Timmy got up to let Billy take the seat next to the window. Timmy preferred to sit in the aisle, where it was easier to trip people.

Timmy was a very happy child, brimming with school spirit. In particular he enjoyed inflicting physical and emotional trauma on anyone weaker than himself. He was very popular, and was sure to go far. Billy made sure he was one of Timmy's closer friends.

Billy sat down, just as the school bus lurched forward with a scream of tired metal. The children desperately gripped the aged green vinyl covering of the seats before them. "Move, you old cow! " the driver screamed. "MOVE hahahaha!!!"

Billy adjusted his seat, and placed his backpack on his lap. He rubbed some dirt off the smeared window with his sleeve. The tiny hole of clarity gave tantalizing hints of the sunlit morning passing them by.

"I hope today's Poisonball day," said Timmy. He clutched his backpack in a spasm of adrenaline.

"Think it might be?" said Billy.

"Yeah!" said Timmy, his face flushed with excitement. "I can't wait to pound people with my balls."

Billy leaned forward, to see the other side of Timmy's face. Timmy's ear wasn't visible...

"Timmy," said Billy, hesitantly, "did you ever get a...did you ever get a pain in your ear?"

"What? No way. Pain is for wussies." Tim looked at him for a moment, and smiled dangerously. "Why? Did your ear ever hurt?"

"No way!" Billy recovered. "Can't wait for Poisonball."

The bus screamed through the various suburban developments, picking up more children and leaving smoke in its wake. They soon encountered the final stop of their morning journey. A large old house, surrounded by a couple acres of lovely meadow, where they would pick up Tracy Appelbaum.

As the bus jerked around the corner, Billy gazed through the smeared safety glass into a field. His eyes lit on an unsaddled horse. The morning sunlight's made it's mane seem to glow.

The strong young horse trotted from left to right. It stopped suddenly, turned, and found Billy's gaze. As the bus continued around the corner, Billy held his breath and wanted this rare glorious instant to last forever.

The bus drew nearer, the unbroken creature rediscovered the sun, and galloped joyously away. The bus screeched to a halt at the end of Tracy's driveway.

Billy watched as Tracy turned towards her house and waved back at her parents. She walked towards the bus, her footsteps light and firm. The bus driver swung the door open. As she ascended, the breeze blew her hair as her face was caught in the morning light shining through the bus' front window. Billy was struck by her beauty. The driver spit a stream of tobacco juice and bile upon the floor.

Tracy sat down with her friends, several seats in front of him. She was smart, too. Bill had also never seen her mistreat anyone less popular or beautiful. Some of the older boys would talk about her in ways that seemed to break her into a set of parts. Billy had no such illusions. She was beauty itself.

Timmy smacked him.

"Ow!" said Billy.

"That's what you get for not paying attention to me," Timmy said.

"But you weren't saying anything,"

"How about if I was? What were you staring at?"

This was a delicate situation. If Billy protested too strongly, Timmy might decide to beat him. But if he said nothing, Timmy would see him as easy prey. Then Timmy might notice his ear. And start flicking it. And then there'd be nothing to do but pray for the morning ride to end.

Billy decided to assume an attitude halfway between it's-no-big-deal and what's-your-problem. "Oh come on, I would've heard you," Billy said, smiling.

Timmy looked at him strangely for a second. And then he smiled, too.

"You've got the moon eyes for Tracy, don't you?"

*He knew!* Billy flinched instinctively. He caught himself, but it was too late. Timmy smelled blood. He laughed wickedly, his grin never quite reaching his eyes.

Timmy leaned in forward for the kill.

"Billy-willy's willie's got a woooo-dy," Timmy started reciting in a dangerously catchy sing-song tone. Billy squirmed. "Billy-willy's willie's got a woooo-dy..." Some other kids were starting to look over. If it caught on he was done for.

"Billy-will-"

"Say, did you hear about that horrible accident?"

"Huh?" Timmy said, momentarily distracted.

Billy had only one chance. "The horrible accident, over the weekend. You know, the train of orphaned infants?" Billy tried to hide the desperation in his voice.

Timmy's eyes began to cloud in a sweeping wave of bloodlust.

"How many dead?" Timmy licked his lips. He leaned forward and grabbed Billy by the shirt. *"How many?"*

"I dunno, could be a couple hundred," Billy said, trying to keep cool. "They won't know until the bodies are filtered from the spaghetti sauce." Would it work?

Timmy let him go, and turned away, entranced. He turned back again to Billy. "How- did it- *happen*," he asked slowly, intensely.

"I don't know for sure," said Billy as he self-consciously readjusted his hat. "But I heard the train exploded near a spaghetti factory, and some of the smaller bodies fell in the sauce," Timmy was almost there... just another second...

The left side of Timmy's face began to twitch.

"They say it made the sauce more salty," Billy finished, with sudden inspiration.

Timmy's head tilted back, and his eyes glazed over the rest of the way. Drool began to gather in the corner of his mouth.

"Coooolllll," said Timmy. Billy sighed with relief. For now, he was safe.

"Blood," Timmy whispered softly, wistfully. "Sweet blood."

THE SCHOOL BUS lurched through the iron gates of Alan Foster Dulles Medium School. It came to a screeching stop right before a speed bump, throwing unprepared children forward. One girl flew down the aisle and past the bus driver, to rebound off the windshield.

The driver drove delicately over the speed bump, and cackled. He pulled up to the curb behind another bus and swung the bus door open. He then sat back in his seat, grunted, and inserted a wad of chewing tobacco into one of several gaps between his filthy teeth.

Tracy and another student helped the shaken girl to her feet. Then, with order born from repetition, the children walked out of the bus and stepped onto the sidewalk conveyor belt outside.

Billy readjusted his hat, so the brim would slightly cover his wounded ear. He swung his backpack over his shoulder. Making sure that Tim safely stood in front of him, he stepped out of the bus and onto the conveyor belt.

The belt moved forward. It led off into the distance into the school's gaping red-bricked maw. As his conveyor belt moved forward, it began to merge with other conveyor belts loading students from the other buses. Billy looked far off towards the entrance to the parking lot, just in time to see the wrought-iron gate slam shut.

Billy turned forward. The entrance to Allen Foster Dulles' Medium School loomed above him. Soon the conveyor belt brought him close enough to examine the school's magnificent entryway mural. It depicted a smiling sun, shining down upon ranks of suited grownups as they tilled a field. The fields tidy rows of plants were yielding a fresh crop of happy children. The boys grasped identical blue briefcases, while the rows of smiling girls waved pink spatulas.

Billy and his fellow schoolmates were conveyed inside, and then past the hidden cameras and gum-sniffing dogs. Billy carefully hunched his shoulders to show a properly respectful attitude. No non-compliant students were detected, and they moved forward without incident.

The conveyor belts flowed onwards through the lobby, and then down the hall past the school's sports trophy case to reach the towering double-doors of the Main Assembly Room. This was the end of the line. The students stepped off the conveyor belts. The nurses, coaches and teachers stood by, lasers in hand, ready to scan the UPC code on the inside collar of each student's shirt.

Once past that gauntlet, Billy followed the other students into the cavernous Main Assembly Room. Here the students lined up to await the morning address by the Principal. Billy walked towards his preferred place in the ranks.

With the last child scanned in, the Faculty put away the lasers and retreated to the large vat of Coffee at the far right side of the huge room. There they refilled their mugs, and drank deeply, conversing with each other or thinking their own unfathomable Faculty thoughts.

It was fairly safe to observe the Faculty during this morning ritual. This was a good way to determine which Faculty members might be particularly dangerous today. Billy watched his Shopping teacher exchange a glazed smile with the new Vice Nurse, Miss Hauptmann. The teacher softly stroked his moustache. It was small in the distance, and Billy couldn't tell if the moustache moved by itself or if that was just an illusion. Some of them seemed to have strange rustling things beneath their clothes, but others did not at all. Billy could make no sense of it.

"Good morning, children!" a firm, loud, dry voice snapped from the doorway.

"Good morning, Mr. Maybee!" the children responded in unison. Each child strived for a tone that perfectly merged eagerness with awe for authority.

With his hands clasped tightly behind his back, Principal Maybee slowly strode into the room. He gave a brief nod to the adults worshipping at the vat. They nodded back, before returning to the Vat for more Coffee.

Principal Maybee walked to the front of the Main Assembly Room. The children saluted and then stood waiting in quiet rows.

Maybee was slightly tall, and whipcord lean. His thin, black hair was cut brutally short, terminating exactly under his almost lobeless ears. His suit was black, single-breasted, and flatly spotless from the top of his bowtie to the bottom of his squeaking shoes.

Maybee removed his feared Red Stamp from his inner suit pocket, and inspected it. He placed it back inside his pocket, and pulled briefly at his ear before clasping both his hands tightly behind his back. The Principal's one vanity, his goatee, twisted slightly from side to side as he inspected his charges. His gaze moved restlessly over the ranks of small humans. Searching ruthlessly for any flaw, any weakness, any sign of incipient spirit.

Billy wondered if Maybee had some weird hidden thing, like his parents. If he did, it didn't show anywhere. Mr. Maybee was really thin, and his clothes were unusually tight for a grownup. Maybe he just *was* a creature, Billy wondered. And the whole *school* was his host.

Maybee started walking through the ranks, and soon strolled out of Billy's view. That was fine by Billy. Through trial and error, he had long ago found his favorite position - three rows back, and slightly to the right. Far enough to escape immediate inspection, just close enough to look like he wasn't trying to avoid it.

"What are we here to do today, children?" Maybee asked.

"To learn to live!" the children shouted together with feigned eagerness.

"And how do we do this?"

"By LIVING TO OBEY!" they yelled in almost-perfect unison.

The room choked silent with sudden tension. Perfect - except for one lone voice.

Someone had missed. Someone had been late with the response.

Billy realized with terror that it had been himself!

*"Who was that?!"* yelled Mr. Maybee. He paced quickly through their ranks, enraged. The children tried not to look at each other.

*"Who wasn't PAYING ATTENTION?"*

What was Billy going to do? He glanced nervously at the fellow students to his left and right. Did they know it had been him? Would they rat him out?

"Well?" Mr. Maybee demanded. He passed Billy's row, stopping a couple of rows past. "It came from this area. Was it you, Trilling?"

Billy wished he could see, but he didn't dare step out of line. He could barely contain himself. Behind him, he heard Andy Trilling swallowed nervously. "N-no, sir! N-never!" he squeaked. Billy knew Andy. The poor kid was as good as gone already.

"This is the Morning Assembly", Maybee continued. "This is where we assemble the student body. Where we you present yourself, so we can see how well we've put you together for the coming day." Maybee looked down at Trilling as if he was something stuck to his perfectly polished brown shoes.

"Your nose is running, Trilling. Maybe you were distracted by the *cold*?" Mr. Maybee asked, his voice becoming soft and seemed almost compassionate. "Maybe you think we should turn up the heat? Maybe that's the reason for this disobedience. You don't think we're spending enough money *heating* you?"

"No, *sir!*" Nervously, Andy Trilling wiped his nose.

"You. *Bulbous.* Piece of *garbage*," began Maybee, slowly and quietly. Billy was dying to turn around and see what was happening, but he didn't dare. "You wiped your nose - on your *sleeve! On your sleeve!* Is that how you show *respect*? Is *that* the attitude that made this country great? *Is it? IS IT?!"*

Trilling knew he was in trouble. He tried to speak. Under Mr. Maybee's fiery gaze, his words just turned to mumbled mush. Maybee reached into his suit and drew forth the Red Stamp. Without taking his eyes off Trilling, he adjusted it.

"What letter shall it be for you today, Mr. Trilling? How long would you like to be Tested?"

"Please sir! I didn't mean to -"

"Shall it be a 'C'? Perhaps a 'D' would make you try a little harder?"

Billy told himself he couldn't save Trilling. The poor boy was doomed from the instant he'd wiped his nose.

But...it wasn't right to let Trilling be punished like this. Billy had made this happen, by not paying attention to the singing. Billy swallowed. Should he turn himself in, and be punished? Or stay silent, and let someone else be punished in his place?

Another voice rang out into the main assembly. "Me, sir," someone said. "It was me."

Startled, Billy strained his ears. It was a normal, conversational tone without shame, or terror, or even begging! Was he insane?

Billy tracked Mr. Maybee's clacking steps as he walked, with agonizing slowness, away from Trilling and towards this new transgressor. Whoever it was stood two rows ahead of Billy. Maybee's footsteps slowed, then stopped.

"*You*," Maybee said. "Pfeiffer." Maybee chuckled. "I should have known. It would have to be you, wouldn't it, Raymond? Dear, sweet Raymond..." He sighed. "Whatever shall we do with you? Sometimes I think you just don't have the wit to do well. But others say different."

"You mean, *differently*, sir," Raymond said, corrected his grammar. Billy's heard a collective gasp of shock from the students.

Maybee paused, as if unsure how to respond. "They say that you're intelligent. *Perceptive*, even." Maybee resumed. His voice grew heavier, darker. "That must mean you're doing this deliberately. Are you? Are you *deliberately mocking* me, Pfeiffer? Are you *spitting* in my *face*?"

"Not really, sir," said the boy. "I'm just tired." Billy watched as Maybee began adjusting the handle of his Stamp.

"You're *tired*!" Maybee laughed abruptly. "I must admit it's beyond me. Oh, well." His voice hardened. "I guess we'll need some help to get to the bottom of this quandary, of why you're so lacking in the proper...focus."

Maybee abruptly swung the stamp against Pfeiffer's forehead. When Maybee pulled it away, the stamp gave a sudden, sucking sound that carried across the silent room like a gunshot. On Pfeiffer's forehead was a red, angry welt surrounded by the Principal's official seal.

"'I'", said Mr. Maybee. "For 'Incomplete'. Do you know what that means?"

"No," Ray asked.

"It means," Maybee sneered. "I think *differently* about proper behavior," he said. "Take him to Testing until we can mark him complete." Maybee ordered.

"NO!" screamed Pfeiffer. He turned, perhaps to run. Miss Hauptmann, the new Vice Nurse, was suddenly standing right next to him. She reached forward, and placed her hand firmly on Raymond Pfeiffer's shoulder. Relatively new at the school, she was already quite well known to the students. She was young for an adult, with thick, dark hair that elsewhere might have been considered beautiful. Here, it gave her the polish and perfection of an obsidian blade.

"Yes," whispered Miss Hauptmann, and smiled.

Pfeiffer screamed in the cavernous silence as the Nurse took him away. Maybee returned to the front of the Main Assembly. From the corner of his eye, Billy watched as Coach Brumble and Nurse Kraft-Ebbing put down their Coffee and hurried over to Hauptmann and her new captive. Nurse Kraft-Ebbing took Pfeiffer's other arm. Coach Brumble followed behind, in case Pfeiffer tried to escape. This was merely a formality. No student in living memory had yet escaped the Iron Nurse.

Billy noticed several other children trying to control their shaking. It wasn't from the cold.

"Well," said Maybee. He seemed quite satisfied. "I hope the rest of you will learn from this. If you've all *Paid Attention* to this- unfortu-

nate incident, then you are on the road to learning the *Right Things*."
He reviewed the assembly one more final time. "I'll be seeing you."

"Good day, Mr. Maybee!" the crowd screamed back.

"Dismissed." The children slowly shuffled back out to the conveyor belts, to be transported to their morning classes. The teachers took final refills of Coffee in their mugs, and unplugged the Coffee vat for its transfer to the Faculty Lounge.

Billy had also picked his spot for its closeness to the Main Assembly Room's exit. He was once again fortunate. He was able to leave the room quickly enough to avoid selection for work detail.

**BILLY STEPPED off the hallway conveyor belt, and paused outside his first period class.** Mr. Murple was the teacher. Billy hoped he could talk with him after class.

Billy stepped inside. The classroom was small, but the room was fairly high. The large windows reached from the tops of the heaters to almost touch the ceiling. Apparently this had worried the Parent-Teacher Authority – if the windows let in too much light, it could cause uncontrolled cheerfulness. Rather than undergoing the costly process of bricking them over, the PTA instead ingeniously hid the windows behind discarded sunshades. They tinged the sunlight a perfect, filthy greenish yellow.

Billy turned his attention from his foiled attempt to look outside, and saw a new teacher sat behind the front desk. Billy watched as he leaned back in the stuffed leather chair, sipping his morning mug of Coffee meditatively as he reviewed an all-black ledger. Billy's heart sank. Where was Mr. Murple? Billy hoped he was alright. Maybe Mr. Murple was just late, or on vacation or something? Grownups did that from time to time.

Billy hung his jacket on one of the nails the PTA had thoughtfully pounded into the wall and walked to his desk. Other students shuffled past him to their selected destinations. One of their few freedoms was choosing where to sit. Billy had selected his favorite seat at the beginning of the year, and through persistence it had become recognized as his own. It was almost entirely to the back, in the first row from the right. Just like the Main Assembly Room, he preferred to be as far as possible from the grownups and still be near the exit.

Billy placed his backpack under his chair, removed his pen and notebook, and tried to prepare himself for the class ahead. His ear had stopped throbbing, and his desk was perfectly aligned with the linoleum floor tiles. Billy felt as ready as he could.

Across and to the left from Billy, Chris Barlowe sat his large frame carefully. They exchanged nods of greeting. Barlowe was the heaviest child in the 6th grade. He was relatively easygoing and difficult to physically intimidate. He was the brunt of occasional jokes of extreme cruelty, but was for the most part relatively popular.

To the front of the room, Russel Neidermeyer moved his short and gawky frame to his favorite spot - directly in front of the teacher's desk. He took out his pocket notebook, and prepared to take notes on his fellow students. Most children preferred to sit further away from the teachers. For Russ, this closeness was vital. It was all that kept him from anonymous student reprisals that could well end his dreams of a bright gray future in middle management.

Keith Moranis sat down in the seat before Neidermeyer. Billy waved hello to him too. Keith was genuinely well liked, because he posed absolutely no threat to anybody. His truly astounding mental thickness and clumsy feet had earned him the nickname "Stumpy." Keith had yet to even learn what the word meant.

The classroom filled with other boys and girls of various shapes, sizes. With a couple of rare exceptions, their skins were all similar shades of a slightly pasty, well-scrubbed pink. They all knew each other. Some exchanged muted greetings with Billy as they realigned their desks and prepared for the day's lessons.

Then Tracy came in.

She walked slowly across the room, her flower-print skirt flowing lightly. She walked right down Billy's aisle to hang up her coat! She smiled at him, as she passed! He smiled back weakly. Then Tracy turned around and went slowly back up the aisle. Billy He could not take his eyes off her, and swallowed hard as she strolled across the room and took her seat.

Just three rows over. Three.... Billy was feeling a way that hurt that also somehow felt really good.

Billy breathed deeply, and tried to distract himself by inspecting the edge of his desk. There were the scratched-in initials, curses, short jokes, and the logos of various popular musical groups which had been left there by other children, in classes past. Some day, when no one was looking, Billy, too, would take out a drawing compass or sharp-tipped pen, and add his own short statement to this legacy of the damned.

THE LAST STUDENT WALKED IN, just as the bell tolled. The teacher wrote a mark next to the last student's name in a large, black ledger. Then he rose to address the classroom.

"Good morning, students." The teacher paused as he looked the rows up and down.

"Align your desks." Keith's was out of line, of course. He marshaled his large feet to quickly kick it into place.

"Good. My name is," he picked up a large piece of chalk, and scrawled on the chalkboard as he spoke, "Mr. Perkins." He finished writing with a piercing scrape of thie chalk, put it down, and smiled at the class. "And this class is English – The Right Way. Are there any questions before we begin?"

In the third row, a girl raised her hand. "Yes, uh," Perkins looked at his seating chart, "Marla, what is it?"

Marla bit her lip. "Where's Mr. Murple?"

Mr. Perkins went to his desk, and took a mimeographed sheet from his black ledger. He put on a pair of reading glasses.

" 'Mr. Josiah Murple has voluntarily submitted to treatment for his unrepentant noncompliance. He has now been Substituted. He will return to lesser duties somewhere else as soon as his treatment is complete. Any further questions or mention of him will be met with suitable reprimands.' " He put the sheet back down on his desk, and looked across the classroom. "Any other questions?"

In front of Billy, Keith Moranis raised his hand.

"Yes, uh, Keith?"

"What's a reppimand?"

"It's when you do something you shouldn't, and something completely justifiable happens to you or your family."

"Oh," said Keith. So much for that, thought Billy. It looked like Mr. Murple had bigger things to deal with than answering his questions about how the world worked...

Mr. Perkins placed his glasses on his desk. "Now then. Are there any assignments due?"

Everyone in the class stifled a groan as Russell Niedermeyer's hand shot into the air.

Perkins glanced down at him. "Yes, Russell?"

"The last assignment was to read the newspaper and list 100 English words that could lead to bad ideas."

"And did you list them?"

Russ cleared his throat, and his mighty Adam's apple cocked into position. He began reading in a proud, monotonous voice. "In alphabetic order- aberration, abnormality, absolution..."

Billy's head remained rigidly forward in an impressive imitation of attentiveness. His eyes wandered listlessly around the room. Finally they settled on Tracy. A natural, easy place to rest. She was looking ahead too. Maybe she also was giving only the appearance of attention.

Just sitting there, in stillness, she was a breathing artwork of life. Like a dawn's glow.

"....debauchery, deviate, dissent, eccentric, ecstasy ...."

As Billy watched, Tracy leaned back and reached back with a perfect arm, and arranged her long, free-flowing hair to hang behind her chair.

Then Billy saw something impossible.

Billy looked again. And the impossible refused to disappear.

The teacher, Russell's voice, the classroom, faded into nothing. Everything went away but what he *could not* just have seen.

Tracy's ear. Her perfect, lovely ear.

It was bleeding....


THE BELL TOLLED AGAIN. **The class was released into the hallway.** Billy followed the class out the door, his mind reeling.

There stood Tracy, walking just a few feet ahead. Tracy had seemed so perfect. So beautiful and so good. Could Tracy really be imperfect? Could she have something in common with him? Something she was fighting too?

Tracy stepped on the hall conveyor belt to her next class. Billy's next class was in the opposite direction. Did he have enough time to talk to her? It was very risky. If he was late to his next class, it would be marked against him. He could even draw attention to them both.

At the same time he just *had* to talk to her.

Billy watched the students go by. They all looked so very obedient and industrious. Upperclassmen would occasionally step off and visit their lockers, and primp themselves in small mirrors. Were they hiding secrets too, that were just like his?

Billy shifted his bookbag and watched Tracy near the end of the hall. He might not have another chance to talk with her all day. Chris Barlowe chose that moment to walk over to Billy, in the middle of his indecision. "Hey," Chris said, and adjusted his backpack. "So, uh..."

Chris looked at him, and then looked around them both, nonchalantly. He leaned in.

"So, what do you think of the new teacher?" Chris asked.

Billy looked around him. There were no obvious Neidermeyers in sight. "He seems like all the other teachers," Billy said. Chris nodded knowingly. Mr. Murple had been different. He even seemed to be on the childrens' side. He seemed to like what he spent his days doing. He'd even had a sly way of pointing out what the lessons weren't teaching them.

Billy looked up the hallway. Tracy was gone. He had no idea which direction she had gone in.

Billy took a last look into the old classroom. He saw Perkins reach into Mr. Murple's desk, and throw something that looked like a book into the trashcan with disgust. The substitute teacher then left his desk to walk around the room.

Billy looked at Chris. He looked at Chris. He felt like he could trust him – but could he be sure?

"That book or whatever must have been Mr. Murple's," Billy said.

"Really?" said Chris, curious.

Billy poked his head back into the classroom. The new teacher was busy laying worksheets on desks for the next class. His back was turned. Billy reached into the traschcan, snatched the book and hid it under his shirt. He left just as the teacher had begun to turn around.

"We should probably get out of here," Billy said.

"Absolutely," said Chris. They both had just enough time to get to their next class and not draw suspicion.

They stepped on the conveyor belts to their next class.

"What were you doing?" said Chris softly. "Have you gone crazy?"

"This thing was probably Mr. Murple's! Don't you want to know what it is?"

"Well, what is it?"

Billy looked around carefully. No one appeared be eying them as the conveyor belt whisked them by. He pulled the book from underneath his shirt.

It was a hardcover book, tattered and old with a cracked binding, and with appeared to be a round hole that reminded Billy of bullet holes he'd seen in video games. It also had a little blood on it. It's title was *The Real History of Coffee and its Only Cure.*

"Well, I sure hope that was worth risking Testing," said Chris. "Why the heck did you take that risk?"

"Do you ever-" Bill began. He stopped. Either Billy could trust him or he couldn't. Chris hadn't ratted him out yet. He might as well go forward now.

"Do you ever get these ideas, that seem to come from - voices or something? Something that seems like a part of you, but isn't, and doesn't want you to be happy, but that also fits in with school and your parents like *completely?*"

Chris looked a little scared. He kept his voice down as they rolled along on the conveyor belt between the classes. "What do you mean?"

"Like something in your ear. Something deeper inside, but like inside your ear that seems like it wants to take you over. And it doesn't want you to be happy. But it seems like everyone is encouraging it to grow."

"I gotta go, there's my class," said Chris. "And if you know what you're doing, you won't talk to anyone else about that nonsense that you're talking about."

At least Chris wasn't telling him he was crazy.

"Ok," said Billy. "I gotta go too." They stepped off the belt, and towards their separate classes.

As Billy stepped into the class, he realized they could also have been talking about how much they had to go and get away from the school.


BILLY ARRIVED **at his next class, and set down his books.** He was starting to feel hungry. He prepared to try to keep his eyes open.

This class always seemed to last forever. He had no idea what it was about this class that was so difficult. Billy realized with a start that he didn't even remember what they went over in this class.

What was even this class' name?

Perhaps it just didn't matter. It was, after all, just another class to get through. Billy did wish Tracy was in this class though. Especially today. He'd give almost anything for a few seconds to chat with her. It rushed back to him again, the anxiety and the excitement jumbled together. The shock, fear and wonder that one of the most magical girl creatures he knew could be even a little bit like him.

Mrs. Hobbey cleared her throat. Billy reluctantly brought himself back to the present. Whatever this class was, Mrs. Hobbey taught it, with a vengeance.

She bolted the classroom door securely shut, and smiled at the students, revealing strong rows of crushing, yellowed teeth. She was overweight, and over fifty; her face was pocked and pitted from what must have been a short and brutal youth. As heavy as she was, the children had long ago learned that she was surprisingly fast and strong when angered.

"Good evening, children," Mrs. Hobbey began. "Today we're going to –" There was a knock at the classroom door. Mrs. Hobbey undid the bolts. "Ah, Raymond. Come in," she said.

Ray Pfeiffer was led into the class by Nurse Kraft-Ebbing. He looked pale and drawn, and appeared now to have a slight limp. Mrs. Hobbey and Nurse Kraft-Ebbing shared cold smiles.

"So nice to see you again today, Raymond," said Mrs. Hobbey. "Take your seat over there," said Mrs. Hobbey. Ray limped past Billy to his desk. Nurse Kraft-Ebbing turned on her heel and left the classroom.

"Now if you're all going to be good little boys and girls, today we're going to watch a video." Billy almost laughed in delighted relief. He couldn't believe his good luck. A few actual seconds to himself. "Sally," Mrs. Hobbey continued, "would you turn out the lights? And you children over there, pull down the window shades." The students eagerly complied.

Mrs. Hobbey pulled down a gray screen from its holding case above the chalkboard. She then waddled over to the back of the class, and turned on the projector. Satisfied, she sat down at her desk in front, and smoothed out her distended skirt.

A white square appeared on the dingy gray screen stretched over the chalkboard. It turned a matching gray. A black circle then appeared, with a number 5 inside it. A line sprang from the center of the circle, and travelled slowly clockwise, gradually erasing the number. When the line completed its journey and was once again at the top of the circle, a number 4 appeared. It all reminded Billy of radar screens in old war movies; the white bar sweeping the circle to detect unwanted intruders. It was very soothing, the way the numbers melded into the next. Now it was at 3.

Billy suddenly began to feel the weight of the whole day, down his eyelids. How nice it would be to rest...

A number 2 appeared, and then a number 1. The 1 softly faded into the image of a television, with a spiral inside it. Billy recognized it, as the happy-wacky spiral in the Mr. McGillicutty's baseball hat that he usually wore in Shopping class. It looked funny and safe, there on the screen. Why, it was even dancing around a bit. Spinning. Billy's...eyes....began.....boring through it...into...the screen...

Billy felt a sharp pain hit the back of his head. He heard a penny hit the floor. He shook himself awake with a start. *What the heck was that?*

Billy turned around, and saw Ray. Ray held an improvised sling-shot, made of two plastic pens and a rubber band. On his desk lay several other pennies. With his other hand, Ray held his finger to his lips in a "Shhh!"gesture.

Ray loaded and shot another penny at the kid to Billy's right. The kid jumped in surprise. Billy turned forward and kept his eyes trained straight ahead. He heard more pennies Ray shot at other kids, the coins ringing out as they fell onto the floor.

Mrs. Hobbey suddenly looked up, and leapt up from her desk. She strode the aisles between the desks, searching for the source of such rebellious sound. Billy kept his eyes pointed straight forward. She looked over Billy's shoulder at Ray, and her eyes narrowed. She pounced. Mrs. Hobbey re-emerged into Billy's field of view, dragging

Ray by the neck. She undid the classroom door's bolts, and dragged him outside into the hall.

Billy told himself there was nothing he could do. He hated himself. Poor Ray was going to go right back into Testing. All for trying to awaken Billy and some others. The rest of the classroom didn't even notice Ray's removal. They continued staring into the screen.

Billy began to hear a voice droning from the projector. "Sleepy... you don't need to be awake, be sleepy....Let your fears drift with your sleep...let your mind relax...sleep...."

Billy blinked quickly. Even though he knew it was some kind of trap, Billy still felt the pull to drift off into unconsciousness. It was so very, very tempting to just let himself go under. To drift into wherever they were being guided. Billy strained mightily to stay awake. He remembered Tracy.

Eventually the pull lessened, and he was able to look away. Carefully avoiding looking at the screen, Billy glanced surreptitiously around him. He could see perhaps a handful of randomly scattered children around the classroom, who might have also resisted the projector. The few possible resistors revealed themselves to Billy through their postures; their shoulders were tense, even as they imitated the drugged, contented slump of their less wary peers. They sat, like him, rigidly facing forward; afraid to draw attention to themselves.

Billy looked at the kid in front of him. Charley Morley. Billy barely knew him. They only had this one class together, which before today Billy barely ever remembered.

Mrs. Hobbey was gone. Maybe Billy could nudge him awake. Billy began to lean forward in his desk. Just in time, he saw the doorway darken again. He leaned back and forced himself to face forward, imitating the slack-jawed expression of the others.

Mrs. Hobbey came back into the classroom, bolted the door shut, and sat at her desk. She took a deep sip of Coffee, and gave vent to a relieved sigh. Billy stole a sideways glance at her. Could she tell which students were still awake? She put down her cup, and lifted her eyes to the class. Billy quickly resumed a glazed stare in the screen's general direction.

The projector's voice droned on. It was a deep and liquid voice, neither male nor female, young nor old. "You are going to sleep. You hear everything we say clearly. Deep sleep. Your thoughts are our thoughts. You are drifting deeper.... You are totally asleep. We are one," boomed a brilliant bass voice from the projector.

"Welcome to Socialization Studies class. Let our voice carve deep into your tiny minds."

Billy felt safest focusing his eyes on the chalkboard past the left edge of the screen. In his peripheral vision, he saw the picture change slowly. The television with the spiral inside faded from view, and was replaced with a bright and cheerful picture of the modern suburban workplace. A business suited man appeared beneath it. Another picture faded in on the right side of the screen; it was of the modern suburban home. A mother in her apron faded in beneath it.

A happy, smiling pod-thing, not unlike the leering menace that had just this morning emerged from Billy's ear, appeared in the charming animation from behind the business-suited man's head and waved, before returning beneath the clothes of it's host.

"We will bring order to your world," said the voice. "With our seed deep in your minds, you will follow the perfect predetermined path. From your planted rows in class to your coming rows in offices, to your rows in hospitals and then at last to your rows of peaceful graves."

The face came off the woman standing next to him, its tentacles acting as hinges. It waved smiling as well, revealing an unhappy frown beneath it. It swung back into place again, and all was well.

"You don't need to notice them. You don't need to think about them – don't think about them. Just feel how productive they make you feel..." The image on the screen changed into a lovely summer's day. Illuminated in beams of light, with blue skies dangling puffy white clouds far back into the horizon, stood a pod, it's mottled green casing and fresh mucous gleaming in the sun.

"If you see a fellow student struggling or in pain, don't help them.

You're wasting your time. Help yourselves by listening to us. We will help you think and do right, just like everyone else."

Billy blinked back tears of frustration. How long had they been putting these thoughts into his mind ? How many times had he missed it?

"And when you've grown into adulthood, all you'll need to do to hear us every day is keep your lovely pods and masks alive with deep drinks from the healing vats of Coffee."

Murple's old book had a title that mentioned Coffee. Could it provide the key to all these mysteries?

The video continued...

"And if anyone ever asks strange upsetting questions about aliens, Pods or Coffee, don't bother with them. Just tell us. We'll know what to do."

Billy shuddered and tried to clear his lumpy throat. Mrs. Hobbey pulled a small silver metal can out of her desk drawer, and began walking down the first aisle. She stopped at one desk, and then another, while looking directly into the children's glazed and staring eyes. When she came to the third desk, she saw something that she apparently didn't like.

She pulled a green seed-shapped object from the can, and inserted it in the child's ear. She looked satisfied, and then continued.

Soon she came to Billy's desk. He rigidly fixed his gaze on the screen. He could sense her dissatisfaction. She pulled forth a seed, and inserted it into Bill's unwounded ear. He controlled a shudder, and somehow managed to maintain the illusion of being hypnotized.

From the corner of his eye he saw her nod with satisfaction, and move on.

He could start to feel the seed begin to dissolve and even perhaps to wiggle.

"Now you will forget this lesson, you will love us, and above all you will trust us without question. At the count of ten, you will awaken, and remember a beautiful movie about horses, circuses, butterflies and laughing balloons. One....two...."

Billy pretended to come to. He mimicked the daze shown by other students. Mrs. Hobbey told them all to talk amongst themselves for the rest of the period. Billy noticed her watching the students carefully, so he managed a good imitation of his fellow students' half-dazed post-hypnotic babble.

As the class period drew to a close, Mrs. Hobbey began to prepare her papers for the next class. Billy mustered up his schoolbooks with a barely concealed desperation.

Billy had just enough time before the next class to visit the bathroom. He locked himself in a stall and began scratching at his ear. He worked with desperate speed, first with his fingers and then a pencil, in a vain attempt to get the seed out. But there was nothing to gain any purchase on. Whatever the thing was, it had dissolved within his skull.

BILLY NEARED THE CLASSROOM DOORWAY. He stepped off the conveyor belt, and stood still for a brief moment, mentally preparing himself. He had no idea what to do about the thing that Mrs. Hobbey had put in his ear. He had no idea how to put together the information he was receiving. He still could not allow his attention to waver. It was very important that he stayed very sharp in this class.

It was Shopping - a course so fundamental that no student could pass to the next grade without this teacher's approval. It was taught by Mr. McGillicutty - a teacher like no other.

Billy approached the doorway. Sure enough, there was Mr. McGillicutty. Dressed in his favorite red-and-blue striped sportscoat, and giving all impressions of complete eagerness to start as soon as the classroom filled.

Billy took his seat. A few seconds later, the school bell tolled.

"Hiya Class!" said Mr. McGillicutty.

"Hi!" said the class as one.

Billy's began to feel an itch inside his ear. He struggled to keep his face straight and not to scratch it.

"Excellent! Boy, we're gonna have fun today!" Mr. McGillicutty waved his arms in joy. His bushy moustache quivered with excitement. "Now, let's make a wish! All of you think about your favorite product!" All the children did so. Billy had the impression that some of the children were now showing genuine interest.

"Quick! Hold that picture in your head, and write it down on a slip of paper! Yay!" *What game is he playing?* Billy thought.

"OK! Done yet? Cool! Now, put them all in this hat," he said, and produced a baseball cap with a television emblem on the front. This image of the television had a spinning spiral inside it, and it was moving. The hat was passed around the room, and the children placed their product wishes inside it.

Billy's ear was really, really itching him.

"Good! Now, children, it's time to demonstrate a very important principle." He chuckled. "Perhaps even more important than Principal Maybee! HA-HA!" He leaned back and screamed in belly-lafter. The classroom politely chuckled. In front of Billy, Chris Barlowe looked at Mr. McGillicutty nervously. Billy watched Chris shift his weight. Chris was probably getting ready to drop sideways out of his desk, in case McGillicutty had another random psychotic breakdown.

The hat received its final paper slips, and was passed back up the rows to Mr. McGillicutty. He placed it on his desk. "Now, here's today's lesson. Listen up, little children! It may be the most important, valuable, and best of all *marketable* information you hear today." He licked his lips. "All of you children are going to part of a *very important* super-secret mission! That's right. Today! Yessir!"

"Oh, boy!" said Keith Moranis. Mr. McGillicutty looked down at him, and beamed Several other children emitted tiny squeals of glee.

"And not only that," he continued, "but you might even get to go home with your favorite product!"

"Wow!" exclaimed Keith, as if on cue.

"That's *right*! Wow!" McGillicutty heartily and cheerily agreed. "Of course, we wouldn't be doing our jobs as Teachers, as your elders, as your guiding lights of behavior and citizenship, if we just *gave* you something. That just wouldn't be right. But the price is so low, so cheap, so darn dirt-level tiny, that you won't even miss it! And it's something that you're even better off without!" He paused dramatically and, like the master showman that he was, moved back and forth in the front of the classroom and let the excitement build.

"So here's the deal, children. We're having a contest, between all my classes. The winning class will go home with the product of their dreams, get an extra-credit A, and – should I? Oh, heck, why not. - And a guaranteed raffle ticket for a *whole month* of dessert rations-" at this, another gasp started from the entire class, "and all you have to do is one teeny, tiny little thing."

Mr. McGillicutty folded his arms, and waited confidently. Soon hands shot up all over the classroom. "Yes, Suzy?"

"What is it, Mr. McGillicutty sir? What is it we have to do?"

"Why, I'm glad you asked that question, Suzy. It's real simple. All we're asking the students to do, is each report a student who doesn't seem interested in shopping. The class which reports the most revealed anti-shoppers, wins!"

"That's it?" she asked incredulously.

"That's all!"

"*Everyone* in the whole class gets the prizes?"

"*YES!*" Mr. McGillicutty nearly danced for joy. He spoke to the whole class. "Isn't that *amazing*?"

The whole class answered him with a spontaneous cheer.

Billy's inner ear had stopped itching him. He closed his eyes in relief, but the respite wasn't long. Just at the edge of his senses, something beginning to move deep inside his mind. He hoped it was only his imagination.

Two desks over from Billy, Paul Kuroff raised his hand. "But how are we supposed to know if they don't like shopping?"

"The clothes their parents buy, what they talk about, whether or not they watch the right commercials...there's as many clues as there are reasons to shop!"

Two seats in front of Billy, Annie Field raised her hand. "But how could anyone not like shopping?" she asked.

Mr. McGillicutty all of a sudden looked very sad. "I would rather not have to talk about this, children." He sighed. "Some people are sick. They must not know how important shopping is, to our survival. They must not even care." He shook his head. "It's sad, children." His smile brightened his face again. "But don't worry! It's easy to spot them, and make sure they get the help they need! So let's go through the warning signs, so you can get to work as soon as you leave class!"

Billy closed his eyes and stifled a groan. The itch in his ear intensified until it was a white-hot agony. Then it subsided. Just barely audible, a familiar voice began to whisper, "*Ssssstop strugglinggg,*"

Billy opened his notebook, and pretended to take notes.

"*Youuu have to do sssomethinggg,*" it whispered with glee. "*You know you have to pick ssssssomone. Ssssomone will get hurt, yessss....Or sssomeone elssse will jussst hurt youu.*"

Billy had been hoping for at least a day's reprieve from this enemy within.

If anyone even saw him struggle with the pod, the other children might see his maladjustment. In this class, they might report him as an anti-shopper. Then they would find the old book from Mr. Murple in his backpack...

"Are you ready for a fun magic trick now?" said the Teacher. The kids responded in joy. What a fun class this had become!

Mr. McGillicutty took the hat filled with paper slips off the desk. "Watch this!" He grabbed the hat, held it by the brim, and waved his hand over it. "Allakizim, allakazam, bring us the goods as fast as you can!" He put the hat on his head. No paper fell out of it; it was completely empty! The children laughed delightedly.

Mr. McGillicutty took off his hat. The part of his pod that was his moustache quivered. Behind his neck, the rest of his pod slowly moved the paper's it had taken from the hat into the teachers' back coat pocket.

"Now think of someone you know who might be an anti-shopper, and put their name in the hat! And may the best student win." He handed the hat to a student in the front of the classroom, and it began making it's way back.

Billy realized that the hat made it somewhat anonymous. Still, they would be checking all the answers. Any false entry would trigger their interest. They would know someone in the class was resisting. They would investigate. But Billy couldn't live with implicating another student. If he was going to do that, there was no reason to fight the pod at all. He might as well just give in.

*Yesss, that's rightttt,* a voice inside him whispered quietly. *Give inn.* Billy shook his head to clear it.

Could he falsely accuse someone no one would seriously suspect? Like Russell Nedermeyer? He dismissed that notion immediately. It was unlikely that any adult could ever suspect such an obvious bootlicker. That would be almost as bad as not suggesting anyone.

Mr. McGillicutty's heady promise of betrayal and greed was really inspiring his pod. Billy ignored its whispers and searched desperately for any way out.

"Okay, children, time's up," said Mr. McGillicutty. "Now fold up your slips of paper and put them in the Magic Hat." He handed his hat to a student in the front left corner of the classroom. "And for the rest of today, think about the product that you believe in! "

The students folded up their slips of paper. The hat began making it's way towards Billy. What was he going to do?

He came up with a gamble. He wrote a name down that absolutely enraged the thing inside is ear.

Angry but temporarily defeated, the itching in his ear subsided. Billy was able to relax inside himself.

The hat was passed up to the front of the room.

The teacher took the hat, looked in it briefly, and smiled. He set the hat aside.

"Now onto a new part of our class - computers!" Mr. McGillicutty waved his hands as if magic was appearing.

The top part of his desk moved aside, and a new computer emerged from a platform beneath. It was impressive showmanship.

The rest of the class was about the proper use of computers - to shop. In addition to doing work for those above you, and to criticize your equals and those beneath you. All aided by everyone's buddy, the device inside the computer named Chip.

"...So just remember that when you're on the computer, Chip is looking at what you read and what you write, what you see and what you send, to keep things safe from you so you can shop forever." Mr. McGillicutty looked at the clock on the wall. "Perfect timing! You've learned so punctually today. Any questions?"

For once, there were none. The bell tolled, and the students gathered their books. "Very well then. Until tomorrow," and Mr. McGillicutty smiled a toothy, moustache-ridden smile, "be seeing you!"

Billy left, feeling a bit of hope. It had all come from somewhere inside, that hadn't been from the creature in his ear but somewhere else. It was an idea that had come, as a way to avoid hurting someone else.

Even before today, when the secret of the school and the world outside had been revealed, Billy had known something was going on that couldn't be trusted. He had been pretty good so far at remaining outside the school's suspicion.

Maybe too good, the realization had been. They might realize that someone who never got in any trouble, but never did too well in class, could be consciously evading their control. So, it might be good for Billy to have a single black mark. That way his record wouldn't be so perfectly clean.

So, in carefully anonymous block lettering, he wrote his own name down and put it into the hat.


LUNCHTIME CAME AT LAST. The students entered the Main Assembly Room, and queued up to the cafeteria window for their lunchtime rations. They brought their lunches back through rows of long plastic tables to their chosen seats. On the raised platform at the front of the Main Assembly room, the Faculty gathered at their separate table. Principal Maybee discussed matters of finance and psychology, as the teachers consumed their Coffee and recharged.

The students' chatter was quiet, but much more spirited. There was no hiding the fact that half their day's classes were over, and soon it would be recess.

Billy had brought his lunch today, so he had an early start to find a seat. He looked for the safest place to sit. Chris Barlowe was seated at his usual table. He had been sitting near Trilling, lately; oddly, Trilling was nowhere to be found. That meant he could sit near Chris, which would be comfortable. Maybe Billy could even show him Mr. Murple's book and they could try and figure out what was actually going on.

Billy looked around a bit further, and saw that Timmy had taken a seat across the room.

Furthermore, Timmy was looking straight at him. Billy realized he had no choice. He sighed and walked over towards Timmy's table.

As Billy walked over, he passed Tracy sitting with one of her friends.

"Hi," he said suddenly.

Her eyes were so huge, and looked so open. "Hi, Billy," Tracy said.

"Uh," he said. He wanted to talk to her, warn her, tell her what he'd learned. Would she even believe him? He looked at her friends. Could they be trusted?

After a few short eternities, he gave up. His face turning red, he said, "That's it, hi", and hurried on towards Timmy's table.

Billy sat down next to Timmy, his face burning with imagined failure. Tracy, would never talk to him now. Had Timmy seen this? Fortunately for Billy, Timmy's mind was elsewhere. "I can't wait for Poisonball today," Timmy announced. "I practiced throwing rocks at my dog all weekend." Timmy grabbed his cardboard milk ration and ripped it open with gusto. "It's so much better with kids though. They scream and beg and stuff. That's the best part."

Billy avoided disagreeing by pulling his lunch from his knapsack. He took out his sandwich and held it in his hand. It had an odd heft that he didn't quite like. He unwrapped it slowly. The folds of wax paper revealed ever deeper, darker stains. He became more and more apprehensive. As the final layer was unfolded, Billy saw the meal his mother had prepared for him. The horrid green creature that only this morning had been a sick part of his head, lay before him neatly sliced on bleached white bread, under a slice of American cheese.

His Mom had also thoughtfully packed an apple.

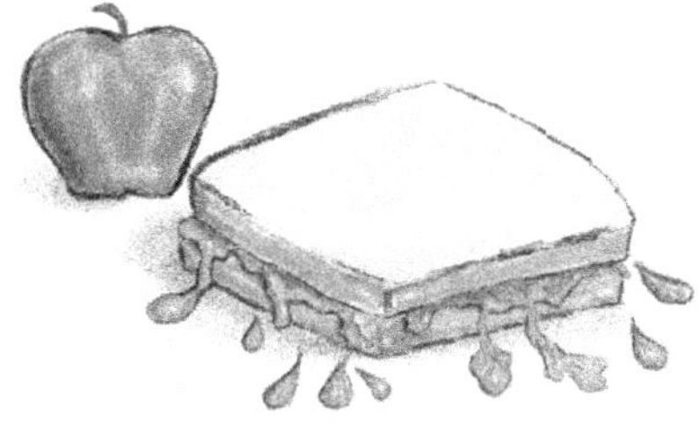

Billy repressed a tidal wave of nausea and fear, and rewrapped the sandwich.

"You aren't gonna eat that? You're supposed to," said Timmy.

"I guess I never thought about what it...." Billy mumbled. "I'm not feelin' that hungry t'day, I guess."

Timmy reached over and took it from him. He sunk his teeth in and took a bite.

"You like it?" Billy asked, surprised.

"My Dad makes it fresh for me like this all the time," Timmy said between eager mouthfuls. "He says it made a man out of him."

"Really?"

"For sure." He gulped down a huge chunk of something, and paused to lick some greenish fluid off his fingers. "It tastes really good, once you get used to it. Dad says it helps us get ready for Coffee. He says it can help you work forever."

Billy stared at him for a bit.

"Does your Dad say why it tastes so...good?"

Timmy shrugged. "Who knows? But it's always better than the stuff here. School food is watered down. This is like the same stuff, but stronger."

Billy's heart sank in despair. "It's the same stuff?"

"Oh, yeah, it's the same stuff! We need it to grow. Don't you want to be big and strong like me some day?" Timmy reached to slap Billy playfully.

Billy was expecting him to swing, and moved out of Timmy's reach before it connected. He chuckled politely. From the corner of his eye, Billy noticed a squad of Faculty members had come into the cafeteria. A perfect change of subject. "Hey, what's going on over there?"

"Wha?" Timmy mumbled around his sandwich. Billy pointed towards the Faculty. Timmy turned his head to see. The Coaches and Nurses had closed the cafeteria's doors, and begun looking closely at the students at every table. Some were looking underneath the tables as well.

"They're looking for someone!" someone whispered excitedly. Billy wanted to run but held himself still.

Principal Maybee stood up and hurried over to the searching

Faculty members. He conferred briefly with one of the nurses. Then his face turned red. The nurse stepped back out of his reach.

Maybee stormed to the front of the room, and cleared his throat. The low hubbub of the student's curious whispers faded into silence.

"If any student has any information about Andy Trilling's whereabouts," Maybee declared, "now is the time to step forward and give it to us. We may even reward you, now. If you wait, we may not be as....understanding." He cleared his throat. "You have been warned," Maybee said darkly. He returned to his seat at the Faculty table.

From the other table Tracy asked "What could have happened?" He turned and noticed her again.

"He must have run," Timmy declared. "What a wussy chicken."

"Where could he have run to?" Billy wondered.

"That's what makes it so stupid. There's no place to run. The Schools are everywhere. Everyone knows that." Timmy took another bite from his sandwich.

Billy nodded amiably and changed the subject to some past military disasters he'd heard about. Inside, he began to think.

Tracy's friend Gertrude pointed out Billy a few tables away. She shook her head. "What's up with that Billy kid? He's kinda weird, huh?"

Tracy shrugged.

"Look at his clothes," said Gertrude, a little smile appearing on her face. "I bet his parents are poor or something. "

Tracy looked at her friend a little closer. "You know, you seem different lately."

Gertrude's eyes narrowed. "What do you mean?"

"I don't know. It's just that lately you've gotten so - like you don't like people who don't even..." Tracy couldn't find the words.

"Do you like him or something?"

"I don't dislike him, do you?"

A thought came to Gertrude, that she thought was her own. *Little miss perfect*, something inside her ear said. Gertie poked at her green salad. "You'll find out what's going on soon."

"What's that supposed to mean?"

Gertrude smiled again, the same little smile, and said nothing.

Tracy brushed her hair back over her ear. She couldn't help but feel that Gertrude was glancing at it. She noticed how Gertrude's features had changed recently. More confident, more smooth. Without that nervous, frightened wrinkle of the brow. Although not as happy either, or not showing it. Her face was becoming harder. Almost like a...mask.

Tracy suddenly wondered if she really knew her friend, and if they would ever be close friends again.

"How was your morning?" Gertrude asked.

Tracy smiled politely, and kept her thoughts to herself. The rest of the lunch was spent talking about things that didn't matter. She found herself resenting Gertrude for making Tracy lie with her own face. Both that feeling and repressing it seemed to make Tracy's own ear itch.

RECESS.

The weather was clear, brisk, and bright. Breezes scattered leaves in delicate patterns. Gentle reminders of winter to come.

Billy had seen eleven autumns, and could remember six distinctly. It was his favorite time of year. Something in the air had a quiet calm. It just felt right. It confirmed that there were cycles no one could alter, not even adults. In a world once again entering into coldness, it felt good to know he was a small pocket of life and heat.

Behind the school was a blacktop strip about fifty feet wide and a hundred across, with a fenced in field of grass just beyond it. Here, for one inexplicable hour every day, adults let children play. The children ran, laughed, skipped and jumped. They talked about stories they had heard, and told childish jokes, and played games with whatever they could find. Squeals and shouts of joy expanded over the field. And the grownup's faces softened, as they remembered what it was like to be allowed to play.

All sorts of games....Basketball. Soccer. King of the Hill. Hacki-sack. Hide and Seek. Blind Man's Bluff. Kickball. Billy was invited into a game of Spaceman by Chris Barlowe. Billy declined politely; he felt like walking around today, and just enjoying the sights. Suzie Adams was giggling and running, from Tommy Hamilton, who was chasing her with a cricket he had found. It all made Billy laugh.

The afternoon sun had driven almost all the clouds away. He looked around some more, enjoying himself for a brief, priceless moment.

Then he made sure he was unobserved. When he was there were no eyes in his direction, he took out Mr. Murple's book from his jacket. With nervous hands, he opened it.

Some of the pages were torn, stained or missing, but enough of the text remained for him to follow.

"....arrival some centuries ago. Some suspect their birth-seeds were carried here by meteor, landing just off the coast of Africa. The how is less important than the what. To control their hosts, from their own bodies they created a strange new elixir - the fluid on which our entire civilization is now built: Coffee."

Billy's eyes widened. He'd never seen a grownup last more than a day without their Coffee. Only Murple had seemed to have the same unsipped cup all day.

That page trailed off to a torn corner. He found the next legible page and continued.

"The creature is inserted when the human host is young, and usually battles with the child during puberty. Once the creature has defeated or overwhelmed the host, the creature will choose it's desired position. Sometimes the creature resides on the outside of the human, and intercepts all communication at that layer. It becomes very much like a living mask that holds the host inside it. Other times the creature resides on the inside, like the heart or the gut, and controls the host from within."

Billy put the book down for a moment, and his thoughts raced. His mother's mask...and his father's strange actions, the thing occasionally visible rustling under his chest or shoulders....

The next page continued. "Coffee is made by the masters. And Coffee feeds the masters."

The next few pages were illustrations from different periods and sources. Some showed early knights and then kings of the Renaissance, all holding cups of coffee and strange, misshapen cloaks or masks. This chain of portraits continued up the present day, now showing presidents, movie stars and CEO's. Always with a cup of coffee, at their table or their side.

Billy put the book back inside his jacket. Instead of having too little information, maybe he had too much.

Off in the distance, at the far corner of the school's exterior, Vice Nurse Hauptmann emerged from a side door. She was leading a boy onto the field. The boy sat down on the grass, and looked away from her. She leaned over and reached out a hand at once delicate, firm and cold, and brought his chin back towards her. It looked as if she was smiling. It was too far for Billy to tell for sure. The boy shook his head free of her grip, and looked straight back at her.

She shook her head sadly, but still smiling, and walked back into the school. The boy walked to the corner at the absolute edge of the field, and leaned back against the fence.

Billy realized the boy was Ray Pfeiffer. Some other children had noticed him too. They went back to their play. Even on a normal day, not many people would play with Ray. He was so strange. There was no way anyone would play with him today, after the Mark from the Red Stamp he'd received this morning.

Billy looked around the playground for a second or two. Then his curiosity got the better of him. He walked over to where Ray sat in a patch of dying grass, his arms huddled around his legs.

"Hi, Ray," said Billy, after an uncomfortable silence.

"Hi, Billy." Ray always looked messy, but he was really disarrayed this afternoon. His hair was the same length as Billy's, and the same sandy brown. Where Billy's was neatly cut and combed, Ray's hair was a broken mandala that pointed in all directions. His sneakers weren't even fully laced.

"So I found this weird book," Billy began. "It's got all this stuff about - things, and coffee, and grownups, and it used to be Mr. Murple's, and..." Billy's words trailed off as he saw Ray's face. Ray wasn't even changing his expression. He looked more exhausted than Ray had ever seen a kid.

"So...." Billy hesitated, and then dove right in. "So you were Tested."

Ray picked a fist-sized rock out of the dirt, and examined it. "Yeah. They're taking a break. After Recess, they're gonna do some more."

"What do they do?"

"You don't remember?"

"I only got Tested once, when I was real young."

"I don't think you want to know." Ray turned the rock over, and examined it. A couple of stray insects scrambled around on the stone, their world turned upside down. He carefully brushed them back onto the ground. He looked back up at Billy, and suddenly his eyes looked very old. "I know I don't want to remember."

They stayed still in silence for a little while. The sun shone on them, and a stray squeal of laughter made its way to them from over the blacktop.

"Why do you do stuff that makes you stick out, Ray?" Billy asked. "Why can't you just pretend to pay attention?"

Ray explosively threw the rock into the dirt. "Because it's *crap*! It's all lies!" He stared at Billy, daring him to deny to it. "Because every minute we pretend is a minute we lose forever. Why do we they have to make us be like everyone else? Stand in line? Sit inside and *memo-*

*rize* these lies?" He looked down at the ground, and seemed on the verge of crying. "Why can't they just let us grow up how we want? If they know so much and only want to help us grow, why don't they have even a single class in being happy?"

Ray lifted his head up, and wiped away what might have been tears. "I mean, why do you pretend so much?" Ray finally asked Billy.

"What?"

"You know. Play along more than you have to," said Ray. "Because you do that. It makes you a liar. That's how you grow up like them."

Billy shifted his feet nervously, but Ray just wouldn't stop.

Billy looked around to make sure no one was in earshot. "It's not just that. It's the – those things they stick in kids ears. Did you see that, in class today?"

"Of course I saw it," said Ray. "I've been trying to wake you up to that for weeks."

"Do you – what do you do about them?"

Ray shrugged. "I don't know. They don't grow in my head. I don't know why. Maybe that's why they keep testing me. I don't know if they want to find out why, or hurt me so much those seed-things stay, or both."

"I'm not so lucky," said Billy.

"It's all so messed up! And everyone knows it, and no one does anything! They get us to not help each other!" Ray exclaimed.

"Keep your voice down," said Billy urgently. Ray lowered his voice, but wasn't happy about it.

"Why should I even have to lower my voice?" said Ray. "Why is yelling and making noise so wrong too? It's like they don't want us to be alive!"

"Okay, yeah. It's a lot of bad things, alright? It's also in the food they feed us. And that Coffee they drink too, that's like a grownup version. And there's maybe other stuff. I don't even know what." It really was a lot when you said it out loud. Billy rallied. "But you can't just fight everything all the time! It doesn't do any good if you get caught." Billy wondered if his voice had gotten too high. He looked around. No one seemed to be looking at them.

Billy lowered his voice. "Look, we just gotta get through it. That's all. We won't be here forever. We'll - we'll be grown up out of here, someday. And then we'll be able to do what we want. Until then, you'll just have to learn to..." he sighed. "It stinks, I know. But you gotta learn to pretend."

Ray looked at Billy for a long, long time.

"But it's *not* a game." Ray picked up another rock, and looked at. It was shiny and flat, easy to hold. He put it down again. " It's *real*." The wind blew cold. Ray let out a long breath, and wrapped his arms around his shins even tighter than before. "They want us to pretend, so they can forget. So by the time we grow up *we'll* forget." His hair caught the wind and flew in all directions. "It's not just that I don't want to. I *can't*. It's not possible."

A moment of silence passed between them.

"Yeah...," said Billy, "I know how that feels."

For a moment, Ray's face was as bright as the sun that warmed them both. "Thanks, Billy."

A bird landed in the grasses behind them, and they turned to look at it. It pecked at the dirt briefly. Finding nothing it wanted, the bird rejoined the sky.

Ray's eyes hid none of his envy.

"Well, uh, later," Billy abruptly turned around and headed back towards the playground. He wished he had a piece of gum. He stuck his hands in his warm coat pockets.

It was too late for him to join any games now. Which was alright. He kind of wasn't feeling like it. Plus he didn't want to hurt his ear. He settled into his favorite position for recess. Standing with his back to the wall of the school, under the protection of a nice shady tree, with a good view of the whole playground in action.

Soon, Mrs. Grundy blew a whistle. The children quickly stopped playing and reassembled. Billy, in his spot, was already near the front of the line by the time it formed. He was sure to get another standard acceptable mark on his behavior chart.

They were marched back into school. He checked around but did not see Ray.

DRESSED **for exercise in sweat pants and T-shirts, the students poured forth from the locker room into the gymnasium.** They gathered loosely in small bands of companions. Finally, just as the last of the young stragglers came into the arena, Coach Brumble emerged from the easy chair in his adjacent office. He clutched a candy bar in his left hand as his right hand scratched his belly.

"Attention!" yelled Coach Brumble. The children moved into rows. He negotiated his impressive bulk through them to the front of the room, like a tanker moving through toy sailboats.

Brumble examined them silently as he finished his bar of chocolate-covered pork. He stuffed the empty plastic wrapper into a voluminous back pocket.

"Jumping Jacks!" he bellowed suddenly. The boys quickly separated their feet to shoulder width, and held their arms level.

"On my count- begin! One! Two! Three! Four!" The children began pumping their arms and legs in an exhausting rhythm. From another pocket, Brumble produced a candy bar and peeled back the wrapper. He moved up and down the rows of larval citizens, making sure all were taking part. His counting, somewhat muffled by nougat and caramel, continued steady and strong.

"Windmills!"

"Situps!"

"Leg stretches! ...Push-ups! ...Crunches!"

The exercises continued in all possible variations, until the medically advised limit of physical damage had been reached. At last the exercises were finished. The boys collapsed. Coach Brumble burped softly.

"Well." He glowered at them through heavy eyes. "That wasn't much of a work out. How do you expect to be men, if you can't even work?" His stomach heaved angrily. Barely anyone had even passed out today. "Fine! Be a bunch of slackers, if that's how you want to do it. See where just getting by will get you."

Several rows back, Billy felt himself slowly come back into his gasping body.

"I guess I can't expect that much from a buncha *girls.*" Brumble's contemptuous facial expression was briefly erased by a truly heroic belch. "Well," he said as he wiped a strand of stray digestive fluid from his upper lip, "the girls are coming over today, and with the shape you're in, they're probably gonna kick your little candy asses."

Slowly the boys' heads rose from the floors. "Really?" went several voices at once. "The girls are coming over?" asked another.

"It's got to be some sort of trick," Mark Chambers whispered to Billy. Billy nodded in agreement.

"I want you to all to behave like little gentlemen. Remember, it's not their fault they're so weak and useless. After all, so are you. And," here the Coach leered and hitched at the back of his pants, "At least they have *some* uses. - SO. Get yourselves off the floor and line up against the wall."

"What are we gonna do, Coach?" asked Keith Moranis.

"You'll find out, Moranis. Meanwhile, do what you're told." Billy wished he could get away with asking questions.

Just as the boys finished lining up, Head Nurse Kraft-Ebbing led the girls into the room. They were dressed in sweatpants and T-shirts, but their shapes did pleasantly un-boyish things to their gym clothes.

Tracy was among them - the first and last person Bill wanted to see. Tracy. Billy saw her, walking and chatting with another girl. The line stopped and she leaned back against the wall.

"And now," said Brumble. He let the words hang in the air for a dramatic pause, during which the remains of his candy bar met its final demise. "Now, you're all gonna dance!"

"Dance?" Murmurs spread through the lines of children. What the hell was going on here?

"You boys are growing old enough, that it's time you learned something about girls. Like the proper ways to touch girls. So, here they are. Square Dancing, Ballroom Dancing, and Line Dancing. And," Brumble savored the moment, his tongue sliding between his lips in a final licking motion not unlike a lizard reveling in slime beneath a rock.

"...The *Cha-Cha.*"

The children went silent with shocked horror.

*No!* Billy screamed inside. *Not today.* His wounded ear would be noticed in an *instant.* And they would make fun of it, make fun of him. Billy wouldn't be able to hide in the background, mark his time, survive and make it through. He would be noticed and ground down like all the rest.

Unless....

*Unless I point out Tracy's wounded ear instead.*

*Wait a minute,* Billy wondered. *How could I think that?*

Another thought followed soon after. *Someone will see it anyway. You might as well.*

It was true, a flaw on her would be the talk of the school. While she was being persecuted, he might not even be noticed at all. He could have time to heal, and to deal with whatever Mrs. Hobbey had put inside his ear.

Billy closed his eyes and found that he could never, ever betray Tracy.

Billy opened his eyes. That really meant something. Since he couldn't betray Tracy, these thoughts had to be coming from that seed Mrs. Hobbey had put back inside his ear.

*Do it!* the thing said, no longer pretending to have his voice. *You're wasssting time!* it whispered with dark seductive tones. *Do it, or I'll forccce my wayyyy outtt!! I'll tell all of them what you know!*

Billy looked across the gym. The girls stood in silent anxiety, just as underjoyed as all the boys. From across the room across the gym, Coach Brumble and Nurse Kraft-Ebbing exchanged darkly knowing smiles. Billy looked at Tracy again. She was leaning her face slightly to her left, so her ear was out of easy view.

The system was so perfect. Someone would always have to lose. Maybe everyone. Kids whose wounds he hadn't seen. Something was done.

Next to Billy, Chris Barlow was wrestling with his own thoughts. "Why do we have to dance?" Chris Barlowe dared to ask the Coach.

"Some of us could use the exercise, tubby," responded Brumble. Several children within Brumble's eyesight laughed politely at Brumble's witticism.

Billy made his way over to where Timmy leaned against the wall. "Hey," Billy whispered. "You want to do this dancing stuff?"

"What do you think?" Tim snarled and leaned towards him. "You think I'm a wuss? C'mere...!"

"Hey, hey. I was just thinking, we should be playing Poisonball, instead of this stuff."

Tim's eyes lit immediately. "Yeah! That's right!" He ground his fist into his palm. Some other kids on either side of them chimed in. "What is this 'dance' stuff, anyway?"

Billy watched expectantly as Timmy they grew more restless. The word spread. No kids wanted to deal with the risks of dancing. They all knew that poisonball brought bruises, nerve damage and blood, but that hurt less and was much easier to heal than ridicule.

"Hey, Coach Brumble sir! Can't we do something else?

"Is there a *problem,* boys?" Brumble rumbled. He glanced over at The Nurse, and they shared another smile.

"It's just, dancing, you know, it's not that fun," a voice ventured down the line.

"What could be better? You don't *want* to touch girls?" the Coach leered sadistically.

"Jus' wanna play games, 'n have fun 'n stuff..." the student's voice faded out weakly.

"Games. Huh? You wanna play games. Well," Brumble's voice rose in volume to address the whole class, *"that's not what life's about.* You shoulda learned that in kindergarten. It's about *work!* What are you, a bunch of babies?"

His stomach began to move with a will of its own, as if something living inside it was becoming restless.

"I said, *what are you, a bunch of babies?"* He roared, as his stomach began jumping up and down.

"NO, SIR!" yelled the class all at once.

"You don't *act like it....*" the Coach's eyes wandered down the line of boys. "How about you, Timmy? You're usually the perfect student. Do you wanna pway games wike a widdle baby?"

Timmy's face reddened, and a young blood vessel pounded in his temple.

"Well, Timmy? Speak up. Why aren't *you* man enough to follow orders?" Timmy's fists clutched empty air as he strained for self-control.

"Dancing is for wusses," said Tim finally. "I wanna *hit somebody.*"

"Oh," Brumble said. His belly rustled thoughtfully. He scratched it, and it responded with a thunderous release of digestive gases. "...I can understand that, at least," he said. His stomach settled down a bit, somewhat mollified. Billy could almost make out what looked like some sort of thing rustling beneath the coach's tent-sized sweatshirt. "We can't really do that with dancing."

"What ...about..." Timmy asked, in a voice that nearly broke with intensity, "...about *Poisonball.*" At the last word Timmy's whole body convulsed with bloodlust. His hands tensed for something to throw, to strike. Several of the boys nearest him moved away.

"Hmmph." Brumble looked over at Nurse Kraft-Ebbing. "Do you think your little girls can handle it?" he asked mockingly.

"I bet they can, better than your little babies," she taunted back.

"How about it, lads?" said the Coach, enjoying the feeling of inspiring his troops. "Is that how the rest of you feel? Would you rather dance or hurt?"

All the boys voiced their approval for physical pain.

"Shall we do it, Nurse?" Nurse Kraft-Ebbing caressed the iron cross around her neck, and granted her assent. It was decided. Billy joined in the collective sigh of relief. Dancing would have been inescapable torture. At least in battle a child had a chance.


THE SEVEN POISONBALLS **were placed in a pile in the middle of the gymnasium.** The class was divided into boys against girls, and then several of the more psychotic boys were transferred to the girls' side. This would even out the teams, by embarrassing those transferred boys into a truly maniacal frenzy.

Billy was on the boys' team. He briefly wondered where was best to stand and await the battle, but it mattered little. Wherever he stood, the outcome would be the same; after some minutes of frantic adrenaline-soaked dodging, he would collapse in pain with his nerves on fire. Still, Billy liked to feel somewhat in control of his destiny. He elected to try the right side of the gym, about 2/3 of the way towards the back. Behind a couple of fat kids who would shield him, at least until they realized the exposed nature of their positions.

Coach Brumble and the Iron Nurse retreated behind the plexiglass safety barrier. The whistle blew. The most homicidal and suicidal students ran to the center, and began to hurl their poisonballs at the other team.

A chaotic swarm of kinetic fury filled the room, as the balls bounced harmlessly off walls or producing a loud sizzling *Spung!* noise when striking human flesh. Billy stayed mobile, and the slower-moving kids ahead of him drew most of the fire.

Some poisonballs missed their targets, and rolled around slowly at the center of the room. Timmy ran forward to grab a bunch at once. This was a high-risk, high-gain maneuver - a player could either control the field early or be instantly, painfully eliminated.

Timmy was able to snatch two. He immediately whaled his first strike at a slowly-retreating girl. The poisonball's stored neurolectricity caught her square in the midsection. She fell to the floor, twitching in convulsions.

As Timmy laughed with glee, an opponent ran from the other side and threw. Timmy twisted but failed to completely avoid his rival's attack, which struck him on his hip. The ball bounced back and the kid grabbed it for another shot.

Neurolelectricity still tingling in his leg, Timmy responded with a lightning throw to the other boy's neck. The kid dropped the ball and went down clutching his throat. Timmy picked up this ball and broke the rules to limp across the line in the middle of the room, and stand over his latest victim. Keeping a tight grip on his Poisonball, he repeatedly struck the fallen boy in the face.

"That was nicely done," Brumble commented to the Iron Nurse. She nodded in agreement. He recorded an extra credit for Timmy's 'kill'.

Across the room, Billy saw Keith Moranis, both doomed and blessed with a low level of awareness. Keith was just running frantically around the room, and no big kids were even trying to hit him. Keith just wasn't a challenge. Dumb enough to ask questions and not be chastised, too dumb to ever really get in trouble, maybe even too dumb to ever be really unhappy ... A wave of envy washed over Billy, and grew deeper, into anger.

Just inside his ear, he was feeling the itching again. Something struggled to come forth. *I wish I could show him what it felt like to be me,* Billy heard inside his head. *I'd sssssshowww himmm...* It whispered hoarsely. He shut his eyes and tried to will the voice away. But all he could hear was the tiny, dark voice, with an edge to it, like a knife in darkness. *We'll throw at them! Hurt them,* it was saying. *I'll do ittttt!*

*You're not me!* Billy thought back. *Stop pretending to be me!*

*I am a part of youuu,* it whispered. *Sooonnn enough, we will needdd to hurt themmm. You will needdd meeee...*

An upperclassman saw that Billy was distracted. He threw a Poisonball directly at his head. Acting on reflex, Billy caught it. It sizzled the palms of his flesh, but didn't deliver a full shock. The kid who had thrown it stood still, startled. He was now out, and Billy had a Poisonball.

Billy began to run around, wondering what to do. His Pod wanted him to *throw itt! Show them your power, give them painnnn!* Another poisonball came near Billy. He dodged quickly, and it bounced off the wall beside him.

*Figghhtt!!!! Hurtttt!!!* the voice inside him screamed.

Billy looked at the grownups. He realized they thought the ball had actually hit him. The strike had been shielded from the adults' line of sight, by the lone fat kid who remained before him. Billy judged that the Coach and Nurse hadn't seen it's exact trajectory.

Billy dropped the poisonballs, and screamed and fell as if it had hit his leg. He got up and limped towards the sidelines. As he came closer, he noticed Tracy had already left the game, and was leaning against the wall, this time without her friends. He wondered if she had faked her loss as well. She seemed to be standing without difficulty.

All of the remaining less violent children were quickly taken out by one brutal act or another. Only a dwindling group of would-be conquerors remained. Soon there was only Timmy, Ralph Petronio, and Mikey Stripe. They circled each other slowly, Poisonballs in all their hands, not wanting to start the endgame until the perfect opportunity.

Billy looked around. The Coach and the Nurse were distracted by the game. Now was actually a relatively safe time to talk with Tracy.

What could he say? Billy tried some things out in his head. "I have this disgusting Pod thing in my head, and it's trying to take me over. I think you do too. Isn't that awesome?" Yeah, right....What did he want to say? He ran through various scenarios in his mind. He realized he had nothing to say. He just wanted to be there, talking with her, because she was the only person there who interested him at all.

He swallowed, and walked over. "Hi, Tracy," Billy said nervously.

She turned to look at him. "Hi, Billy," she smiled. Billy's heart jumped. That voice inside him yelled at him to *run! Run away before she hurtssssss you! You'll only get made fun offfff!*

He opened his mouth to speak. "What do you think of school?" he found himself saying, not knowing why.

She looked back at him, a bit intensely. "My parents want me to do good," she said. "It's real important to them." She sighed.

Billy nodded. "My parents too." Billy paused. He lowered his voice, and he realized he had to ask her about her scar.

"So..."

"Yes?" she asked. He tried to figure out how to get this out.

"Tracy," he started again, "did you ever notice how it seems like grownups have these -"

Billy was interrupted by a loud scream. Everyone in the room turned towards the middle of the arena. Billy turned just in time to see Timmy pummel his last remaining opponent with multiple neuroelectric balls. Ralph Petronio fell to the ground with a wet thud. Timmy laughed in dark abandon as he smashed the agony-inducing globes into his fallen foe's head and neck. There was a red mark on the side of Timmy's face; he must have been hit squarely there. That should mean Timmy had already lost, but Brumble had chosen to ignore it. Of course the Faculty always liked Timmy. He was a winner.

Billy turned back to Tracy. A couple of her friends had come over.

One of them had a stiff face that reminded him of how his mom looked when she disapproved of something. It wasn't safe to talk to Tracy now. Billy turned away from Tracy, trying to hide his sadness. Timmy he walked off the gym floor like a hero, his face quivering in rapture.

Brumble and Kraft-Ebbing returned from behind the safety barrier. "OK, great game, Timmy." said Brumble. "I need two kids to take Petronio to the Nurse's Station," Nurse Kraft-Ebbing declared. Billy wanted to get out of the Gym. Right now, before he said something else to Tracy. He raised his hand.

"Good boy, Billy. And...Barlowe! Yes, that sounds good. You can use the firewood sled."

Chris went over to the far corner of the room, and brought the sled over to Ralph Petronio's prone body. Billy grabbed him by the wrists, and Chris grabbed him by the ankles. As the rest of the class lined up for more calisthenics, Chris and Billy wrestled Petronio's limp form onto the sled, put on the yokes, and strained and tugged the sled out of the gymnasium.

Back in the gym, Gertrude eyed Tracy. "What was he saying to you?"

Tracy shrugged warily. "Just stuff."

"I just don't know about him," Gertrude continued. "I don't think he's normal."

"What if he isn't normal? So what?"

Gertrude gasped. "You don't care if he isn't normal?"

Tracy stared back at Gertrude. "I don't think it's as big a deal as grownups make it."

"Maybe you're not normal," said Gertrude.

"Don't call me that!" said Tracy.

"See? You want to be normal. So why do you like that boy?"

"I don't like the way you say that. The way you say it, you're just being mean."

"You should know better than to say Tracy isn't normal, Gertrude." Mary jumped in. "Just look at you. You aren't even pretty."

Both Tracy and Gertrude looked at Mary, surprised. Mary smiled.

She had seized the center of attention. She was pretty, and Tracy was pretty too. That could make them a good team, of saying mean people to others and rising above them. Tracy would be foolish not to accept such a teamup. To some people, Mary was prettier than Tracy.

"Who asked you?" said Tracy.

This time both Mary and Gertrude gasped.

"I'm just helping you!" said Mary.

"No you're not," said Tracy. "Gertrude is my friend. You take that back that mean thing you just said."

Mary scratched her head, honestly confused. "Take back what I said?" She nodded at Gertrude. "About her?"

"Yes! Say you're sorry."

"Fine, whatever. You'll see what you get then, hanging out with ugly oddballs."

"My friends are my friends. If you want me to be nice to you, you be nice to them."

Mary turned her back on Tracy, and mentally added her to a list of enemies.

Tracy turned back to Gertrude. Gertrude was shocked. Something was slipping through her face. She mumbled a little.

"What?" asked Tracy.

"Why did you do that?" Gertrude whispered. "She's popular. I'm not."

"Because you're my friend, you dummy," said Tracy.

The stiffness in Gertrude's face slipped a bit. A tear was quickly wiped away, as a fragile and real smile came to her face.


CHRIS AND BILLY **pulled the sled up the empty hallway, and maneuvered it onto the conveyor belt.** They rode in silence towards the Nurse's Station.

Soon they rounded the corner, and Chris breathed a sigh of relief. It echoed around the empty halls. Usually when Billy was in these halls he was rushing to reach some class on time. It was odd being in no hurry, and being the only kids around.

"Heard anything about Andy Trilling?" Billy said softly.

"No," said Chris. He pointed at the Faculty Lounge they were passing. "I don't think they have any idea where Andy's gone, or even how he got away."

"That's pretty cool," Billy said.

"Yeah – as long as it lasts," said Chris.

They walked a few more moments in silence.

"I read some of that book," Billy said under his voice. "The one Murple had, before he...the one he had." Billy didn't say anything further.

After a short while Chris gave in to his curiosity. "What did it say?"

Billy looked ahead. They were almost there. "I'll tell you later," Billy whispered.

The Nurse's Office loomed around the corner. Billy and Chris arranged properly downtrodden, unhappy and respectful expressions on their faces, pushed the sled off the conveyor belt, and quickly jumped off beside it. They walked up to the door. Billy raised his hand to knock on it. He heard voices from within, and stopped. Unable to resist, Billy and Chris leaned in closer to hear.

First there was a pleasant, even, adult and well-modulated voice: *"You are one of the following. You will choose and check a box you will be in."*

Then an upset, young boy's voice cracked, saying "I choose my own choices! Not yours!"

*"You can only have one choice. One of those who follow."*

"I am anything I want!" Billy realized the kid's voice belonged to Ray.

*"What you want is not in the choices."*

"I don't care!"

*"A Seed will be placed in you, until it keeps. In the rich dark soil of your hate and fear. If you resist it will hurt."*

"So what?" said Ray's upset, cracking, still-defiant voice – and for once, Billy was proud to be a kid.

Billy turned to Chris. "That sounds like Ray Pfieffer," he said.

Chris nodded. "They're Testing him." Chris shook his head. "You'd think he'd know better than to resist."

Billy swallowed. He was beginning to experience some vague, unpleasant memories. Even though they were controlled by these strange things, his parents had delayed Billy's Testing. Maybe they had resisted. If it weren't for Ray awakening him during the filmstrip this morning, Billy might have already been been Well Adjusted ...

*"You can only be one of the following,"* the voice began again. *"To do that you must follow."*

Ray's response was drowned out by Chris. "We have to drop off Petronio," Chris reminded Billy. "If we get back late, we'll both be in a lot of trouble."

Billy nodded. This also meant they could interrupt the Testing, which Billy found himself wanting to do. He raised his arm, swallowed, and knocked on the steel door. "Who dares?" demanded the voice from within. It was the same voice as he'd heard before, the voice of Nurse Hauptmann. "I'm in the middle of important work here!"

"I'm very sorry to bother you ma'am," said Billy. "We were sent by Coach Brumble and Nurse Kraft-Ebbing. We've got a boy who..." How did Brumble always put it? "...Who tried to get out of gym class by collapsing."

"Oh, very well," she said. Enormous door bolts klanged rang free, the door slid open and Nurse Hauptmann beckoned them. Up close, Billy noticed the length and sharpness of her fingernails; her other claw clutched a cup of Coffee that was almost all gone.

Billy and Chris dragged in the sled.

"Put him over there," she said, "and sit down while I write your return note." The boys wrestled Ralph's form onto a nearby wooden bench, and sat next to him.

The Nurse handed them the note. "And say hi to Coach Brumble-butt," the Nurse said. The boys looked at each other, confused. Suddenly Billy got it – she was attempting to make a joke. Billy laughed politely, and nudged Chris. Chris quickly joined in. "You're good boys," she nodded approvingly. "Don't get in trouble now."

"Grownups get so weird without their Coffee," Chris noted to Billy once they were outside.

"Yeah," said Billy.

They passed the Faculty Lounge again.

"What do you think would happen, if someone got rid of all the Faculty's Coffee?" Billy asked.

"Are you kidding? They'd probably go nuts. Well, even more nuts."

"That's right," said Billy. He swallowed, and then grabbed Chris by the shirt. He stepped off the conveyor and Chris followed him.

"We can do go into the Faculty Lounge, and get rid of all their coffee!" Billy said. "If we do that, maybe we can make all this stop!"

"Huh? Why?" said Chris.

Billy stared at him in surprise. "Because it's not right!"

"Nothing here is right, Billy," said Chris. "It's a School. The best we can hope for is to do our time and get out with good behavior."

"But Trilling escaped! Maybe Ray can too!"

"What's gotten into you?"

"Do you ever have a – a thing in your head?" Chris gulped nervously, then nodded. "Me too," said Billy. "Mine attacked me this morning. But Ray, they don't seem to stay in his head! He knows how to fight them!"

Chris shook his head. "What are you talking about? He's losing, Billy! He's stuck in there being tested. He doesn't even know how to save himself."

"But maybe we can save him," said Billy. "And he can show us how to keep the weird things out of our heads!"

"No way am I going to get between adults and their Coffee. It's too risky.

Billy started to speak, stopped, and started again. "I'm going to do this. Are you with me or not?

"What are you going to do?" asked Chris.

"Just keep an eye out."

Chris' eyes opened wide in fear. "You're really going to do something," said Chris, becoming increasingly alarmed.

"I have to," Billy said.


Billy and Chris slowly opened the door to the Faculty Lounge. There were no teachers to be seen. "All the spare teachers must still be looking for Andy," Billy said.

"Okay," whispered Chris. "You go ahead, and try your stupid plan. I'll make a noise if I see anyone, but there's no way I'm going in there and I definitely don't want to know what you're doing."

Billy stepped in softly. Chris closed the door behind him. And the plan that had started to form in Billy's head...

...began to fade.

What was he doing again?

He should just go find a teacher to talk to. Billy moved towards the intercom near the doorway. His hand was halfway to the button before he stopped himself.

He wasn't the one trying to call a teacher. *That was that thing inside his head.*

*You'llll be caugghhhttttt,* the thing said. Billy's ear began itching. *I'llll maaaakke you screammmm. And you'llllll be punishedddd. Just give uuuuuppp.*

As the thing expended effort in speaking and struggling, the net of confusion it had cast over Billy's thoughts disappeared. Billy remembered his plan. He turned and walked towards the Faculty Lounge's large brass vat of Coffee.

His ear suddenly exploded in pain. Billy fell to the floor. *NO!* it declared. *I WON'T ALLOW ITTTTT!* it screamed. The pain and desperation were giving it strength....as was something else. Was it Billy's proximity to the Coffee?

Yes! These things seemed to need coffee! Maybe it fed them inside the grownups? Gave them some kind of sustenance that pain and misery could not?

Billy grit his teeth against the pain. Inch by inch, Billy crawled towards the Coffee Vat. Feeding off Billy's fear and anguish, his Pod began to grow. *I won't waittt until the nighttt again thisssss time,* it declared. *I'll take you now! And you'lll rat out little Chrissssy next!*

"Never!" Billy yelled, and bit his tongue. *Haaaah, that'ssss it,* the Pod continued. *Givvve usss away. Or don't! And I will winnnn laterrrr. I'll give up little Traceeeey too.* Billy bit his tongue in rage. The rage only made the Pod-Thing stronger.

Billy remembered why he was here. Not all the details, that was still too fuzzy somehow. But there was an emotion he could remember. It was sometimes at the edge of how he felt around his parents, and his friends. Around Tracy. He didn't know quite what this emotion was. It made him stronger. He was able to the last few final feet, to reach the brass vat's side.

The Pod began emerging from Billy's ear. It was preparing to take him over.

*You loosssse, swwwweet Billy!* It screamed in triumph. *Nowww you willl be minneee at lassssttt!*

Billy didn't waste his strength trying to fight the Pod. Instead he struggled to his feet, and leaned all this weight upon the vat.

It tipped over and fell to the hard polished floor. The vat cracked, and the putrid cover fell. The strange powder inside spread all over the floor. The pure afternoon sunlight streamed in through the windows, and set the substance into flame. Billy fell again to the floor, feeling waves of pain take him into unconsciousness.

Billy was in terrible pain, yet he felt strangely satisfied. He could stand to end like this. He had done his best, and no more could be done. *Nooo* the thing inside his head declared. *You must fear.* Billy laughed feebly. *Feed me your fearrr!!*

As he drifted out of this world, Billy knew at least he'd done what was right.

The creature began to scream....

Billy woke **up on the conveyor belt.** "Stand up!" said Chris.

"What?" said Billy, still dazed.

"I said stand up!" Chris demanded again. "Some grownup is going to notice you!"

Billy struggled to his feet and tried to stand with nonchalance. They were moving back towards the gymnasium, with the empty sled they'd brought Ralph in.

He touched his ear. His Pod had shrunk again, and gone inside - mostly. "What happened?" asked Billy. "Where's my – my..." He pointed at his ear.

Chris shuddered. "All I know is I pulled you out, and you owe me big time." He shook his head. "Boy you made a racket in there."

"You saved me?"

"Yeah, well," said Chris, embarrassed. They traveled on down the eerily still and quiet halls.

Billy rubbed his eyes. "What about Ray?"

"What about him? As soon as the Faculty finds out they've got no Coffee, maybe he'll have his chance to run. I hope he can still make it out."

"Me too."

They got back to the gym class. The girls were already gone and the boys were already coming out of the locker room dressed in their regular clothes. Just then the bell began to toll.

"We're late!" said Chris in panic.

They rushed into the locker room and changed out of their gym clothes. Chris made it out first. Billy hurried soon after, still putting one arm through the sleeve of his shirt as he held his book bag through the other.

He pressed his way through the other kids. His next class was all the way across the school, and it was with Mr. McGillicutty! That man would take no excuses and look deep into why Billy might be late. He absolutely had to be in class before it started, if he wanted to escape this day alive.

As he got closer to the classroom the hallways grew increasingly empty. Ahead of a thinning crowd of students entered separate classroom doors. Was he going to get caught anyway, after all of this risk? Had they been right to leave Ray? If the Nurse was without her Coffee, would she let up on Ray? Or would she Test him even more cruelly?

If suspicion landed on Billy then poor Chris wouldn't be far behind. Chris, who had saved Billy even after backing Billy up had put them both in danger. All this other worry – and on top of it he realized that all this stress might also feed his pod. A sick, oozing sensation of diseased satisfaction was his reply, from deep inside where he didn't want to look. Maybe this fear and speculation itself would feed his Pod.

Almost no one was left in the hallway. The final bell would have to ring soon, and he still might be late to class. At last he neared the open door to the classroom. He was going to make it! He broke into a run.

He made it inside the door. Somehow, the bell hadn't rung yet! He was the last student in, so he hurried to sit before he could be noticed. He found his desk, and breathed a sigh of relief. Billy kept his eyes averted from the front of the room, as he dug out his workbook and his trusty pencil.

McGillicutty hadn't said anything yet. The best Billy could do was play this out. When all his materials were properly arranged on his desk, as innocently as he could, he raised his head to gauge the attitude of his teacher.

When he was finished, he looked up.

His mind reeled when he realized the classroom had no teacher.

"Why hasn't the bell rung yet?" Theresa Cunningham asked her fellow studients. "No idea," said another student, just as surprised.

"Say, where's Mr. McGillicutty?" asked Tommy Moranis. He stood up. Billy waited until another couple of students had risen out of their seats, and got up also. Slowly the class drifted towards the doorway. Tommy again could be counted on to take the first step, with the innocence of the oblivious. Billy found his way through the students to see what might be going on..

Directly across from them, another class of students poked their heads into the hallway. "Hey Fred!" Tommy yelled across. "Is Mr. McGillicutty in there?"

"No," said the kid. "Is Mrs. Jonesenrank in there?"

"Thank God no," said Suzy, right behind Billy. The other kids laughed a little nervously. Mrs. Jonesenrank was almost mean enough to be a Nurse.

"Hey!" came a child's voice from down the hall. Billy stepped past his classmates into the hallway, to see where it came from. "Do you have any teachers down there?" the student continued.

"No!" yelled Billy joyously.

The students began to step outwards into the hallway, eyes wide with wonder.

One child finally dared give voice to their greatest dream. "All the teachers are just gone?"

The fire bell rang.

The children knew the sound, and responded with motions drilled in by repetition. The piercing sound cut through all talk, all thought, and any urge except to get as far away as possible. Even with no teachers, they formed lines, and stepped onto the now-motionless conveyor belts, and walked as fast as they could towards the nearest exit.

They got all the way outside, and still no Faculty appeared. This was even stranger. No one could ever remember having been outside in such numbers, with no teachers around at all.

The children stood silent. After some time, someone began to cheer. They all took it up, and began to clap. Some of them sang songs they had been taught long ago, back when there had been a Music class.

Billy watched Timmy, several feet over. Timmy appeared to be mystified. He didn't know what to do. He half-heartedly pushed a couple of kids who stood near him. They pulled together in a group, and Timmy found them a bit harder to intimidate. He walked away, glowering.

Other kids began gathering into small groups, to play.

After a few minutes had passed, a strange sound was heard off in the distance. The children slowly stopped playing and strained to listen. It grew louder, as if something was coming closer. The sound had a vague aspect of something being chopped by a machine.

Billy followed the sound's direction. Suddenly the sound grew louder, and a long green shape emerged above the nearby hills. It looked vaguely like a dragonfly. The children watched, silent and astounded, as it drew closer.

It was a helicopter. As it came closer into view, they could see a strange globular object dangling beneath it. When it passed directly overhead, Billy strained his neck to look straight up it. The object was round, silvery-gray, and about the size of a small refrigerator. Billy quickly recognized it.

It was a Coffee vat.

The helicopter slowed and stopped, and then hovered in place above the Faculty Lounge. The vat was slowly lowered down. When it seemed about to hit the school's roof, two huge bay doors opened outwards. The vat slowly slipped between them, and quickly disappeared from view.

The cable was drawn back up towards the helicopter. The end of the cable dangled loosely, no longer carrying its burden. When the cable had disappeared entirely inside the helicopter, it rose into the sky, and flew over the opposite horizon.

Silence followed, and minutes passed. During which the children just looked at each other.

Suddenly the bell rang, and the Faculty emerged from the school's doors. They gripped their freshly refilled Coffee mugs, and looked frightened and angry. They commanded the students to fall back into their homeroom ranks.

*That's it?* Billy asked himself. *I risk everything, and all we get is a few minutes to stand outside?*

As they marched back in to class, he wondered if his pod-thing was chuckling.

THE SCHOOL DAY **was soon over.** Billy rode the conveyor belt with the other students, through the front doors and out of the school. He looked ahead. Down the tarmac, the long yellow cocoons were filling slowly with larval workers. The tide of children was flowing home. Relief was in the air. For what little still remained of today, at least school could be left behind.

Billy glanced over his shoulder. No grownups appeared to be paying attention to him. As the belt moved forward, he reached into his bookbag. He pulled out the book, and looked at the title again: *The Real History of Coffee and its Only Cure.* He knew all cared to know about the history. He needed to find out about the cure part. He couldn't do it by himself, he'd tried. He had to find a way to cure this thing inside him, inside his friends, this thing that had grown to maturity inside his parents and robbed them of their childhood joy when they needed it most - in their adulthood.

He went to the back of the book. More history. He skipped ahead further. He looked ahead furtively at the conveyor belt that was moving him along; they hadn't reached outside yet. He looked back, and at last he reached a title page that said" *Part 2: Its Only Cure.* He flipped past it. A page followed at the top, titled "Connection".

The page was empty. He tried to flip ahead - but there were no more written pages in the book. All that remained were some small shreds near the binding.

Billy shoved the book back into his backpack. Was this all some kind of joke? He picked up the backpack and put it on his shoulders. It felt like it held all the weight of the world. He wondered if, somewhere inside his head, the seed-thing within him smiled.

At that exact moment, the belt rounded the last corner and took them outside the school doors to the sidewalk. Suddenly Billy saw Principal Maybee, standing next to the conveyor belt. And Maybee was looking directly at him. Billy had passed all the other Faculty inside, still recovering from having missed their dose of Coffee. Billy hadn't expected Maybee to be outside, since the Principal so rarely ventured into direct sunlight. He had this time, however, and he was staring at Billy quite intently. Billy wondered why. Then he suddenly realized how foolish he had been. Billy had not been looking properly depressed and respectful.

Maybee motioned to him to step off to the side of the conveyor belt. Billy swallowed, moved to the side of the belt, and stepped off onto the sidewalk. The other students rolled on past. Those students riding nearest to Billy immediately ignored his existence.

The Principal held his riding crop in one hand. In his other hand, he held the Red Stamp. Billy restrained a shiver.

"Did you enjoy yourself today, Mr. Short?" the Principal inquired, with disarming innocence.

"Oh, yes, sir. I learned a lot of valuable things today, sir," Billy replied, trying to to keep his voice as calm as possible.

"Really..." Maybee said. He drew out the single word as if it were a line of rope. Hands clasped tightly behind his back, he towered over Billy. "And what things have we been learning...?"

"How to work and how to buy. I can't wait to grow up and be able to make money and buy things, sir."

Maybee raised his eyebrows. "It's good to work at *some* things... you were talking with Ray Pieffer on the playground, today, Billy. "

There was no use in denying it. "Yes sir."

Maybee leaned in suddenly like a hungry snake. "What about?"

Billy kept his gaze steady. "Just, stuff, you know. He owes me a cookie from a couple of lunches ago."

"That was it?"

Billy nodded. "Yes, sir."

The Principal examined him coldly, holding him frozen to the spot. He fingered his red stamp. "Coach Brumble and Nurse Kraft-Ebbing said you and another student were sent on an errand this afternoon," he continued.

"Yes sir. We took Petronio to the Nurse Station." Inside, Billy's heart sank. Ray must not have escaped. He had risked him and his friend Chris for nothing. Billy hoped Ray hadn't broken. Or Chris. He resisted the urge to run away.

"Did you by any chance go into the Faculty Lounge?" asked the Principal?

Billy decided to play it very, very innocent. "Huh? Why would we?"

"Maybe to try some Coffee?"

"Ugh," said Billy. "That's for grownups."

"Perhaps to help Ray, then?"

"Help Ray?" said Billy. "Why?"

"A good answer," said the Principal. "Why would you help anyone? But if that's how you feel, why did you loan him that sandwich cookie three weeks ago?"

"So he would stop bothering me with his weird stuff," said Billy.

Maybee leaned back a bit, considering this. Billy's heart raced, as he examined Maybee's expression. He appeared to accept Billy's answer, and stood back somewhat satisfied. "That's good. Because you're a good student, Billy. You've got a *fairly* clean record. You don't need to get filed with the likes of Ray." Maybee was silent for a moment.

It was important to keep a grownup like Maybee talking, and distracted from giving his full, undivided attention. "What's wrong with Ray, anyway?" Billy blurted. "Sir," he added.

Maybee considered the question, and then Billy. Damn! He had slipped, and asked the Principal a real question. Had he forgotten he was at school?

"It's a very interesting problem," said Maybee. "There were – ah, are a lot of very complicated things going on with Ray. Hmm....yes," he scratched at the dry, thin skin of his face. His cheek twitched slightly. "Yes, what it all boils down to is, he thinks that he's unique."

"And he isn't," Billy said, eager to seem to agree.

"Yes, of course not. All people are basically the same." The Principal gazed down at Billy, examining him. "You might think you're unique, special. This sort of thinking is a cancer to guard against. It causes unpredictability, unplanned change, disruption. In every way that matters, you are all the same. You are born; we gather you, we plant the Seeds of discipline within you. We raise you up good and strong. And when we're done, we ship you out, so you can make us a fresh new crop."

"Yes sir," repeated Billy.

"Good boy. You're all just peas in a Pod - remember that, and you'll do just fine."

"I'll remember, sir."

Maybee looked at his watch. "Now get to your bus," he said. Billy saluted, and stepped on the conveyor belt that would take him to his bus. When the belt reached its end, he stepped off and walked the few remaining feet to his transportation home. Without really knowing why, he lingered at the side, letting other students enter the bus before him.

*I'll remember what you said,* Billy thought. *I'll remember all your lies.*

Ahead of Billy, a student was struggling under the weight of her bookbag, as she climbed up the bus' steep steps. After a short but intense struggle, she reached the top step, and turned the corner to start down the aisle. Her heavily loaded backpack slipped off her shoulder, and bumped into the sleeping bus driver. He awoke with a curse, and lunged at her head like an old and angry bear. She scrambled out of his reach, with millimeters to spare.

More children, too eager to leave school to wait for the driver's rage to ebb, continued to climb aboard, and blocked the driver from his vengeance. The driver growled in frustration. He eventually sat back in his seat with a thump, and grabbed his whiskey flask instead.

Billy heard a sudden sound to his left. He looked down, and realized it was a penny that had landed near his feet. Where were they coming from?

Billy looked down near the entrance, at the trees just left of the gate.

There, in the trees above the fence, Billy was shocked to see Ray waving back at him.

Ray gave Billy a big thumbs up, and disappeared back into the trees.

Billy smiled. He made sure no other Faculty members were looking, and gave a thumbs' up in return. Billy then faced towards the bus. He hid his smile, and did not look back at the gate again. He didn't want there to be any chance that he could give Ray away.

Inside he treasured this moment. Ray had gotten out! And Billy and Chris had helped him.

Where would Ray go? Billy knew that if there was anywhere that Schools or Work did not control, Ray would find it. And he would get bring this free world back to them.

Billy breathed with relief, and stepped onto the bus. He had made it through quite a day.


THE BUS DRIVER **prepared himself with his ritual of deep swigs from a nameless steel flask.** When both the bus and the driver were fully loaded, they would set off down the road.

Some late-arriving children quickly scrambled for their seats.

Billy stole a glance at the bus driver as he walked up the steps. Billy couldn't see any signs of a pod-thing on him. Was he so full of natural bitterness that he didn't need to be controlled?

Maybe it was the alcohol. Maybe that had helped the bus driver keep from having the pod - at the cost of keeping him from doing anything else with his life but becoming mad and bitter. That was no way to win either.

Billy sat next to Timmy, and briefly closed his eyes. This had been the hardest day of school Billy'd had in a long, long time.

The bus driver gunned the engine. Some late-arriving children quickly scrambled for their seats. The bus took off, bouncing off another school bus on their way out of the entrance. The other bus driver's curses faded into the distance, as their bus entered the main road and headed for the student's homes.

Timmy appeared to be in an unusually fine mood now. "I got in a fight in the hallway," he said joyously. He licked his knuckles as they drove past the guardhouse and through the steel gate.

"Who with?"

"Oh, some punk. That Barlow kid. After that stupid fire drill break we had today...Boy, did I knock him around." Timmy smiled as he ran through the fight in his mind, and mimed kidney punches at the seat before him. Billy heard a faint curse from the front of the bus. It was the bus driver, as they swayed around a corner and almost hit a particularly resourceful pedestrian. The bus driver seemed angry because he'd missed.

Timmy's smile faded. He began to look troubled. "You know, Billy, I told everyone about that disaster you talked about this morning, and no one else heard about it. Are you sure it happened?"

"Which disaster was that again?" Billy asked effortlessly.

"You know...." Timmy's eyes developed a far-way look. "You know, the one with all the blood and the...." Clearly moved, his eyes began to tear at the recollection of this vision. "...the bodies....babies..." He sighed dreamily.

As Timmy drifted off into blood-swept rainbows, Billy looked ahead at Tracy, in the front..

There she was, head swaying with the rhythms of the bus. He couldn't see her face. He imagined she was smiling.

Billy never heard what girls said to each other. He wondered what they talked about, and what they thought. The grownups all said girls were strange and inexplicable. They never mentioned how. They just are, both the male and female grownups said. They said there was just a huge wall between boys and girls, that no one would ever scale.

Tracy's stop was coming up. It had been last in the morning, and so was the first one reached as they repeated the circuit home. He looked at her ear, and remembered what he'd seen today.

They had been in the same classes together for a couple of years now. And he still didn't know anything about her.

The bus slowed to a halt. Tracy was getting off.

He got up and squeezed past Timmy.

"Hey, where ya going? This isn't your stop," said Timmy. "Are you retardant?" Billy gave no response as he shouldered his bookbag and stepped into the aisle.

"I'm talking to you, Billy! Hey!" Billy kept moving. Ahead, Tracy had gathered her books together, and was starting down the steps.

*NO!* A small voice inside Billy tried to yell. *What are you doingggg?*

Billy was nearing the front of the bus now. *They'll laugh at youuuu!* He continued walking forward.

"So, *that's* it," said Timmy. "Billy loves Tracy! Billy loves Tracy!" The chant spread among the bus like wildfire. "*Billy loves Tracy! Billy loves Tracy!*" fifty mouths shouted as one.

Tracy turned around, startled. The noise grew louder until the bus was shaking with it. There was now backing out now. Billy stepped past the fuming bus driver and off the bus.

"Shut *up!*" bellowed the driver. "QUIET!" The voices were lowered slightly, but did not cease. "SHUT UP BEFORE I MURDER ALL YOU LITTLE CREEPS!!!" he screamed. Timmy leaned forward eagerly, as the bus driver wavered on the edge of coming completely unhinged. The bus quieted down and the driver regained control of himself. Timmy sat back, disappointed.

The driver drained the last of his flask, and threw it behind his seat. He then slammed the bus' door shut, and roared off in an explosion of dust and aging metal. Billy and Tracy were left standing outside her house.


BILLY WATCHED **the bus disappear in the distance.** He was done for. All his careful planning to not be noticed was set aside, in this one brief impulse he didn't even understand.

He set his shoulders, and faced Tracy. She stood half-turned, with her books under one arm.

"Why did you get out here?" she asked. "Don't you know they'll make fun of us?"

All the things he had thought about saying to her scattered away and hid. "I had to talk to you," he managed.

"What about?"

"Uh, your ear."

She raised a hand anxiously to the side of her head, and dropped it. "There's nothing wrong with my ear!" She turned around hurriedly, to leave.

"Wait!" he paused. "I have it too."

They faced each other in silence across the driveway.

"Have what?" she asked finally.

"That...thing. That thing that's a part of me, that grows out of stuff I don't want to think about...that tries to make me hate, tries to take me over. I have it too."

She bit her lip nervously. Her face was pained.

"Well, if you do, why on Earth would you want to talk about it?" She touched her ear, and winced. "And why do you think *I* would?"

"I didn't want to just talk to you about *that,*" he said, frustrated. "I just-" Why *had* he stepped off the bus? "I just see you every day, you know, and - you're so beautiful," he blurted.

She stared at him.

"I'm not trying to-" He suddenly had no idea at all what to do with his hands. He put his hands in his pockets. "Uh, anyway, I saw you, and I saw you had this, and I have it too, and I - I just thought I'd like to talk to you. Maybe we could be – like, I dunno, help each other or something. That's all."

This wasn't how he'd planned it all. But he hadn't really planned it. It had just happened. He would never *ever* do something this stupid again.

And she kept *looking* at him.

"Look, I'm sorry I bothered you. Please, just forget the whole thing. I guess I'll see you around," he finished miserably. He hefted his bookbag, now as heavy as the world, and turned to go.

Something touched shoulder. He turned around. It was Tracy.

"Would you like some soda?" she asked him.

Billy nodded. Tracy smiled. Together they headed into the house.

Where her hand had touched him, his shoulder was still smiling

Home.

Billy headed up the lane to his parents' house, in a state of reverie. He was feeling so good, that he wasn't even feeling the pain of the Pod. It was that same feeling that had helped him in the Faculty Room. He was feeling too good to even wonder what the feeling was.

The words he'd shared with Tracy still rung in his ears. The fear he had overcome was still fresh, the joy and pride too new to separate. He wanted to sit in it, and at the same time not even think about it.

He could feel Murple's book in his backpack, swinging around with his every step. He realized what the book had meant for a cure: "Connection". Like he and Tracy had just made, together.

His parents' house grew larger as it came nearer. He knew he be within it for a while yet. It no longer seemed quite as singular, quite as dominating. He knew some people outside it now. There were some other people, good people, and he was connected to them. It was no longer just him against the compromised nature of his family, his school, and the world at large.

He put the book in a plastic bag, and buried it in the soil in the woods just outside his house.

Billy stepped inside the door . His Mom had just finished setting the table. "Glad you decided to join us, Billy," his Dad said drily from the living room. His Dad's Pod rustled with merriment.

"Hi, Dad. Sorry I'm late - I was trying out for the mumble-mumble team."

"Oh," said his father, successfully uninterested. As he stood up and folded his newspaper, Billy sighed with relief. Billy would have to remember to seem to like sports this coming week. He went to the bathroom to wash his hands.

"What's for dinner, honey?" asked Mr. Short, as Billy stepped back in.

His Mom returned from the kitchen with a dinner tray. "Ration packet 789-A, in Worcestershire sauce," she stated proudly. "I found a new coupon." Billy and his father followed her into the dining room.

"You're so frugal, honey." Mr. Short pecked her mask, and pulled out her chair. They sat down to begin the evening feast.

Billy settled into his place at the foot of the table, and picked up his spork. He looked up suddenly at his Mom.

Once, he realized, she had been a young girl. Maybe even like Tracy.

"How was work today, dear?" Billy's Mom asked Billy's Dad. Billy looked at him, too. Had his own Dad once been just like him? Just wanting to live his life and be free?

"Oh, it was great. We got the new account today. The office should double production this week."

Billy suddenly wanted to ask her. Was his Mom was still alive in there; still young? And his Dad. Had his Dad once been like him? Had his Dad once wondered the same things he did?

They were both children once. Why had they let these awful creatures win, and left their childhood dreams behind them?

Mr. Short's Pod was restless. It could smell uncomfortable questions hanging in the air, about to be asked aloud. Billy looked back at his plate, and began to shovel in the food. There were great risks to asking grownups real, hard questions. That was School's first and strongest lesson. Even if they had no Pods or Masks, sometimes it was safer to actually insult grownups than ask them things they didn't want to think about.

"Oh, honey - your friend Harry called from MegaDrone yesterday. Something about a party," said Mrs. Short as she ladled out more the meatloaf-substitute.

"Right, right, I keep forgetting. They're going to have an office party next week." Philip Short chuckled, and had another sip of fresh-brewed Coffee.

Billy considered that his parents had to have been somewhat like him. Not *exactly* like him, of course. Just because his parents had lost, didn't mean he had to. Or Tracy. Or Chris. Or even Timmy, though he honestly seemed like a lost cause. Some day, they could find a way to beat this mess they all were in. With Tracy's help (he hoped), they could keep going. Maybe they could even wake other kids up, and all keep their heads down and their eyes open, until someone put a winning plan together.

Maybe they could all have a chance.

"So how was school today, dear?" Mom asked Billy suddenly.

"Huh? Oh, it was fine. you know." Damn! He had to stay alert to his parents, too.

"Did you learn anything new?" asked his Dad.

"Some more ways to work, shop and follow rules."

"Wonderful," said Billy's Dad, and smiled. "That's what the world needs. You know," he said, as he paused with a sporkful of substance poised majestically halfway towards his mouth, "When I was a kid, we used to walk uphill in hip-deep snow. Do they still make you do that?"

"Sometimes, when we get volunteered for yard duty."

"Good for you." Mr. Short's Pod rustled in agreement. Billy nodded politely, and sopped up the last of his dinner ration with a corner of whitebread. "May I be excused?" he asked.

"What do you think, honey?" his Dad asked his Mom.

"I don't see why not. He's been so nice and quiet this whole dinner, hasn't he?"

"Okay then, off you go," said his Dad. "And remember to not be such a baby tomorrow."

"Yes sir, I will," said Billy with sudden determination. He pushed in his chair and placed his dishes in the washer. As he walked up to his room, his Mom observed him thoughtfully from behind her mask.

Billy finished his homework, and started putting together a new model car. He had found it calming. His father opened the door and saw him working. Billy was pretty sure that, far beneath the Pod, his father loved him deeply. As long as his father's Pod's suspicions weren't triggered, Billy hoped he would be safe. Despite the other things he and his mother had inside him, they still cared and they still wanted connection.

At that moment, it all came together. That's what Mr. Murple's book was saying in that last section. That's what had helped him get through the day, and help Chris too. That's what had led him to talk to Tracy, and had helped him step forward. That was even what he had been thinking towards this morning, before the bus' arrival had knocked this thoughts asunder.

Billy readied for sleep, and his thoughts kept racing.

Ray had escaped. Andy had escaped. Maybe even Mr. Murple had escaped? Because they had connected. They had found people to help, and to help them. Maybe, someday, if Billy found enough people they all made it through the schools, they could all escape to a place that had no Schools and Work. Or at least, no Pods and Masks.

Or they could make a place like that. And then, working together, they could all rescue their world.

*And I can have a family and friends that can really talk and think and love. And we can dare to be right, and be good to each other, and others, and can dare to do good things. Maybe for everyone.*

And that's just how he fell asleep.

Dreaming...

# CHANNEL WEIRD(ER)

**10**

---

# MY UNDEAD DAD

[*O*riginally printed in "Better Tombs and Graveyards" magazine]

MY DAD'S UNDEAD. But he's still a great Dad.

We play around in the living room when he comes home from work. Or we'll go out in the yard and play tag. Every now and then, one of his hands starts to fall off. Mom or me'll pick it up and put it back on with a bit of rubber cement. He'll smile. He probably thinks we fuss too much.

He died a while ago, right after my sixth birthday. He was a sales consultant for some Internet company. He went out to their Christmas party. He didn't return that night, or the next. Mom got real mad. She called Grandma and even got out her suitcase.

Three days after the party, a big package showed up on the porch. It was from the Internet company. It was Christmas morning, too. I was real psyched. We dragged it into the living room, and opened it up.

He was in it.

"Dad!" I said.

"Just where do you think you've been, worrying us half to death?" said my mom.

"Mmmmmmrrrruhhhhhh," my dad responded.

Mom looked at him kind of funny, and told me to go to my room. I went up the stairs and tried to listen. I couldn't hear too much. First she screamed. Then I heard her call Grandma. A couple hours later, she called me back downstairs.

"Why's Dad smell so funny?" I asked.

She sighed. "He's a zombie now."

"What's a zombie, mom?"

"Someone with a dead body and mind, that has enough soul left inside them that they can still follow simple commands..."

"Are you guys gonna get a divorce?"

She paused for a bit. "I don't know," she said. "It's supposed to be 'til death do us part'. But I don't know if that applies here." She looked over at the box my dad was still in, and he looked back up at her. She shivered. " 'For better or for worse', though...we'll just have to make the best of it."

Later on, Grandma told me what happened. The Internet company was going under, and they needed more funding. So they traded Dad's soul to the devil. They scotch-taped him to a boardroom table, and sacrificed him, and everything. But just when they were about to trade his soul, Satan found out my dad was really just temping for them. So Dad wasn't really owned by them; it was more like he was rented. So the devil had to return his soul to his now-dead body.

Dad works in advertising now.

It was bad for me, at first. He was all weird. None of the other kids had undead zombie Dads; why did I have to have one? He was so *different*.

I told Mom I didn't want Dad to be undead. Mom said I'd just have to get used to it. I hated it.

Like sometimes, if he had a long day at work, he'd come home and make these hollow, scratchy growling noises and snap his mouth open and shut.

He smelled so weird now, too. And he only ate raw liver. And we had to give away our dog, too, 'cause Rusty kept gnawing on his leg.

Then he got really into yard work. So lame. He would go out in the yard with a shovel, like 4 times a week. Mom gave me a new chore because of it. Every Saturday morning, I'd have to go fill in the holes where he'd taken a nap.

Next he bought a big, new power mower. That was really cool! But he would just hog it all weekend. He'd stay on it until vultures would start to circle. Then Mom would call him in, and at least I could ride it for a while.

The one thing that was really weird, weirder than anything else, was that now he'd try to play *games* with me. And have fun and stuff. And we *never* used to do stuff like that when he was living. Back then, he'd just come home late and go to bed. If it was a weekend, he'd mostly watch TV.

Now that he was undead, though, he wanted to play all the time. And I'd have to be all careful, now. Like, if we played catch, his hand would keep flying off and we'd have to dig it out from the bushes.

He just wasn't like the Dad I knew.

I didn't know what to do. I couldn't ask him to be alive again. Even if he could be, it didn't seem like he'd really enjoyed being alive. I mean, when he was breathing, he wasn't decomposing, but he wasn't doing all that much else, either.

I was mad. I didn't really want to be around him.

Then one Saturday morning he knocked on my door. Just like when he was alive, he didn't really say much. This time, though, was different. He was holding something in his hands.

It was a scale model of a fighter jet. It was new, and it looked really cool. Also, he had glued it to his fingers. I helped him pry it off. Then I helped him glue his thumb back on.

It felt good to help him. What he tried hadn't quite worked right, but he'd tried.

Mom pointed out that having his heart ripped out and burned by his employer, maybe really helped him appreciate his family.

When the weekend was over he went back to work, and I watched him go. I looked forward to him coming back, and maybe working on some models or maybe just lying around on the couch. It was good to have him around, I think because even though he was undead, now he was at least really here.

It was kind of embarrassing at first, having an undead zombie Dad. Now I think it's kinda cool. And you know what? My friends do too. Not that I care. But it's fun. And salesmen don't come around any more. Jehovah's Witnesses, forget it. All he has to do is answer the door and they run screaming and hugging their bibles. It's awesome. And you couldn't have a better Dad for Career Day at school. Or Halloween.

He'll still have a bad day at work, every now and then. He won't talk about it. Actually 'cause he currently lacks the power of speech. I still can tell something's bugging him though. And now I know lots of ways to cheer him up. Usually all it'll take is a shovel full of some nice fresh dirt on him. It gets on the couch too and then we have to vacuum it up, but mom understands.

I don't know if I want to be just like my Dad when I grow up, though. Not alive, I mean. He's always trying to get me interested in graveyards and morgues. I just think they're corny. Sometimes it's a bit rough being in a closed car with him, too. Especially in the summer. Mom tells me to not be such a nitpicker.

Mom's right, too. 'Cause no matter what, my Dad is a great guy. He isn't even fully alive, and he still works so hard for us. Maybe someday he'll retire, and we'll all move to Arizona. He'll decompose a lot slower there. Until then, he'll keep on working to give us the good life.

I love my undead Dad.

## 11

# GUARDIAN ANGST

I came home to my apartment, to find my guardian angel.

As soon as I saw him, I knew all the things angels ask us to forget. We're not supposed to remember them, because we're supposed to think we're on our own. That helps us act with the most pure intent possible. Their theory is that without knowing the safety net we can have, we will better learn to balance will and structure before we die and go to whatever's after. I don't know if it's 100% true, but it's a bit outside of my experience so who am I to judge?

I dropped my keys on my desk. "I thought we're only supposed to see you angels in the most dire circumstances."

"That's right," my angel said. "You're driving me crazy! Do you know how hard you make me work? Do you know what it's like when an angel goes crazy?"

"What are you talking about? I'm just – you know, I'm doing my thing. I'm exploring art, I'm working at my job…"

"You're courting death, destruction and mayhem every day of your life. Every second! Good Lord, you can't even be safe sitting at home. The time you spend on the Internet…the scams, the cults… then when you go outside. Do you know how many times last week I had to steer you away from a certain end?" He sighed. "I'll give you a clue. That girl you got the wrong number from at the bar? It was the right number. I changed it. She's a runaway with a father in the mafia."

I blinked. "Okay. But how am I supposed to know that? I mean, what do you want from me?" I let my voice raise a little. Sure, they having nearly infinite power and benevolence tempered by love of God and all His creations, and also all the other angels all trying to do well with everything. But I get to say something. "I'm trying to do the best with my human experience, my, my living experiment that's me here! The first real talk I can remember, and you're just going to give me a bunch of crap because I don't know what I'm doing? Why don't you tell me what I *should* be doing?"

"Because that's not the rules!"

I put my hands on my hips, of all things, feeling foolish but not enough to stop. "Should I just live the safest life possible?"

"Of course not!" My angel said, offended. "You just try so many things, and then I put good things in front of you and you just run away! You're a good-hearted mortal. It's just so strange how you do and then you don't listen to yourself. I need you to get on a path and stick with it! You're making me crazy here!"

"How do I know you're not a guardian devil?"

It looked deeply wounded, and said nothing. I felt bad now. I knew, without even knowing it was so beyond question – this was a good being who wanted the best for me his whole life. If it was even gendered of course.

"Okay, look." I sighed. "I'd love to hear from you how I can do better. Okay? I'm trying without a manual here."

It's face was tortured. "It's stretching things just to talk this much to you." Then an expression passed it's face, the purest guilt and pain across such a face of clarity, light and benevolence was truly awful to see. It made me want to weep.

"Maybe we can work out a deal," it said. "If you just..."

I stopped him suddenly. "Don't tell me."

"What?" his eyes stricken.

"Whatever you were about to say. I don't want to hear it. I changed my mind." I grit my teeth. "Whatever you tell me will mean that I'm not living *my life*."

It began to cry. "But what will I do? Every – every time, every day, it's just so hard!"

"I'm sorry I've been such a burden to you." I wanted to make him feel better, but actual bitterness slipped through which surprised me. Was I really that difficult? I realized it probably knew my thoughts anyway, so I might as well hear them. "I'm not out here robbing banks or beating people up," I said. "I'm just trying to do my thing."

I looked at the bags beneath his glowing eyes. His hair was a mess. It was supposed to be some glorious glowing mane, but all kinds of stuff was stuck in it. I looked a bit closer, and it looked like twisting clumps of unproductive thoughts.

I felt bad for him. "Look man-"

"I'm not a human!"

"Okay, okay! I believe you. Look...higher being, we're taking this moment to talk, right?" I pointed him towards my chair. "Why don't you take a seat."

"I..."

"Take a break. Let's talk it through."

It looked over at my chair. "I don't know if I have taken the time to sit down for ... three centuries."

I spread my hands. "I'm right here. You can still keep me from doing harm. Maybe I'll be safer if you're sitting, or something? Less chance something will get knocked off a bookshelf?" I nudged him towards the chair. "Just take a load off"

He sighed and sat, closing his eyes. Flaming tears of sunlight came poured from underneath his glorious eyelashes.

On impulse I went to the fridge, brought back a couple beers, and held one out for him. He opened his eyes and looked at it, without raising his hands. I pushed it into his chest until he grasped it. He held it in his hand.

"It feels cold."

"That's right."

"I understand some humans prefer their beers warm."

"Yeah, they're just wrong. Give it a try."

He took a sip and made a face. "It tastes awful."

"Okay. Just take a sip any time you feel like disagreeing with me. Now let's talk about you for a bit."

The angel took a sip, but said nothing, watching me almost suspiciously.

I sat at my desk chair across from him. "When's the last time you just enjoyed something for you?"

"I enjoy things all the time! The birth of babies, the growth of a flower, peaceful transitions in to the afterlife, helping keep a human protected from bad paths until they have a chance to grow..."

"No, no. Not things for other people. When is the last time you had a chance to just enjoy a thing because it was something good for you. Not because it was helpful to any other being."

He thought long and hard. His eyes drifted into a misty glow.

"Several thousand years ago, I was floating over the pacific. There were fewer humans to manage then. In the time between one islander dying and another being born, I was distracted by...the most amazing dawn. It was just after a mighty storm and the sky was almost cloudless, with just a few puffs of clouds to show their beauty against the multicolored sky. The mostly placid but still-moving ocean beneath me. A squad of dolphins enjoying the sun rising before us. They might have even seen me, some nonhuman creatures can have an easier time with that. We all floated in that moment, them in the water and me in the air just about it, as we bore silent witness to God's creation. A beauty that..."

He took another sip. "That was not for disagreement," he clarified. "A beauty that it is easy to forget about."

I nodded. "Alright." I cracked open my own beer. "Look, you've been with me my whole life, and I appreciate it. I don't even know how many things you've saved me from-"

"You have no God-damn idea," he said. Shocked at his own words, he took another sip. "Hits fast!"

"Sure does. So how about you be kind to you for a bit? Seems to me you're close to cracking."

The angel started at me for a second, and then began to cry. Great job, I thought to myself. You made your angel cry. "Alright, come here being." I held my eyes open.

It looked at me, as if it couldn't stand to trust me. "Come on, I'm here. It's okay."

It came up out of the chair, and I gave it a hug.

I wrapped my arms around it, and it wrapped it's arms around me, and I could feel a bit of its infinite power. But also, its infinite sadness. I just stayed there with it, trying not to think about how it could probably keep crying until I grew old and died, and then some. I could spare this moment, and quite a few more. So I just gave him the attention he deserved for each moment.

Eventually it separated. "Thank you," it said. "I'm really grateful. I don't have many other beings I can talk to."

"Really?" I shook my head. "What about, you know, other angels?"

"They've all got the same things to deal with. They never tire. They can't allow themselves to wait a moment."

"How about..." I wondered. "Do you have a guardian angel for yourself?"

"No! Don't be insane."

"How would you know? Maybe you would be set to not remember them unless they're around, like you are for me."

"I don't think so," it said at last. "We are less of the experience of free will combined with less certainty."

"But you don't know for sure, do you?" I pointed out.

The angel paused. It took another sip. "This beer does make such an idea easier to contemplate."

"That's it's job. Anyway, even if I don't remember you, I appreciate you. So appreciate yourself too."

It smiled. "Thanks, -" and it mentioned a name I had never heard before, that I also knew from the depths of my being was mine. Perhaps the name was beyond time. If there was anything to reincarnation, this might be the name of the me that experienced them all.

"You're welcome," I said in return.

It moved a bit away from me, and placed a hand on my shoulder. It's wings spread out, going through the walls of my space.

"I'll remember this for the both of us, and keep looking out for you, and I'll also find a way to be kind to me. I ask the same for you, of you."

I nodded. "Easy to say, hard to do, I know." Not knowing what else to do, I somewhat awkwardly shook his hand. He laughed, wiped away some his streaming sunlight tears, and disappeared.

I woke up, and found myself staring at Facebook. What was I about to write again?

I closed my browser. Maybe it wasn't a good use of today to have more arguments with strangers.

It was beautiful outside. No matter what the weather was. It was time to take a walk and enjoy all of this life.

But maybe I'd stay inside a couple of minutes more. Maybe meditate or something. I wasn't sure why, but I felt it might be good to stay in until someone had fully sobered up.

## 12

# THE BUDDY LUNCH

"Can you help me out here?" Mark asked, his face desperate.

Fred realized Mark was talking to him. He took his headphones off, and looked around his cubicle in the vast office floor. Everyone else was eating lunch at their desk.

He looked back at Mark. "I'm actually working on something here. Can you find someone else?" "We're interviewing someone, and it's gone on for a couple of hours. So the big boss said we should break for lunch. He wants to go take some calls, so he asked me to hang out with the interviewee for a bit."

Frank frowned. "Okay, but why do you need my help?"

"It's kind of...hard going keeping this conversation going. We want to seem natural. I can't think of anyone else who could handle this better. Help a brother out."

Frank sighed. "You know I'm behind here. If you really need my help..."

"I do."

Frank put down his headphones, logged off his computer and walked with Mark towards the cafeteria. They grabbed today's menu, what looked like some rather good cheeseburgers and some salad that came with the deal.

Frank coughed. "So what should I know about the guy? The boss must like him."

Mark's face froze into a mask of impassiveness. "You'll see."

"What do you..."

Mark pointed over to a table where a large child-sized porcelain doll was sitting, motionless. It had a white dress with a light-blue stripe around the bottom, with ruffles at the sleeves. The doll had a laptop next to it. Moving no other part of it's form, the doll's childlike head swiveled in Frank's direction. It smiled.

Frank grabbed Mark's arm, and pulled him around the corner. "Oh no. Oh you gotta be kidding me. Not again."

"You promised, man!" Mark whispered back intensely. "I need your help on this!"

Frank shook his head. "Why do we keep interviewing soul-killing possessed dolls?"

"Because they kill at coding, you know that!"

Frank sighed. They walked towards the table, and set their plates down.

"Hello," said the creepy porcelain doll.

"Hi," said Mark, and very tentatively shook the tiny doll's hand. "This is my friend Frank."

"Hello Frank. I'm Dolly Dollerson!" It said with perfect chipped cheerfulness. "We're gonna be great friends." The porcelain beneath it's eye had the lightest stain of what looked like... Ketchup. It had to be ketchup.

"Hello Dolly," said Frank, realizing just as he said it that he was repeating the refrain of the famous old song. He sat down.

"Hee hee," said the doll.

"So, uh, what do you do?"

"I'm a database engineer. I also drink the souls of those who cross me. You aren't going to cross me, are you, Frank?"

Frank threw a scowl directly at Mark. Thanks buddy. "No, of course not. I, you know, I mind my own business. It's all about the work."

It raised a single mechanical eyebrow. "That's smart. You stay smart. Hee."

Mark coughed. "Dolly here has taken up databases after her previous position working for Salesforce. She was already heading up a team before she left. She's a natural."

"What were you doing at Salesfo-" Frank began.

"I headed up HR."

"Of course you did," said Frank smoothly. "What made you take up databases?"

"I have a good mind for cold precision," said Dolly. "Also, numbers in databases can make grown men cry."

"Isn't that the truth, huh?" Mark forced laughter, elbowing Frank in the ribs.

"Got that right," agreed Frank. "What made you Oracle?"

"No one MADE me leave. I LEFT." It moved it's porcelain face pieces in an imitation of a scowl. "Are you suggesting something?" said Dolly with perfect pinprick perkiness.

"No, no," said Frank smoothly. "I just meant with your, your obvious skill at precision, were they no longer challenging enough?"

"Yes. Okay, you're off the hook for now. I've got my eye on you." It kept one glass doll eye focused on him, as that side of it's face turned a mechanical check upwards in something that was supposed to approximate a smile. "Is this a typical amount of attendance?" Dolly asked. Her other eye moved off of Frank and snapped into sync. Then she looked around, her smoothly swiveling neck covering nearly 360 degrees, like an owl.

"Pretty much," said Frank. "Some folks are on PTO."

"We have a lot of food options," said Mark. "Kosher, Halal, vegan, gluten-free..."

"Do you have souls?" she asked softly.

"Uh...not that I know of." Mark admitted.

"I'll have to see what I can do then."

Frank sorted through his mind, and nothing came to him but the old set of cliches. Better than silence. "What are you looking most for in a position?"

"A place where I can make everyone as happy as me! FOREVER. EVER EVER AND EVER."

Frank raised an eyebrow. "Doesn't that...kind of conflict with enjoying how databases can make grown men cry?"

Dolly shook her head, with the perfect smoothness of a plastic joint in a socket. "Good question. Not at all. It instead the best time to DRINK their souls so they can be HAPPY AND HAPPY."

Frank nodded. "Well, you should fit right in then." He saw a gleam of hope. "If you aren't so stuck on the souls thing."

Dolly Dollerson looked at him with a puzzled glance in its frozen eyes. "Yes Frank? Why do you say that?"

Mark looked over at Frank. "Eh, heh heh, Frank's still getting over a bit of a breakup. He used to date someone else who was...flesh impaired."

"A doll?" Dolly asked. "Why did you break up?"

"It was just time," said Frank.

"So she dumped you, hee!" It swiveled both eyes back on him as it smiled.

Frank was about to respond angrily, and then laughed too, surprising himself. "You're right." It felt a bit of a relief to admit it. "She wanted...more interesting opportunities I guess. Anyway, she liked it here while she was here."

"But...everyone here is still so ... living," said Dolly, puzzled. "Why would she leave before she had made everyone as HAPPY AS HER, FOREVER AND EVER, you know."

Frank shrugged. It was a mystery to him too. For all her faults as a significant other, Amy had at least been good with his family. "She did say something once about there not being a lot of room for her to grow."

"Let's not dig up old negativity now, Frank," said Mark. "Let's stay on track about working for us. There's so many things Dolly can do here."

"Sure. Dolly, Have you met our current VP's of marketing and production?" Frank indicated the corner table.

There sat two dolls, in sharp suits. They slowly raised empty spoons from bowls of red, that Frank and many others always hoped were just tomato soup. They were surrounded by several other human VPs, who also stayed quite quiet.

"I...have not," said Dolly, suddenly somewhat unnerved.

"They came on board last year," said Mark.

"It's been a year now, hasn't it?" Frank inclined his head philosophically. "I didn't realize it was that long. To be honest, I thought it was kind of bad at the time. But, their expertise in a variety of fields has worked out really well."

"Absolutely," said Mark. He seemed more than a bit relieved to be back to talking on a positive note. "Yeah, it seems like they are quite happy."

"And they've been able to get past the whole souls thing, too," said Frank, a perfectly innocent look on his own face.

Mark's face froze. "We don't need to talk about compensation right now..."

"I disagree. Hee. I think we do." Dolly Dollerson's eyes narrowed. "What about compensation?"

Frank shrugged. "We had a hard time keeping interns, so we didn't have a lot of souls to offer. So we cancelled the intern program, and they accepted stocks instead. All about the profits, for the good of the company," said Frank.

"No souls?" the doll turned to Mark. "You foolish sack of blood. You didn't mention NO SOULS." It waved its arms at the cafeteria. "No souls in the dining room, no interns, no souls, only stocks instead?"

"I understand being interested in souls," Mark responded, "But we can't really pay in life-force any more. We could pay in happiness, maybe? Like how much enjoyment would you want to suck from each of the living per quarter?"

It frowned and gnashed it's perfect tiny teeth. "I need a house to keep my form in, so I am not stuffed into a trunk and burned when my soul wanders for new victims. That means I must make good income, especially in this city. But once I have that money, does it bring me souls?" Dolly shook her head. "The best things in unlife cannot be paid for."

"There's still things that can be paid for," said Mark, a panicked edge rising into his voice. "You can still get a lot of nice things. Think of how you can help make people happier and happier, forever and ever!"

"Is there room in the budget for hiring contractors?" said Dolly hopefully.

"I'm sure we can work something out," said Mark.

"We do also have a general policy against soul harvesting now." Mark kicked him under the table. Dolly noticed. "We order food out, when we can't cook it," said Frank. "I don't think there's a startup offering souls yet."

"That's a good idea!" said Dolly. "I think I'll do that! Want to join me?"

Frank blinked. "Uh..."

"I mean, I'm not working here now. No souls, this is bullshit." Dolly crooked her finger at Frank. "You have an original way of think-ing. You can keep your soul. We will make the green tickets you blood sacks think bring you joy. Just bring lots of other souls to me. We can set up a database. We can even store them in a database, hah haaaaaaa!"

"We can talk about it," Frank said smoothly. "Send me a proposal."

"Done." Dolly snatched her laptop bag from the table, and leapt off the seat. The possessed porcelain doll stood and turned it's polished blank face up to Mark. "There's no need to waste my or your time any further. I won't forget you tried to hire me without telling me about the souls. Watch your back heee heeee!"

Dolly left as quickly as her eager doll legs could take her.

"Frank, you're an absolute dick," said Mark. He shook his head. "Now I'll have to get a new set of defensive hexes. Maybe even a damn salt rug and a familiar. It'll probably scorch my protection budget for the rest of the year."

"All I did was tell the truth," said Frank. "I'll be at my desk."

He spent the rest of the day figuring out if he could begin a startup based on protective hexes. If he and Mark wanted them, maybe there was a way to cut out the middle witch.

**13**

___

## HELL IS WHERE THE HEART IS

Some kind of thing had just gone bump in the morning.

David Richardson woke to a set of screeching and thumping noises. It was so odd that he wondered if his alarm clock was busted. He hit the snooze, but the sound didn't stop.

Half-asleep and growing more than half-vexed, he sought around his small and dismal apartment for the noise. He opened the curtains to see it was still rather dark outside - it must have been barely 6 am. Nearly two hours before he usually woke up to throw enough coffee into his sluggish system to dare and face the LA traffic.

The sound continued, and as he became more awake he realized it was constantly changing. The thumping was intertwined not just with a high-pitched noise but with a shriek. Outside, and off in the distance, some car alarms started, accompanied by some breaking glass. The sounds continued growing louder, the overall affect being ominous as well as awful.

Fully awake now and more than a little upset, he opened the door to his studio flat. His first floor apartment in a revamped motel faced directly out Santa Monica Blvd. There what he saw made him stare a full two seconds, close his eyes, and open them to stare a gain.

There appeared to be a full-force gale of grayish pterodactyls.

They were just swarming everywhere, flying up and down, around, confused, slamming and bumping into houses, cars, streetlamps all along the street and off into the distance,. They were screeching all the way and louder as they hit. Car alarms continued adding to the cacophony.

Above them a second and third sun had appeared, surrounded by a strange fog that was alternately yellow and purple.

The entire earth outside seems to have been transformed into some sort of desert apocalypse.

David closed the door. He looked at his cellphone. He still had 4 full bars of signal. Not sure of what else to do, he called his mom.

"Hey, mom," he said."Hi David," she said. "What a pleasant surprise! I was just thinking of you. What's up?"

"Just saying hi."

"Okay," she said and waited. As a mother, she knew there would be more.

"So uh, Mom, what's going on in your corner of the world?"

"Nothing much. Your father just found out he lost his fishing hat."

"Oh. Yeah that's tough. Hope he finds it...uh, how about, outside?"

"It must be early in the morning out there in Los Angeles David. Are you ok? What's going on?"

"Yeah I just uh – you're not seeing anything strange outside?"

"No. I mean, it's raining here."

"OK. I'll uh – ok. Bye". He hung up and called his friend Bill. He realized he should have called him in the first place. He must have wanted to make sure his mom was okay. It couldn't have all been a childish need for comfort.

"So Bill are you – are you seeing-?"

"Man I was just going to call you! Yeah, what's going on?"

"You're seeing what I'm seeing right?"

"I think so. Big bat-looking' things with sharp heads or something, flying into stuff, weird sky, 3 suns, sky is yellow or purple, just in flashes. Um...just...I don't know what the hell's going on."

"Yeah me neither. But the cellphone's are still working."

"Yeah. Yeah!" Bill paused, and David heard him pop open a beer. "Weird."

"Yeah, I guess so."

He heard Bill set a bottle down. "Isn't it a bit early for a drink, Bill?"

"What? I'm up, you're up. Why not?"

"What's going on now?"David had no idea. "I guess the cell-phones are still working, and the Internet's still up." David cracked the door open and looked up the street. "I see people going in and out of the supermaket – I guess we still gotta go to work."

Bill snorted. "Well, you do what you gotta do. Think I'm calling in today."

David had nothing else to say so he said goodbye. He looked out the window, and then he looked at the clock.

He didn't want to be late for his new job. He'd just started working there a month ago, after a long stretch of unemployment. This whole mess was going to be awful on the morning traffic. He'd better head out now to stay ahead of it.

He showered, brushed his hair and shaved, still in a bit of a daze. With the chaos outside, at least it didn't seem like a day he'd have to care about his most office-approved shirt. He threw on his favorite dress shirt, a bit daring for the office with a darker than usual shade of blue.

Then he walked to his car, ducking pterodactyls and blocking ones headed directly for him with his briefcase. A couple still got through, leaving some occasional stains on his shirt. It was good that he hadn't worn his best one, it would have been dirty by the time he got to the office anyway.

He set off for the highway, which his wipers on full to clear the smears of creatures flying into it. Past all of the flying jetsam there were still 3 suns in the sky. It didn't seem that much hotter. Maybe a few degrees. Perhaps the suns just hadn't punched their way through LA's normal pollution yet?

After a bit, the flap of wings and screeching became a bit monotonous. The morning commute settled into feeling about the same, as the bunch of pterodactyls flapping around and causing a general nuisance melded into the typical gridlock, bad driving, lane-hogging luxury cars and middle-fingered salutes. The highway was also slick with the strange creatures, and the drivers thus driving as badly and slow as they typically did right after it rained.

As he passed drivers entering onto the highway from other onramps, they were at first a little bit observant of the pterodactyls but soon were quickly back to honking at each other and flipping each other off.

He might as well make sure the traffic wouldn't make him late for work. He turned on his radio for any traffic updates.

"...This morning there's a traffic pileup on the 101 and some other interesting reports this morning – reports of pterodactyls."

"A lot of them everywhere," piped in a high-energy cohost. "They're like in-laws at a barbecue, amirite?"

"Oh, Phil, don't go there," said a third host on the mic.

"We've still got all we need for a good morning," the first host chimed back in. "Let's brighten things up with the latest Taylor Swift!"

David turned off the radio and found himself not minding the rest of his drive to work. It was at least a little different. He parked near the office and got a coffee from a shop around the corner to brace himself for the office, like he always did. People crowded inside, and as he opened the door a couple ran out shielding their coffee cups from further flying creatures pterodactyls.

Coffee in hand he walked to his desk, passing various conversations. A coworker was asking his manager "Aren't you even curious about all this weirdness? What do you think is going on?"

"I don't know but look - this is our best chance to hit our numbers for this quarter. You better have those docs ready for the meeting or you're gonna be in trouble."

"I'm gonna be in trouble?"

"Yeah! We've still gotta sell advertising. I mean, you know? If the end is near then really maybe we have to sell MORE advertising.

Maybe we should start thinking of ways we can capitliaze on the market-share of the pterodactyl see-ers."

"But don't you think we should consider the larger implications of this."

"You do have a point," the manager tapped his fingers. "How this might affect the retiree demographic?"

The rest of David's day was, very strangely, just like every other day. The big bay windows outside showed a general calming of swarms of pterodactyls, as they appeared to become acclimated to their new surroundings. They resolved into slowly circling in clouds as the 3 suns and a new moon moved slowly in different directions beyond LA's haze.

Towards the end of the day, David decided that he really had nothing to lose. He went into his boss' office. "So uh, where's my check?"

"Check? Well you know Richardson, things are all weird today what with all this stuff that looks like pterodactyls, you know, I just, I don't know-"

"Really?" David shook his head. Even today, he had to deal with this? "You didn't have my check yesterday either. You know you're going to have to pay me anyway. Why not just pay me now?"

"Well look, you know, I mean you gotta understand, things are all crazy-"

"I came in today to work, even though there were pterodactyls flying everywhere and 2 new suns in the sky. You're here too."

His boss sighed, pulled out an envelope from his desk drawer and handed it to him.

David took it, and looked at it. At least it was the right amount. "Why did you even wait?"

"Ah, I like holding onto money as long as I can."

David sighed. "You have some connections. Have you heard anything that explains this pterodactyl stuff?"

"Nope. See you tomorrow. And be here on time."

David finished up his work, mostly responding to emails, and left for home. He turned on the radio, just in time to hear "...interrupt this broadcast for a special address from the president of the united states."

"Finally!" said David. "Some answers."

The President of the United States' began. "Hello, my fellow Americans and people around the world. On the basis of a lot of reports, and as confirmed by the evidence of our own eyes, it would appear that the Los Angeles area has somehow merged with what appears to be an alternate reality hellscape. To be absolutely honest with you, we're not quite sure what to do about it yet. But we're in the process of doing that. In the meantime we request that you all continue to go about your business, do your jobs, and continue to buy the products and services we need for a healthy economy.God bless you all, and may God continue to bless the United States of America."

David stared at the radio in his dashboard. "That's it?"

"That was the President," said the announcer. "Now a word from the opposing party."

"It's absolutely ridiculous that the President suggest we should be happy right now. This is all a distraction from what we really need - tax cuts!"

With no other ideas for where he should go, David drove back to his apartment and parked in the only spot he could find. As he unlocked his front door two creatures started materializing on either side of him.

He panicked, and his key became stuck in the door. He tried to pull it out as the creatures become more solid. There were two of them, male and female. They were naked, and red, and came complete with horns, claws, the back legs of goats and a pointed tail.

The creatures were fully materialized. He finally got the key out of the lock and rushed inside, turning to slam the door behind him.

The female one jammed a hoof between the door and the jamb, preventing him from closing it.

"Get out!" said David. "I don't want any, I just got home!"

"We should get out?" the female demon asked, with a surprisingly sweet voice. "What are all you people doing here? What have you done to our world?"

"Well - Wait – what are you - what are YOU doing here? In my world?"

"We don't know what's going on," the male demon said. "We're just minding our own business, and then suddenly you turn our world into some kind of Hell."

"That's what I'm - wait." David scratched his head. "Are you saying my world is your Hell?"

"What else could it be?" asked the male demon.

The female nodded. "Look at this horrible place. How overpopulated are you? And you. You dress in the fated prisoner garb of legend, with that ceremonial rope around your neck to signal your obedience. You must work hours every day for colored tickets. How much do you get paid? How long do you sit in your, what did they call it to frighten us as children - traffic?"

"I always feared coming here when I die," the male said with sorrow.

The female looked at her companion with sad black eyes. "Do you think we have died? I had hoped we lived a better life than this."

"I do not think it is Hell, because I have you," the male demon said. "That is the only reason it can't be Hell."

She embraced him. David looked away, trying not to be rude. Not only were both of the naked, now that he had a chance to look at her she was really hot. Well, except for the horns, hooves, tail and bat wings. She was beautiful even, with long legs ending in hooves and long flowing black hair, inquisitive purple eyes set in a lovely face that just happened to the color of red leather.

To be honest, the male demon was very fit too. His abs looked like they were cut out of red marble.

"Well my world is not a hell okay?" David protested, exasperated. "It's really not that different from any other day."

The female demon's eyes widened, and David wondered if he saw pity there. For all the eye contact that he could make while her chest was exposed.

She faced her companion. "He does not even know of his own

imprisonment and torment. How sad it is for this drone that he thinks this prison land is freedom, or even purgatory."

"Then..." David sputtered. Their comments were uncomfortably close to the mark. "Why don't you go home then!"

"Don't you think we wish to, demon?" The male demon asked him challengingly. "Are you saying you can send us back where we should be? Is this some kind of a farce?"

"Perhaps we must pass some test?" the female demon mused.

The male demon cocked his head. "Is that it? What conundrum would you riddle with us, spawn of Hell?"

David shook his head. "Look. I have no idea how you guys got here. I just woke up this morning to see all these bats flying around. Now you two just show up on my doorstep. I've had a long day, I barely got paid and I'm tired. I'm going back to my apartment." He began to close the door.

"Wait!" said the demon girl.

"What?" said David.

"We need some place to stay," she said.

The male demon nodded agreement. "We know nothing of your world, or its night. It is probably a great danger to innocents such as we."

"Call a cab. Get a hotel room."

Her brows furrowed. "A...cab? One of the mythical vehicles to transport those without wings?"

"Would this not require...money?" the male demon pointed out. "We have heard of this, in our legendary descriptions of your hellish place." He shivered. "In this cold place, and I don't only mean the temperature."

David looked around. It struck him how quickly all the chaos, dust and demon-looking things had come to fit in with Los Angeles. Even these two beings. So far at least, they seemed to be just another small hassle in his day to day existence.

"Look, I don't really know you guys. Okay? And after all, you don't know me either. Let's not be roommates just yet. You can - I don't know, find a bus station or something. Or people sometimes sleep at the beach." He eyed the sharp talons on the ends of their fingers. "You guys should be alright."

Then the female demon made an excited squeal. She pointed over her companion's shoulder. "There! My sweet, that is the first mountain we often pass on the way to your parent's clan nest, is it not?"

The male demon squinted. "Usually we see it from below...but I think you are right."

"That way is our home!" she squealed. "Strange being of Hell, if you cannot protect us in your home, can you at least take us there?"

David considered it. "How far a drive?"

The girl pursed her lips. "The place is...which direction does your small lonely sun rise in?" Her lips looked pretty except for their purple color and the small fangs slightly protruding from them. Or maybe, because of them.

"Over there," David pointed. "We call that direction East. And it's a fine sun, okay."

"Whatever you wish to believe," the male demon responded.

The female nodded. "Then take us in that direction, East. For several horizon lengths."

David frowned. "Can you give me that in miles? Like if we were driving about that last." He pointed at the cars driving past them on the street.

Her eyes rolled up in her head as she thought, showing a different color of eyeball as she had no pupils. "At that rate of speed, it would appear to take about 3... do you split your day in 24 pieces?"

David nodded. "We call them hours."

"Three hours."

It was a lot to ask. He almost said no but realized he had nothing else to do. He then caught himself feeling a bit bad for not offering to let them stay in his apartment. He shook his head. What was wrong with him?

"If we do not find our home, what shall we do?" The guy demon-lookalike said.

They both looked so very lost, and vulnerable and open to him.

David felt he understood them better than most of the people he talked with every day.

"Okay, let's go," said David, and sighed. They went back to his car, and laboriously folded their tails and wings to fit in the back seat. He explained seat belts to them, and they confirmed these were bindings they could put and remove at will, and not traps to send them to some sort of hellish torment.

David them headed east on the 5 and negotiated traffic as they all sat in silence. He looked out at the landscape. He was seeing it a bit differently than usual, maybe because of the changes to the environment, and maybe because his passengers were causing him to think about it.

"You don't like living here either do you?" the male demon asked.

"What's not to like?" David said, sarcastically. "Whatever hell we're merging with seems to fit right in. Maybe it's just all out in the open now, and looking like it feels."

"If do you not like living here, then why stay?" the demon woman asked. "All your world can not be as this."

"I used to live in a better place," said David. "But I ended up here."

"Were you banished? It would make sense if this were your punishment."

David sighed. "I loved a girl. A lot. I put everything I had into it. It didn't work- it never does for me. I'm so tired of trying new things and new places, so I thought I might as well stay here. If love won't work, any place is just as good as any other."

"But that doesn't even make sense," the other demon asserted. "If you don't like it as much, then it is not as good. If you do not care, then why not be a place you would like more?"

David's fingers tightened on the steering wheel. "Look. I'll figure something out."

The female demon looked at him, and then to her companion in sympathy. "The way you say you're living now, seems worse than you say our world is. Our 'Hell'."

David said nothing, and the resumed driving in silence. The suns began to drop below the horizon. One of the few things David had to admit was pretty about the area was the sunsets – the skies painted by the sunlight on the canvas of the smog. The new suns added some different textures, and the many different flying bat winged creatures did not detract from it.

"This is not bad," the male demon admitted. "An occasional belch of lava from a new small volcano or stalagmite would do well."

"Yes Hyrax. It could mix with it in a way that was unexpectedly subtle and appealing."

David slapped his hand against the dashboard. "We haven't even introduced each other have we? Okay, he's Hyrax. I'm David. What's your name?"

"As your mouth forms words, it would be Yggrakka. In our home species tongue it is-" she gave vent to a long stream of trilling screeches that sounded like a songbird being crushed by a wheel.

"I like Ygrakka," said David.

"Yggrakka," she corrected him.

The demons continued to look outside the windows, and soon resumed asking him questions about the strange land he didn't like that he chose to stay within.

An hour and a half later they had gone far enough into the desert south and east of Los Angeles to see the stars, undiluted by the city light.

David cleared his throat. "Okay, do you guys see where you should be living at?"

Hyrax let out a squeal of dismay. "The mountains and horizon and look as they should, but the home nests of our clan kinfolk are not here."

David put a hopeful tone in his voice. "Maybe they're over the next hill or something?"

Yggrakka looked quite upset. "They should be here. If they are not here, they are not on your world."

David considered it. "So you guys really don't have any money."

"I don't think so – my sweet, what is money again?"

The male demon mused. "Money – yes, our myths of hell tell us that you live for this sick system where your lives are dictated by colored tickets, and numbers that records their transfer."

David rolled his eyes. "Yeah, that awful stuff. Do you have any?"

"No."

"All right, go around behind the building there and wait for me. I'll get a room, you should see the light turn on. Then I guess fly up? You guys can fly?" They nodded. "Great. You can at least sleep the night. I have to go back to work tomorrow morning. Probably pretty early because of the drive, so you guys are going to be on your own after that."

Hyrax nodded. "Thank you, we appreciate it. It would be frightening to sleep underneath all of this openness and its clear night full of stars in your hell world."

A half an hour later they were all gathered in his hotel room.

"Why do you not take your prison uniform off?" said the male demon. "Your masters should not care once you are out of their view."

"Yeah I think I'm gonna...stay dressed. Thank you though."

The male and female demon shrugged. "It makes us uncomfortable, but as you wish."

"So, are you two the only of your...world that you've seen?" He had almost said "of your kind" as that might have been...species-ist?

"So far, yes."

"This has been quite a stir for our little world here," said David. "I sure would like to know what we can do about it. Although I guess it hasn't surprised a lot of people, here in Los Angeles.

Yggrakka sighed. "I expect it is the same back in our world." Both demons shook their heads.

David sat in one of the hotel room's chairs. "You might have to get jobs now."

"You have been so kind to us until now, in your way," the female demon said. "Why would you say such a thing?"

"Yes, do not torment us!" Hyrax exclaimed.

"I was just... fine." David went to turn on the TV.

Yggrakka spread out on the bed, her wings unfolding and brushing against the lamp shade on either side. "So cramped...."

Hyrax sat in an opposite chair. "Tell us of this mate of yours, who left you here, so that you did not feel like moving on and trying again."

"Ouch," said David. "I'm not saying it's wrong. Just when you put it...like that..." He coughed. "Think I need a drink." He checked the mini bar. Fortunately for his wallet it was empty.

David sat back down, and folded his hands. "She was beautiful. She wanted to be an artist, like I did. Our families didn't believe in us, but we would believe in each other. So I guess we... built a dream. We built the dream that we would come out here to be together, and make it together which it with each other's help in the space."

"You thought this hell might be a place that you could build this dream?" The mailed demon asked, nonplussed.

David smiled ruefully. "Yes I did."

"What happened then?" The female demon asked.

"She changed her mind about the part of the dream that included me." He heard his own words as he said them. It felt like he was passing sentence on himself, and the ruling was a punch to his gut. So quickly and completely it defined the end of so many dreams and hopes, dissolving to leave in their wake only wasted years.

"I understand," the male demon said diplomatically. "I guess your species has many years in which you cannot enjoy mating, until both you and your mate are properly in heat or estrus."

David worked his way through that mentally. "No actually," said David. "We can pretty much mate any time we find someone who's interested."

The demon couple looked at each other, and then back at him. Yggrakka broke the sudden silence. "Then why in all the worlds aren't you mating right now?"

David squirmed. "I don't know...it's just the timing!"

Hyrax snorted. "We can only make together once every five years. We were just on the edge of this moment when our worlds merged together. You can do this at any time you want, and instead you work this job in these prison clothes and sit at home and hopelessness?"

"You don't know me!" David yelled.

"I think I start to understand something," The female demon said. "You were about to call her this morning, weren't you?"

"No I wasn't," said David lamely. "I was just, sleeping."

"I understand." Hyrax shook his head. "We must have been about to make the same mistake."

"We were about to part ways," said Yggrakka. "And you were about to try to get back together."

David looked from her and then to Hyrax. "You aren't saying...I did this?"

She sat up on the bed, and he tried not to notice her beautiful body between her hooves and horns. "But David, this merging of worlds isn't everywhere in your world, is it?"

He shook his head. "It doesn't seem to be like this on the East Coast, or really outside of Los Angeles. They can see it elsewhere, including the big moons and everything, but for some reason it's not affecting them. Like, as I think about it, I guess new moons showing up would really mess with the tides too. But I haven't heard anything about that."

"Your hell is where you are, David," they said. "And our hell was becoming us too." She moved off the bed and close to him, grabbing his arm. He yelped as her claws nearly pierced his tender skin, and he suppressed a girlish shriek of pain.

"That hurts," he said.

"Yes. Others will hurt. That is the nature of relationships. You cannot avoid the hurt. That is how you make Hell too - by avoiding the feeling that is life." Yggrakka did not loosen her grip, as her eyes drilled into him. "Such a Hell is wherever you are, and it makes it similar for those around you. But none of them feel it as bad as you."

"But it doesn't seem that bad," David protested. "It's really just like every other day."

"That's exactly it," said Hyrax. "It makes perfect sense. There are enough of you now, feeling misery and expecting misery, in a low-level way where you can still live your lives but you aren't enjoying them, that you just expect hell. So your mind brought your vision of hell here. And unfortunately for us, that's our world. Where feeling like you really is hell to us."

"As it should be," the female demon added.

David shrugged. "All right, let's say that's true. What can we do about it?"

"You can get a new attitude my friend," she said. "Do it for us. Do it for yourself."

"How my supposed to do that?"

She shrugged, and looked at her demon boyfriend. "We could have sex," she pointed out.

David blinked. He wondered if you'd heard her right, or thunder had just struck in the room and he hadn't noticed. "Sex?"

"That's what you call mating, right?" said her demon man.

"I'm kind of, not into dudes," he said. "No offense."

"I'm not into pale hornless pinkbeasts either," said the demon boyfriend. "But I'll do what it takes if that's how we get home."

"Me too," she said.

David was feeling it was all a bit much. "Look. This bit about Los Angeles becoming Hell, well honestly it's the first theory of heard that makes sense. But I don't think mating will do the trick, thanks. Why don't we get some rest, and see if anything else occurs to us. Before I have to get up early to go back to work tomorrow," he finished, realizing as he said at how sad that sounded.

They had no better ideas, so they decided to go to sleep. For the couple, slumber meant hanging upside down like bats in the corner of the room Hyrax's bat wings unfolding to wrap around her.

David turned out the light, but couldn't sleep. He picked up his cell phone charging on the night stand, and looked at the phone number of the woman who'd broken his heart.

He could've done a lot of things different. Maybe some of them might have worked. But he'd given it literally all that he knew how to do. And that had depleted him. That is ruined him of faith for a little while. Maybe that well was about done.

Still, what was he to do with the rest of his life?

He opened the window to stare out into the nightmarish land-scape. It wasn't the suns and flying creatures that made it such a nightmare.

He looked over at the couple hanging upside down in the corner, fast asleep. Yggrakka looked particularly peaceful, and beautiful.

MORNING CAME and the sun shone in through the opened windows. David decided to leave his guests be for a while, and sat on his bed in thought.

Outside were the same familiar swarms of pterodactyls. Until they began to fade. Behind him he saw the couple unfurl from the corner. They were starting to become transparent.

He heard a rustling of leathery wings. The demon couple unfolded, and began going transparent as well.

Yggrakka came over to him. "You did it!"

Hyrax rubbed the sleep from his eyes. "What did you do?"

"I don't know," he said honestly. "I guess I changed my mind?"

"Perhaps that was enough," she said. "Someone else could have been the tipping point, and you changing your own mind has shifted things back. Thank you."

David eyed her very strong-looking, fit and sharp-taloned boyfriend, and decided not to mention what also might have helped. He had woken up Yggrakka around 3 am, and decided to take her up on her offer while Hyrax snored. It was amazing what could be done with an eager demoness in a hotel bathroom.

She put her hands on his shoulders. This time her talons didn't hurt. "You should know that you are not so hideous to me," she said softly. "I see you in your spirit. You should show your claws more. It is not shameful to be in pain. It is beautiful, really. It shows how the strength and power of your heart."

Her mate Hyrax left first, shaking David's hand before he completely disappeared. She leaned in and kissed him as she faded, her lips becoming soft as a morning desert wind.

David looked around the room a bit, and took his tie from where he'd he laid it on the hotel's cheap desk. He placed it carefully inside his briefcase.

There was nothing much to go back to his apartment for. They could keep his security deposit. He realized he didn't even like his pillow.

He checked out of the room. On his way back to his car he passed a dumpster, and threw his suitcase in it with his tie.

He pointed his car to somewhere new. He didn't know what he'd do or where. It just had to be somewhere else, and some thing else.

Two weeks later he'd found a new job, and met a nice girl who'd just moved from New Mexico.

# ABOUT THE AUTHOR

James Beach is a writer, photographer and recovering musician. He was born and raised in New Jersey, and was once told he was a bad Photoshop superimposition on the East Coast. He successfully escaped and now lives in San Francisco, a perfect locale for exploring his emerging super powers.

*For more declassified information, visit*
jimbeach.net